CONTENTS

CORGI CASE FILES

Case of the Pilfered Pooches

Corgi Case Files, Book 4

J.M. Poole

Sign up for Jeffrey's newsletter on his
website to get all the latest corgi news:
www.AuthorJMPoole.com

True happiness is being owned by a corgi!

Case of the Pilfered Pooches
Published by Secret Staircase Books, an imprint of
Columbine Publishing Group, LLC
PO Box 416, Angel Fire, NM 87710

Book layout and design by Secret Staircase Books
Cover images by Yevgen Kachurin, Irisangel, Felipe de Barros

First Secret Staircase paperback edition: December 2020
First Secret Staircase e-book edition: December 2020

* * *

Publisher's Cataloging-in-Publication Data

Poole, J.M.
Case of the Pilfered Pooches / by J.M. Poole.
p. cm.
ISBN 978-1649140258 (paperback)
ISBN 978-1649140265 (e-book)

1. Zachary Anderson (Fictitious character)--Fiction. 2.
Pomme Valley, Oregon (fictitious location)—Fiction. 3. Amateur
sleuth—Fiction. 4. Pet detectives—Fiction. I. Title

Corgi Case Files Mystery Series : Book 4.
Poole, J.M., Corgi Case Files mysteries.

BISAC : FICTION / Mystery & Detective.
813/.54

ACKNOWLEDGMENTS

Welcome back!

There are several people to thank for our return visit to Pomme Valley, OR. High on that list would be my wife, Giliane. That woman has a super stressful job — which works her to the bone — and she still has the time to go through the book, looking for errors. She's the love of my life and I am damn lucky to have her at my side!

I also need to thank the members of my Posse, most especially Jason, Gina, Michelle, Elizabeth, and Diane, my mother. Thank you for taking the time to go through the book with a fine tooth comb. Trust me, it is much appreciated.

The cover illustration was once again provided by Felipe de Barros. Not only has he demonstrated exceptional skill in catering to my crazy ideas for the cover — like adding my father's dogs and my mother's dogs — he's been a delight to work with. Thanks again, Felipe!

And, of course, I have to thank you, the reader. There are many titles of books to choose from. Thanks for selecting mine!

I hope you enjoy the story! Happy reading!

J.

Giliane —
These stories are for you. I love making you laugh,
whether intentional or unintentional! Thank you
for being there for me! Love you always & forever!

PROLOGUE

G et back here, you knuckleheads. I'm not gonna go runnin' off after you. I'm too old for that. You know it. I know you do. Stop being a little toad. Casey, don't you even think about running away from me. I'll put a leash on you. So help me, I'll do it."

Loud, joyful barks indicated the recipients of the threat were in no way ashamed of their actions. Before long, the sharp, piercing barks echoed noisily throughout the park. Three chocolate Labs were out enjoying one of the first sunny days Pomme Valley had seen since Christmas. It might've been only 55°F, but one would think it was a warm tropical day judging by the number of people who were in one of the city's two downtown parks.

The owner of the three brown dogs smiled politely at the people he passed as he followed his dogs around the park. There have always been leash laws in place in Pomme Valley, but the dog owners knew it was rarely enforced. It was a generally accepted fact that, if your dog caused problems, or else ran off, then any damage the dog caused was the responsibility of the owner. Thankfully, the PVPD had yet to be called in to negotiate any crises.

The Labs' owner, a man in his early seventies, wearing a blue windbreaker, jeans, and work boots, had his hands full keeping an eye on his three dogs. All three were running around, off leash. Thankfully, two of the dogs were immediately distracted when the owner produced a knotted three-foot section of rope and threw it up into the air. Within moments, a dog had attached itself to each end of the rope, and, in less time that it takes to say 'pull' a fierce game of tug-of-war was on.

Satisfied that at least two of the dogs had become preoccupied, the elderly dog owner turned his attention to the third. Youthful, spirited, and displaying an excess of energy, the third chocolate Lab started running circles around her owner in eager anticipation of what each of them knew was to come. A tattered tennis ball was produced, sending the young dog into fits of ecstasy. Her sharp, enthusiastic barks echoed raucously throughout the entire park.

"Okay, okay. Calm down, Chip. I've got the ball. Here. Go get it."

He threw the ball as hard as he could. Chip was back in less than ten seconds. She proudly spit the soggy ball at his feet.

"Yuck. That's disgusting. Do you have to make it so slimy? Fine, here you go. Go get it!"

The man lobbed the ball a second time. As before, the ball was returned in just a matter of moments. A quick check of his other two dogs confirmed that neither was willing to relinquish their end of the rope, so the game of tugging continued. He threw the ball a third time, but just as he released the ball, he heard a growl come from behind him. Distracted, he turned to look. The game of tug had been settled. The victor was trotting victoriously toward him, holding her prize with her nose lifted high. The other, the man noticed, was looking as though she was trying to ascertain the easiest way to get the rope back.

The ball he had thrown landed on an exposed rock and immediately ricocheted off, angling straight toward the nearby woods. Chip barked enthusiastically, signaling she was in pursuit. Within moments, she was gone.

"Chip! Get back here! I don't want you going in there by yourself. Do you hear me? Chip, I'm serious! Get back here right now!"

The other two Labs abandoned the rope and appeared by their owner's side, concerned by the firm tone of voice he was exhibiting.

"It's okay, girls. You're not in trouble. Chip ran off after the ball. Let's give her a few minutes. She'll be fine."

Several minutes later, and growing uneasy, the man entered the woods with his other two dogs shadowing him. He pushed through a row of shrubbery bordering the woods and called again. When there was no forthcoming response, he put two fingers to his mouth and whistled.

Still nothing.

A whine caught the man's attention. He glanced down to see one of his other girls, Casey, staring straight at the dense woods. She whined again. Abby, the third and oldest of the trio, had settled to the ground. Her tongue flopped out of her mouth and she was panting contentedly.

"Are you okay there, buddy?" a voice interrupted.

The concerned dog owner turned to see a much younger man holding a leash to a golden retriever. His dog, identified by his tag as 'Buster', was pulling at his leash and was also looking in the same direction as Casey. Both dogs barked, almost in unison. Abby leapt up from the ground, as though she had been sleeping on a hot plate that had just been turned on. Within moments, all three dogs were barking their heads off.

"One of my dogs has gone missing," the elderly man stated. "I threw a ball, and it bounced in there. She hasn't come back yet."

"If you'd like, I'll watch your other two while you go look."

"Will you? Thanks. I'll be just a moment."

Leashes were produced and clipped into place. Both chocolate Labs whined when it became apparent they weren't invited to accompany their owner. Right about then, Buster, the golden retriever, came up to sniff noses with both of the Labs. Once the introductions had been made, all three settled to the ground to wait.

Ten minutes later, the Lab owner returned, holding the tattered ball with a look of concern on his face.

"You didn't find her?" the Good Samaritan asked.

The man shook his head no. He looked worriedly down at the ball he was holding. A crowd of concerned dog owners was gathering.

"She's gone. I found the ball, but there was no trace of Chip. She'd never run off like that. I think … I think someone stole my dog!"

ONE

Well, what about this one? It's furry and has an obnoxiously loud squeaker. It's sure to annoy the hell outta me. Would this one work, Your Excellency?"

A long tri-colored snout poked into the bin of plush animals and started nudging them around, much like a toddler would do when looking for his favorite toy. With an exasperated snort, the owner of the snout extricated itself from the first bin and shoved it into a second. And then a third. Within moments, the entire aisle was covered with strewn toys.

"Really? Come on, Sherlock. Must you go through each and every one?"

"It's okay," a voice assured me. "I can have my son clean all those up. Don't even think about it."

I turned to look at the pet store owner and smiled apologetically.

"I'm sorry about all of this. I should have warned you; Sherlock is a smidge on the picky side when it comes to toys. I've been trying to get him to replace that nasty, ripped up toy pheasant of his for a while now. Nothing seems to spark his interest."

"Don't worry about it. I'm Justin Roesh, the

owner of the store."

"Zack Anderson."

"Of course. I know who you are. You are well known around here, Mr. Anderson. But, probably not as well-known as your dogs, am I right? Well, isn't this a treat? I've been wanting to meet your dogs ever since I first heard about them. We don't get many corgis in here."

"They're an interesting breed," I confided with the owner, "no doubt about it. Highly intelligent and highly stubborn. Sherlock, come on, buddy. Make up your mind."

"Your other dog appears to have made a selection," Justin announced.

I automatically glanced down at Watson, my other Pembroke Welsh Corgi. The timid little red and white dog had selected a long-necked purple giraffe and was proudly carrying it around the store by the neck, as though she had killed it herself. I squatted down to give Watson a friendly pat on the head.

"Good job, girl. At least someone was listening to me while we were in the car. Come on, Sherlock. I didn't want to be in here this long. Pick something, you stubborn goober."

Sherlock trotted over to the next aisle, which contained all manner of treats and chew toys, and paused, as if he was a fox and had just discovered the hidden hen house. He promptly thrust his nose into a half whiskey barrel and came up with an irregular, triangular-shaped piece of … I blinked at the thing. I really didn't know what it was. It looked like leather? Rawhide?

"An excellent choice," the owner told me. "Pig ears are a favorite chew toy for many of our customers."

I looked over at Justin and raised an eyebrow.

"Did you say pig ears? That's just the name for that rawhide thing, right? It's not an actual pig ear, is it?"

Justin grinned at me. He slid his hands into his pockets as an unreadable expression spread over his face. I groaned aloud and my forehead wrinkled with disgust. Sherlock had picked out a pig part? I pulled one of the ears out of the barrel and studied it.

Yep. It was an actual, genuine, pig ear. In fact, I could even see a few veins showing through the skin. A look of horror appeared on my face as I suddenly imagined a whole sty full of pigs without their ears. How nasty could you get?

"I think I'm gonna be sick."

Justin waved a dismissive hand at me.

"Oh, don't worry. Everyone says the same thing. It's completely natural, organic, and believe-it-or-not, it's perfectly healthy. In fact, we have a wide variety of pig ears, cow hooves, and…"

"What's this?" I interrupted, holding up nearly a foot long elongated, shriveled piece of rawhide that looked like it had been left in the oven for far too long.

"That's a pizzle. They're very popular, too."

I held it up to my nose and sniffed.

"It smells terrible. What's it made of? Do I want to know?"

Justin's smile threatened to split his face in two.

"That would be one of the chew toys we sell here that are composed of 100% organic ingredients."

"And that would be...?"

"Dried bull penis."

I dropped the thing as though I had just discovered I was holding a live rattlesnake. I looked at my hand in disgust. An automatic swiping of my hand down my pant leg assured me that no trace of pizzle remained anywhere on my skin. However, a quick sniff of my hand had me looking around for a restroom since I could still pick up lingering smells from that nasty thing. Then I saw both Sherlock and Watson lift their noses, sniff a few times, and then collectively turn to stare at my pant leg.

Aww, nooo.... I do believe it was time to change. Or burn these pants. I had been holding dried bull penis? That was a secret I would willingly take to the grave. I think I was gonna be sick.

"Do people know what these things are when they buy 'em?"

Justin nodded. "Of course. Naturally, their

first reaction is similar to yours, but I assure them that everything is perfectly healthy and safe. The dogs love them! You really ought to let them each have one."

"In a pig's eye, pal. Oh, no. Let me guess. You sell those here, too?"

Justin laughed. "No. Tell you what. The first one is on me. If either of your dogs doesn't like them, then at least you won't be out any money. Samuel, would you please start ringing up Zack?"

"You're that sure of yourself?"

"I am. Just step over there to the counter and my son will take care of you."

I glanced at the young teenager with the severe case of acne. It was the same kid Vance and I had seen in here last year when we went looking for that missing glass tiger. It had been hidden in plain sight in this store. The kid, if memory served, had tried everything he could think of in order to keep us away from its hiding spot.

It hadn't mattered. Sherlock had honed in on that thing the moment his paws had hit the ground. The simple fact that this store was still open suggested that Justin, the kid's father, had made peace with the police. That, and paid back all the money he had owed his distributors.

We were given the pig ear and the (shudder) pizzle, free of charge. Justin had insisted. He was yet another fan of Sherlock's and was thrilled to death to say that Sherlock and Watson frequented his little shop on a regular basis.

"Mr. Anderson."

I had just pushed open the door to head outside when I hesitated. Justin was approaching from behind. He nodded his head, encouraging me to continue moving outside.

"I just wanted to say, once again, how sorry I am about how Samuel behaved with that damn tiger. He really is a good kid."

"He was just trying to protect you," I reminded him. "He thought that reporter was going to turn you in and that you'd be arrested. No one wants to see that happen to their father."

The shopkeeper's head fell. "I know. We had hit some rough times. However, all is good. I squared up with my distributors, apologized to the police and am hoping I can put this unpleasant business behind me. If it wasn't for your little Sherlock, I think I'd probably be in jail."

Sherlock promptly sat and reverently raised a paw as he looked at Justin.

"Is he trying to shake my hand?" the store owner asked, bewildered.

I shrugged. "Sure looks like it. You'd better humor him. Go ahead. Shake his paw."

Bemused, Justin knelt down and gingerly took Sherlock's paw. After giving the stubby leg a firm shake, Justin regained his feet, but continued to stare curiously at the corgi.

"I never knew dogs could be that smart."

"Not all of them are," I said. "These, however, are as sharp as tacks."

Satisfied that peace had been made, Sherlock turned on his heel and strode toward the street. Two minutes later, I had loaded the dogs back into my Jeep. The brown paper bag holding the dogs' new toys/treats was sitting on the passenger seat. The bag had been stapled closed, but even with it sealed shut, I could still smell the foulness that emanated from within. No wonder both of the corgis were staring at me from the back seat. I honestly didn't think I'd be able to stay in the same room when I gave them those disgusting things.

My cell rang. Or, rather, my car's stereo rang. It was Jillian's cell. I rolled up the windows to cut down on the outside noise and took the call.

"Hi, Jillian! How's your vacation going for you? How are your parents liking Flagstaff?"

"Hello, Zachary! It's wonderful here. I never knew any part of Arizona could be this beautiful, or this green. There are trees everywhere! And do you know what? I can even see some snow dusting the tops of the nearby mountains!"

"Didn't I tell you that you'd like it? But, the million dollar question is, what do your parents think? I'm the one who suggested they should stop by on their trek to the Grand Canyon. Did they like it?"

"Not only do they absolutely love it, they won't stop raving about it. Oh! I should also in-form you that we followed your advice and went to One-Eyed Bill's Steak House last night for dinner. My father would never admit it, but I know he had a fantastic time. I even saw him tapping his foot several times when the wait staff began singing."

I do believe a little bit of context is in order here. One-Eyed Bill's is a restaurant in Flagstaff, AZ, that employs local music students as its waiters and waitresses. Northern Arizona University has one heck of a music program, and it actively encourages its students to seek jobs at the restaurant so they can get a taste of performing in public. One-Eyed Bill's has an old west motif about it, complete with saddles, bridles, and all manner of bric-a-brac from that time period. Plus, they can—and do—serve one wickedly awesome ribeye.

"That's definitely good to hear. Your father concerned me the most. I couldn't quite tell if that would be his type of thing, but I decided to take a long shot."

"Well, it worked. I just think it might've worked too much."

"Oh? Might I ask why?"

"My parents now think you're the best thing to happen to me since Michael passed."

"I'm not sure how to respond to that. Is that good?"

"Yes."

"Ah. Then I'm glad. I think if it were up to our

parents, then they would have already married us off."

Jillian laughed. "I know. I think your mother has my mother on speed dial."

"Just what I didn't need to hear."

"What did you end up doing today?"

"We just stopped by the pet store. I am really hoping I can get Sherlock to abandon that ratty pheasant he carries around. The squeaker died long ago. It's more pathetic than anything."

"Zachary Michael, you will do no such thing."

"Whoa! Why are you middle-naming me?"

"Do you have any idea how much that toy probably means to Sherlock? That's the first toy that you bought him. I've seen him carry that thing around all over your house. In fact, I've even helped patch it up when it was torn. If you'd like to give him a new toy, so be it. However, you need to promise me you won't take his treasured toy away."

"You're suggesting that dogs can get sentimental over their toys?"

"I'm not suggesting anything. I'm informing you that I know they can. You've given Sherlock a second chance in life. You're his daddy. You gave him that toy. He won't want to part with it."

"Well, now that you've completely made me feel like a jerk, I guess I'll stop trying to replace it."

"Good. What new toy did you pick out for

him?"

"He turned his nose up at all the plush animals I showed him, and let me tell you, Fur, Fins, & Feathers has quite a selection to choose from."

"See? Didn't I tell you?"

"Yeah, yeah, score one for you." I heard Jillian laugh. "Do you want to know what he picked out instead? One nasty, disgusting, I'm-doing-my-best-not-to-puke pig ear."

"What do you have against pig ears? I hear they're perfectly safe for dogs. My father used to give them to our dogs back when I was growing up all the time."

"Do you know what else the owner suggested I get for the dogs? A pizzle." I heard a distinctive snort, followed shortly thereafter by a gasp of surprise, and then a bout of coughing. "Jillian, are you okay?"

"Do you know… cough, cough … do you know what a … cough … heavens. Excuse me. As I was saying, do you have any idea what a pizzle is?"

"I do now."

"And you bought one? Willingly??"

"Well, no. The owner of the pet store gave me one free of charge to split between the dogs. I don't know if I can do it. I don't know if I can give dried bull dong to the dogs, let alone cut one in half." Jillian snorted again and her coughing resumed. "Find this funny, do you?"

"Oh, you have no idea! I have such a clear, vivid picture in my head of you with a look of utter disgust on your face as you give that thing to the dogs. You just made my night. Thank you!"

"I'm glad I amuse you."

"If only you knew how much."

I felt my face flame up. She wasn't even here. How could she possibly make me blush?

"You're blushing right now, aren't you?"

WTF?

"Now, how in the world did you know that?"

"Because I know you. What are your plans for the rest of the day?"

"I've got both dogs with me. I don't need to go back to the house yet, although I wouldn't mind losing the bag of animal parts sitting on my passenger seat. I was thinking that maybe I ought to go for a drive."

"That sounds nice. Where would you go?"

"I'm not sure. Do you have any suggestions?"

"You could always take I-5, toward Grants Pass. It runs along Rascal River for at least ten miles. It's a pretty drive."

"That sounds like a plan. I think I will do that. Thanks!"

"You're welcome. I hope you enjoy your afternoon. I'll call you tonight."

"I look forward to it, Jillian. Say hello to your parents for me."

"I will. Goodbye, Zachary."

The Rascal River in southwestern Oregon stretches nearly 215 miles and flows in a general westerly direction. It starts at the Cascade Range and flows all the way to the Pacific Ocean. People flock to the river for its salmon fishing, white-water rafting, and its gorgeous rugged scenery.

Some of the best examples of the rocks that form the Earth's mantle can be found in the Rascal Basin. In fact, the only dinosaur bones that have ever been discovered in Oregon had been found in the Otter Point Formation located in the extreme southwestern corner of the state. And if you're wondering, yes, I do sound like I'm reciting from a tourist's map. That's because I am. I picked it up the day I moved here. In fact, it's still in my Jeep.

Twenty minutes into the drive, I came across one of those roadside fruit stands. The bright, appealing specimens of fruit had me pulling off the road so that I could make a few selections. An older couple smiled politely at me as I approached.

"Hello, young man," the older woman began. "Might we interest you in some fresh straw-berries?"

I nodded eagerly, "Absolutely. The fruit in the grocery stores is nothing compared to this. How is it this fruit looks so good? I didn't think this would be the time of year to harvest anything."

The old man grinned. "Greenhouses. Who says you can't teach an old dog new tricks? We're the only farm this side of the Rascal to have over half our crops protected from the elements."

I nodded appreciatively. The woman handed

me a basket and I proceeded to select several flats of strawberries, some blueberries, a few nectarines, and even several plums, even though they didn't look like plums to me. The plums I was used to were small, purple, and weren't more than several bites. These things were large, nearly the size of lemons, and had skins that were mottled light red. The man saw me studying the plum and clucked his tongue. He pointed at a small, handmade sign which indicated what they were.

"Freedom plums. They're sweet and juicy. You'll love 'em."

"Can I interest you in a jar of honey?" the woman asked from my left. I turned to see her holding out a large mason jar filled to the brim with some of the best-looking honey I've ever seen in my life.

"You have your own bee hives?" I asked, impressed. "It looks fantastic. Sure. I'll take one." A thought occurred. I knew Jillian loved honey. More than likely, she'd like a jar, too. "You know what? I'll take two."

Smiling approvingly, the elderly couple began assembling my order.

"Oh my goodness!" the woman suddenly exclaimed.

Alarmed, I looked up.

"What? What's the matter?"

"Aren't those two of the sweetest looking dogs I have ever seen in my life?"

I looked over at my Jeep. Two canine faces were plastered to the windows. Four ears were sticking straight up, and each dog had two lines of drool running down the window to presumably collect on the sill. How they knew I was buying food was beyond me.

"Are those corgis?" the woman asked.

I nodded. "Pembroke Welsh Corgis, if you want to get technical. I adopted both of them last year just after I moved to Pomme Valley."

"You live in Pomme Valley?" the elderly man asked, surprised. He nudged his wife and pointed at the dogs. "Honey, I'm willing to wager that one of those pups is the famous Sherlock we've heard so much about."

My eyes shot open. Wow. I couldn't go any- where anymore without someone recognizing the dogs. Me? I'm an unknown, but the dogs? Royalty.

The woman turned to me with an imploring look on her face.

"Is … is one of them Sherlock?"

I smiled, nodded, and held out a hand.

"I'm Zack Anderson. That's Sherlock, on the right. He's the one with black on his face. The other is Watson."

The woman clapped her hands in delight. "Oh, Sherlock and Watson. How adorable!"

"Would you like to meet them?"

"May I? I would love to."

I walked over to the Jeep, opened the door,

and carefully set each of the dogs on the ground. Making sure the leashes were tightly wound around my wrist—we were still on the side of a road after all—we approached the fruit stand.

"Sherlock? Watson? I'd like you to meet … umm, I never caught your names."

The woman ignored me as she hurried out from behind the counter to squat down next to the dogs. I heard a sigh and looked up at the old man. He took my hand and gave it a firm shake.

"Peter Boone. This is my wife, Dora."

"How have you heard about Sherlock, if you don't mind me asking?"

"We may not live in Pomme Valley, but the exploits of this little dog are the talk of many in our town."

"Which town is that?" I wanted to know.

"Wimer. We're about twenty-five miles north of Pomme Valley."

"That's a long way to come to sell fruit, isn't it?"

"We don't mind the drive. We're both retired. This gives us something to do. Wait until everyone hears we met the famous Sherlock and little Watson, too!"

Dora was still cooing over the dogs, who were loving every second of it. Butts were wiggling, nubs were wagging, and each of the dogs was vying with the other to see who could get the most attention. I felt a tap on my shoulder. Peter was holding out another Mason jar, only this one looked to have peanuts in it.

"Here. These are dry roasted. They're safe for dogs. I'll throw these in at no extra charge."

I smiled and thanked the shopkeeper. The dogs were definitely better known than I would ever be. They had procured another freebie just on their looks alone. Oh, well. At least it wasn't dried penis.

I thanked our new friends and promised to come back soon. We returned to the road and continued west until I could see the outskirts of Grants Pass. I made sure no cops were in the area —and no traffic, for that matter—and executed a U-turn.

I was going to have to admit it. I was bored. After Samantha's death, I had become accustomed to remaining indoors in Phoenix and shunning all human contact whatsoever. I had become absorbed with my work, even if my writing was nowhere near as good as it had been when Sam had been alive.

That was the past. This was the present, and it was definitely a different story. I was startled to learn that I enjoyed going out and talking to people. I enjoyed going out on excursions with the dogs. I was also surprised to discover I enjoyed hearing how complete strangers were fans of my dogs.

Oh, and I mustn't forget to mention how much I missed spending time with Jillian. Don't get me wrong. I'm still not ready to get married again. Neither of us are, for that matter. However, we each had managed to fill a void in our lives that neither of us realized needed to be filled. We enjoyed each other's company so much that, for the first time ever, I'm contemplating taking a cruise. Me. Hater of boats. I'm actually thinking about paying someone a lot of money to see how sick I could become out on the open water. What was this world coming to?

Now, you need to understand something about me. I've never understood what the fascination was with cruises. You spend all your time on a boat. Eating. Drinking. Partying. Well, two of those three were activities that held little to no interest for me. Sitting around on my rear, day in and day out, didn't sound like something I wanted to do. I mean, if I wanted to sit around and read a book, then there were certainly more economical ways to do it.

Jillian had assured me there were other things to do. According to her, these ships had everything on them. Theaters. Live shows. Shopping. Even rock climbing, although why someone would want to do that in the first place also escaped me. The one thing that did hold some promise was something called 'excursions'.

I had started to turn my nose up at this, too, when I suddenly realized I was being selfish. I could see this was something Jillian really wanted to do. Samantha had never expressed any interest in taking a cruise, either, so the subject had never come up. Jillian, on the other hand, had brought the subject up several times. Later that night, I had begun my research on why anyone would spend thousands of dollars on one of those floating hotels. You want to spend the night away from home? That can certainly be accomplished by ...

Sorry. I should stop harping on that. The fact of the matter was, thanks to Jillian, I was willing to give it a shot. I don't know where we'll end up going, but if we ...

My phone rang again. This time the screen showed that the caller ID was unavailable. Do I answer? I did know a few people who purposely had their numbers blocked. However, I hadn't heard from either of them in over a year. There was only one person that frequently called me with a blocked number, and I've never heard them speak. And, it always happened super late at night. Or very early in the morning. Whatever. Oh, the hell with it. I'm not afraid of a damn phone call.

"Hello?"

No answer.

"Is there anyone there?"

Still no answer. Hmm. Was that the sound of someone breathing? If this was my mystery admirer, I've never heard them make a noise before. My cell was resting in one of my Jeep's cup holders. A closer look was warranted. A check of the display confirmed that a call had connected, only I still couldn't hear anything. I deactivated the hands-free option and held the phone up to my face. Nope. I still couldn't hear anything.

"Last chance, sport. If you don't say something, then I'm hanging up."

Silence.

"Very well. Adios, amigo."

I tossed the phone onto the passenger seat. Stupid cellular technology. In this day and age, they still couldn't guarantee your call would be completed properly. There's gotta be a way to block those damn calls.

As I drove back toward Pomme Valley, enjoying the breeze from the open windows, I decided I wanted to do something. Something fun. But what? Maybe see a movie? Go out for a pizza? It was approaching noon. I could go for a bite to eat.

I tried Harry first. Unfortunately, I got his voice mail. He was probably tied up at his vet clinic. The discovery of Harry's role as Pomme Valley's only veterinarian still ranked in my top five surprises of all time. It also meant his schedule mirrored that of a typical banker: 9 to 5, Monday through Friday. Weekends were no better. He had two kids, and spent the vast majority of his free time with them.

Well, I could try Vance. I never knew what his schedule was like. He might have the day off.

"Hey Zack. What's going on?"

"Vance. How's it going, buddy?"

"I've had better days. What's on your mind?"

Suddenly, my feelings of boredom felt supremely insignificant. Here I was, calling Vance, to see if he had an hour or two to spare so he could hang out with me, when it sounded like he had more pressing matters on his hands. Not only was he a detective in the Pomme Valley police department, he had a family of his own. I clearly had caught him at a bad time.

"You know what? It sounds like you're busy. Sorry. I shouldn't have bothered you."

"It's okay, Zack. I appreciate the distraction. I've been working on this case that came in last night, and it isn't going well."

"Case? What kind of case? Hopefully nothing bad."

"It isn't. No one was hurt, if that's what you're wondering. A dog has been reported missing."

My ears perked up. There had been a dognapping? While deplorable, it just might be what I needed to get me out of the funk I've been in lately.

"Good timing, pal. I've got Sherlock and Watson with me right now. Where are you? We'll get to work."

"Thanks for the offer, Zack. I appreciate it. However, these types of cases pop up all the time. The dog has undoubtedly wandered off. Give it a few days and they'll turn up somewhere. So, at this time, we don't need you."

Damn. Vance had dangled the carrot, and I

had taken the bait. Now what do I do?

"That's okay. I guess if you need our help, you know where to find us."

"I do. Thanks, Zack. I'll keep you posted."

We were driving through town when Sherlock suddenly perked up. He stepped up onto the window sill so he could look outside the window. The little corgi gave a soft woof. Within moments both corgis were looking through the windows, only they weren't looking at the same thing. Sherlock was looking back at the street I had just passed. I checked the mirror. We had just passed Oregon Street. I waited for the traffic to clear before I executed a U-turn. Once I turned down the street, I saw that there was a small park nestled in between several large lots. Did Sherlock want to go outside and burn off some steam? Why not? I think some exercise might do us all some good.

I was setting Watson on the ground when I noticed a tennis ball wedged up under the back seat. Perfect. This was definitely meant to be. Holding the ball in my right hand, with the leashes wrapped securely around my left, we headed into the park. I saw a group of old ladies sitting on a picnic bench nearby, chatting amiably. They ignored us as we passed by. I stepped through the chain link fence, dropped both leashes onto the ground, and threw the ball. Both dogs took off like a shot.

My cell rang for a third time that hour. A

quick glance confirmed it was Vance. Had he changed his mind and wanted some help after all?

"Zack. Hey, pal, I wanted to apologize for being so brusque earlier. If you'll pardon the pun, I had just been hounded by the captain. You remember the dognapping I told you about?"

"Yeah. What about it?"

"Well, the owner has just posted a reward for the safe return of his dog."

"Okay. Why would the police have a problem with that?"

"Because the owner is willing to offer one of his prized John Wayne collector rifles to whomever returns his dog, no questions asked. Zack, do you have any idea how many nutballs are going to respond to this? Captain Nelson wants the case of this missing dog solved. Now."

"Wow. How much could a rifle be worth?"

"This one is estimated to be worth over $10K."

"For a gun? Damn. That's crazy. Is this guy loaded?"

"I don't think so. The captain was telling me about the conversation he had with the dog owner. In his words, it boils down to what he values most. If the loss of his gun would mean the return of his missing dog, then that's a price he's more than willing to pay."

"So, where did this theft happen?"

"At one of the city parks."

TWO

Y ou're kidding, right? If you tell me that this dognapping happened at the park off of Oregon Street, then I'll … I'll … I'll eat one of these pig ears I just bought for the dogs."

"As much as I'd like to see that, no. This happened at the big park on the east side of town. Actually, it's at the end of 8th Street. Why do you ask?"

Talk about foolish wagers. I'll have to be more careful than that. I made Vance uphold the promise he had made to me last year, about finding a missing Egyptian pendant. Vance had unwisely bet that if Sherlock would find the missing necklace, then he would wear tights to his first dance class.

I should backtrack a bit further. Tori, that'd be Vance's wife, is a teacher at PVHS, as well as a dance teacher. Some time ago, she mentioned she was thinking about teaching an Irish dancing class. Jillian expressed interest, and naturally wanted to sign up, dragging Yours Truly along with her. Time passed, and I was dismayed to hear that Tori was ready to start the class. Now, the only way I'd agree to volunteer to participate for that class was to have Vance suffer through it right along with me. Thanks to an ill-conceived wager my detective friend made a few months back, he had to take the class wearing a Peter Pan costume, complete with a set of neon green tights. It was a night I would never forget.

Yeah, go ahead and laugh. If you can imagine a 250 pound sack of potatoes in tap shoes, then you have a pretty good idea what I looked like as I tried to duplicate the moves Tori was teaching us. Seeing Vance in his ridiculous getup was icing on the cake and made the whole night worthwhile.

With that being said, if I would have made a wager about eating a pig's ear, and then lost, then you better believe Vance would be handing me a bottle of ketchup as he whipped out his phone to record the scene for posterity. The moral of that story would be for me to keep my big trap shut. Thankfully, this dognapping happened at PV's other park.

"Sherlock woofed at me, as if he'd picked up the scent of something. We literally just stopped at Oregon Street Park to check things out when you called."

"Nope, wrong park. That's okay. If any developments arise, and I need the three of you, then I'll be certain to give you a call. Keep your cell handy, Zack."

"Will do, pal."

For the next half hour, I threw the ball for two overjoyed corgis. They barked, they ran, they saw squirrels, and then they ran some more. I couldn't figure it out. How much energy could two small dogs have? They were wearing me out and I wasn't even the one doing the running.

It took a while, but the dogs finally ran out of steam. Watson spit the ball at my feet, only to have Sherlock dart in and snag it, as if he didn't trust what I'd do with the ball should I gain possession of it. By the time we made it home, both dogs were out cold. I had to carry them inside, much the way a prince would carry a sleeping princess inside her castle.

I grinned at both of my dogs, who were now snoring on their beds in one of the guest rooms upstairs, and decided to retire to my office so I could work on fleshing out my next novel. I had already completed the rough draft—in record time, I might add—and I just needed to read through it so I could check for errors. Sure, I have an editor. A very expensive editor. However, I would like to appear as though I don't need to take an English 101 class, or else demonstrate that I have more than a three-word vocabulary.

You see, I have learned that, when I write, my brain tends to operate at a speed in which my fingers can barely keep up. As a result, errors creep in. And we're talking some serious, what-were-you-thinking errors. Granted, I might not be able to catch all of them, but if I could just set aside some interruption-free time to read through my manuscript, then I know I could typically catch at least 90% of them. So, I booted up my laptop, opened my latest manuscript, and began to read.

Thirty quick minutes later, my cell phone rang.

A glance at the display showed it was my mother calling. Knowing full well that a call from my mom could last well over an hour, I silenced the call and went back to reading. I made a mental note to call her when I was done. After all, thanks to Jillian's influence, I was trying to be a better son and not appear like I was avoiding her calls. Okay, I was avoiding this call, but it was for a good purpose. The completion of my manuscript trumped anything else at the moment.

Tryst in the Gardens, by Chastity Wadsworth. My editor had claimed it would be an automatic bestseller, since my last three books had all sold amazingly well, and the number of preorders continued to increase by leaps and bounds. My 'unique edge' was back, Barbara—my editor—claimed. I needed to 'ride this wave' as long as I could. So, she had quite literally told me to get off my butt and finish the story.

My cell chimed, announcing the arrival of a new voice mail. I ignored it, slid the cell over to the left side of my computer, and returned to reading. I had to make it through nearly 70,000 words, and at the rate I was going, I wouldn't be done until next Tuesday.

My phone chimed again, although this time

it sounded different. Curiosity getting the better of me, I checked the display. A new email had arrived. Apparently, my mother had decided to try her hand at contacting me via an alternate means. Skimming through the message, I saw that she had purchased a new cell and had some questions about some of the 'new-fangled' apps that were included with the phone. Her words, not mine.

I groaned. The phone was returned to the desk. Sorry, Mom. You're gonna have to wait.

Back to my manuscript. I read through a dozen pages before the blasted phone went off again. Looks as if now she was trying her hand at texting.

That's it. I am now officially tired of all the interruptions. How was I, as a writer, supposed to work when I kept getting pulled out of the Zone? For all you non-writers out there, the 'Zone' is the frame of mind writers strive for, where the words just flow out of you and you can't seem to type fast enough. The Zone was only accessible—for me—when I wasn't being interrupted every five minutes.

A simple flick of a switch effectively silenced all alerts from my phone. Whoever invented the mute button on a modern cell phone should be awarded the Nobel Prize for genius. Now, for the third time, back to work.

* * *

Faster and faster Annabeth hurried. She spurred her stallion on, as much as she dared. After all, it wouldn't do to run the poor creature to death. However, if she didn't make it to the train station on time, then the likelihood of missing Evan became an uncomfortable reality. She had to tell him how she felt. He had to know that he was her one true love. If those words remained unspoken, then...

"Awwooooo!"

Let me tell you something. Nothing will yank your sorry butt out of the Zone faster than having two dogs sneak up on you when you're not paying attention. It's a good thing I wasn't taking a drink. I'd be cleaning vanilla-flavored soda off my monitor right about now. Those two little boogers had just scared the snot out of me.

I turned to look at the newest set of distractions. Sherlock and Watson had apparently woken from their nap and now wanted to play some more. In fact, Sherlock had brought me his tattered pheasant.

I squeaked the bedraggled bird a few times and then tossed it out the door, into the hall. Both corgis yipped excitedly and tore off after it. I had just turned back to my computer when both dogs returned, carrying the small, ratty toy between the two of them, and having a minor tug-of-war at the same time. It was as if both dogs wanted to be the one to present the toy to me, only neither was willing to give up their portion of it to the other.

"Be careful," I warned the dogs, remembering what Jillian had told me about Sherlock's favorite toy. "You don't want to damage that thing. Why don't you two grab one of those knotted ropes? They're much more suited for a game of tug, okay?"

Watson blinked her eyes a few times at me, promptly spat out her half of the toy pheasant, and then trotted out of the room. Bemused, I waited to see if she would actually return with one of the ropes. There's no way that could happen. Dogs didn't understand that much English, did they?

Watson trotted triumphantly back into my office with a thick, knotted, two-foot section of rope. Parts of the rope were fraying and parts looked as though they had been nearly chewed through. Sherlock took one look at the smelly, thrashed, chunk of rope and immediately dropped his pheasant. A split second later, he snagged the opposite end of the rope and a fierce game of tug-of-war began.

Leaving the corgis to their snarling, jerking, and tugging game, I returned my attention to my book. As I started to read, my thoughts drifted to dog toys, of all things. The corgis could really use a few new toys. I'm sure I could find what I needed on Amazon.

It started out harmlessly enough. I don't know what happened. The next thing I know, I was sitting back in my chair, rubbing my eyes, and eyeing with amazement a shopping cart holding at least $200 worth of dog goodies. A glance at the clock told me I had lost over an hour. I don't even remember opening up a browser window so I could surf online.

"This is getting me nowhere," I grumbled as I carefully saved the items in my cart and closed the browser. I had to laugh. If Samantha had been here, then she would have called me one of her favorite nicknames for me: Squirrel Boy. You know. Easily distracted? That's me, no doubt about it.

I tapped the Wi-Fi key on my keyboard, which promptly kicked me off of my own wireless network. That meant no more Internet. Then I made certain the dogs were preoccupied, which they were. Both were taking naps in the hallway, laying in such a way that the dogs could keep an eye on me should I try to sneak out of the room.

Once more, I returned my attention to my manuscript. I really needed to buckle down and get through it. I had at least two-thirds to go. I was sure I could do it.

The doorbell rang. Both dogs were on their feet in a flash and sprinted down the hallway. I hurried after them, determined to make it to the door before them. Call me silly, but I swear it was an on-going competition between the three of us. The dogs were determined they could outrun a lumbering human, and I was prepared to defend the human race.

I don't know if you've ever chased after a dog, but if you haven't, rest assured that 99.9% of the time, the dog will get away. The corgis were low to the ground, had short, muscular legs, and could move like the dickens when they were properly motivated.

Sherlock and Watson came to a sliding stop at the top of the staircase. I preferred to carry each of them up and down, 'cause I really didn't want either of them to hurt themselves going up or down the stairs. However, I really shouldn't have worried. Both corgis hesitated only long enough to verify I was still in pursuit, then began what I could only describe as a 'hop' down each stair.

They were quite good at it. Makes me think they've been practicing whenever I'm not there. Needless to say, there was no way I was going to be able to make it to the door before they were.

The doorbell sounded again, sending both dogs into frantic fits of barking.

"I'm coming, I'm coming. Hold on. Guys, is that really necessary? It's not the Boogeyman, okay?"

Sherlock must have thought otherwise.

"Awwooooo!"

It was my winemaster, Caden Burne. He was in his early thirties—although his face looked much younger—had thick curly black hair, and was stick thin. He told me once that it was because of his high metabolism. I seemed to recall stating something about not trusting skinny people. Thankfully, he had a sense of humor and laughed off the comment.

Today, he was wearing a black tee shirt with a gold embossed logo of some heavy metal band, blue jeans, and black sneakers. A red baseball cap completed the picture. He was also holding a small suitcase. My eyes zeroed in on the case. I couldn't help it. I groaned aloud.

"No worries, Zack," Caden told me as he came inside. "I don't have anything for you to try today."

I immediately brightened. That was the best news ever. Thanks to my propensity for hating wine, Caden viewed me as the best guinea pig ever when it came to taste-testing newly created recipes. I, on the other hand, was always less than thrilled.

"Whatcha got there?" I asked. "Is it something for me to sniff? Is it something you're looking to try?"

Caden followed me to the living room, set the case down on the coffee table, and gently opened it. I edged closer to see what was in it. The case, I noticed, was lined with felt, as though my winemaster had been transporting a miniature Ark of the Covenant. What was nestled within the suitcase, however, brought me up short.

It was a trophy. Two trophies, actually.

They were made of crystal, were elongated, and shaped like monoliths, with one being several inches larger than the other. It was the kind of award you'd expect to see at car dealerships for winning national recognition. I should also mention that these two objects were green, resembling nothing more than giant emeralds.

Caden gently pried the first from its sunken nest, produced a small square of white cloth from somewhere within a pocket, and reverently polished the surface of the seven-inch crystal award. As soon as he was done, he held it proudly out to me.

"So, what is this for?" I asked as I rotated the commemorative object in my hand.

There, etched onto the surface of the crystal —in gold-leaf writing, no less!—were the words, "In Recognition of 25 Years of Excellence in the Art of Winemaking: Lentari Cellars".

I whistled loudly. "Twenty-five years? Really? Is that how long Lentari Cellars has been in business?"

"It's actually longer than that," Caden explained. "But, since PiNWO rarely gives out these awards, we'll take it."

Confused, I pulled my eyes off the case trophy and looked at Caden.

"Who is 'Pinwo'? I've never heard of him."

"Hmm? Oh, sorry. That's right, you wouldn't know. PiNWO is a what, not a who. It stands for Pacific Northwest Wine Organization. They cover Oregon, Washington, Idaho, Montana, and even Wyoming. Come to think of it, I think PiNWO oversees parts of northern California, too."

"Okay. Well, that's great, right?"

Caden nodded and then pointed at the second, larger trophy still in the case.

"That's the one I'm really excited about."

My winemaster pulled the second object from the case. It was a larger version of the first award, and just as green as its smaller counterpart. This trophy underwent the same polishing process before it was placed into my hands.

"From the same place as the first?" I asked.

Caden nodded again. "Yup. This, Zack, is the Holy Grail of privately owned wineries here in the Pacific Northwest. Read what it says."

The blasted thing was heavy. Caden seemed to think this thing was worth its weight in gold? Maybe I should use two hands. It probably wouldn't be good if I dropped it, so I pushed aside the empty case and gently placed the larger green crystal trophy on the coffee table.

Now that I was staring at it, I rotated it until the front of it came into view: 2017 PiNWO Grand Champion—Lentari Cellars.

"That's really cool," I exclaimed as I gave Caden a congratulatory slap on the back. "I didn't even know we entered any contests."

"We enter contests all the time," Caden pointed out. "Or, should I say, I enter these contests for the winery all the time. We might not always win, but I feel our wines are good enough to try."

"What wine earned this?" I asked.

Caden returned to the carrying case, opened a side compartment that I didn't even know was there, and removed a velvet drawstring pouch. I heard the clink of metal striking metal as he opened the pouch and reached inside. Three medals were produced. Two were gold and one looked to be silver.

"Two of our wines took gold," Caden proudly informed me. "The Syrah and the gewürztraminer."

"What took silver?" I asked as I pointed at the third medal.

"Silver? Pah. What you're looking at is platinum. It's the same wine that earned us Grand Champion. The Syrah."

"Nice," I decided. I looked admiringly up at Caden. "You're doing a heckuva job, amigo."

My winemaster grinned back at me, "Thanks, buddy. I can't tell you how happy I am that you inherited the winery and not Abigail."

"You're definitely pulling your weight around here," I told him. "I think you've just earned yourself a raise."

"No arguments there," Caden decided. "Hey, on that note, I have a request."

I glanced at the case, then at the medals, and finally, at the two trophies. Is that what he's been doing to me? Buttering me up so that he can make some outrageous request?

"Oh, stop frowning," Caden scolded. "At least hear me out before you shoot me down."

"Fine. What's up? What do you need? Money for something?"

Caden nodded. "As a matter of fact, I do. I was hoping you'd make an investment in the winery. Several investments, actually."

By this time, I'm sure I was frowning. Caden wanted me to make several investments? That could only mean he wanted me to part with thousands of dollars. Yes, I could afford it, provided I didn't go too crazy, but before I approved anything, I wanted to see what my winemaster had in mind.

I crossed my arms over my chest and sighed. "Hit me with your best shot. What's on your mind?"

Caden pulled a brochure from his back pocket and handed it to me. It was from the John Deere dealership in Medford. This particular brochure was advertising a new line of tractors.

"You want me to buy a tractor?" I scoffed. "Seriously?"

"Hey, don't laugh. We used to have one here."

My eyebrows shot up. "We did? Where is it now?"

Caden scowled. "Take a guess."

"Abigail talked her mother into selling it, didn't she?"

"She felt the tractor was an added expense, and her mother shouldn't have to worry about maintaining a piece of farm equipment."

"This is a small winery," I pointed out. "I really don't think we have enough land to warrant buying a tractor."

"I'm really glad you just said that, Zack."

"Oh, no," I groaned. "I just remembered you said, investments. Plural. Now what? You're looking to add more land?"

Caden nodded excitedly, "Yes! Zack, you're not going to believe this. Old man Parsons has finally decided to retire and give his farm to his kids. The first thing his oldest son told me was that they were planning on down-sizing the farm 'cause no one really wants to farm any more. Besides, they have plenty of money. I asked him how much land he was looking to sell. Zack, he said he'd be willing to sell us twenty acres."

"Twenty acres," I slowly repeated.

"His land borders Lentari Cellars to the north and west. It'd be perfect! We'd have room to grow!"

"Correct me if I'm wrong," I slowly began, "but we're not even using all the acreage we have at our disposal now, right?"

"True," Caden admitted, "but…"

"How many acres are we up to?" I interrupted.

"We've got ten acres planted right now."

"And how many acres does Lentari Cellars have?"

"You still don't remember?" Caden scolded.

"Just answer the question, pal."

"Fifteen."

"Okay. We have fifteen acres to work with. You're suggesting we more than double our existing acreage?"

"Hence the request for a tractor," Caden said, a little more smugly than I would have liked.

"Let's talk money," I replied. "How much are we talking about?"

"Well, if you want the honest truth, he hasn't told me a number yet."

"Uh huh. Is this where I'm supposed to call him and wheedle him down?"

"We might not ever get another chance to expand the winery like this, Zack. I'd seriously think about it."

"Fine. I will."

"You're a good man, Zack."

"And this tractor?"

"If you've been persuaded by my remarkable charm to add on to the acreage, then getting another tractor would definitely come in handy. All good wineries have them."

"How in the world could you possibly drive a tractor through those vines?" I asked, bewildered. "There's not enough room between rows. You'd squish 'em all flat!"

"The rows are a little under five feet apart

from one another," Caden informed me. He held out a hand, indicating I should pass the John Deere brochure back to him. "You're right. Most tractors wouldn't fit. However, you'll notice here that it says that these three models are narrow. Zack, they're specifically built for use in orchards and wineries."

"A specialty tractor?" I asked, amazed. "What will they think of next?"

"You'll think about it?" Caden asked.

"If I decide to approach old man Parsons and inquire about purchasing some land, and we end up buying it, then yes. I will consider it."

Smiling, as though he were the victor of a long, drawn out battle, Caden left, humming merrily. My winemaster wanted to add another twenty acres? Did we really need to consider expanding so soon?

My eyes fell on the two awards standing proudly on my coffee table. I hadn't even known Caden had been entering any contests, and I certainly didn't expect him to tell me we had won anything. Yet there they were. There was no doubt in my mind that Lentari Cellars produced a fine bottle of wine. Well, more than one bottle. The winery produced several different types of wine, with more in the works, from what Caden tells me.

Our waiting list was growing, the prices seemed to keep going up, and it didn't look as though we'd be slowing down anytime soon. We were turning a hefty profit every time we harvested, so, what could it hurt to plan ahead? More than doubling our existing acreage would certainly be a wise investment. And I couldn't even begin to imagine how much income the extra land would bring in once they were all producing grapes. We were up to ten acres now, producing nearly four tons of grapes per acre. Caden's goal is to hit the perfect '15'. Fifteen tons of grapes per acre, producing two barrels of wine per ton.

See, Caden? You can teach an old dog new tricks. I actually remembered.

It couldn't hurt to inquire what the Parsons family was asking for the acreage. I had already convinced myself that, if reasonable, I'd place an offer. I'll make the call just as soon as I sent my completed manuscript to my editor.

Back to the salt mines.

I trooped back up the stairs and placed their Royal Canineships into the guest bedroom I've nicknamed the Dogs' Room. I even lifted them up onto the bed. Curious, Sherlock eyed me, wondering what I had in mind. I flipped the television on, changed the channel to a station dedicated to all things animal, and let them watch.

I had learned long ago that, oddly enough, some dogs do enjoy watching TV. My corgis were two of them. Put on a show that had animals in it —any type of animal—and they'd become completely distracted.

Confident that Sherlock and Watson were taken care of, I returned to my office. There was my book, still waiting for me. I had no sooner sat down and resumed reading when the barking began.

"For the love of Pete," I grumbled. I hurried over to the dogs' room. "What's up, guys? Now what?"

What I saw had me laughing outright. Both corgis were standing up on the bed and had moved as close to the TV as they could without falling off. Sherlock was barking his fool head off while Watson would occasionally add her two cents. When she wasn't growling, that is.

Surprised, I leaned toward Watson and double-checked. Yep, sure enough, my quiet, timid girl was growling at the TV. For the record, I should mention that little Watson rarely growled at anything. So, what was she growling at?

It was a show about training dogs—tiny poodles, of all breeds—to do those doggie obstacle courses that the border collies typically won. I shrugged as I looked back at my dogs. I have never cared for poodles. Sure, I've been told they are one of the most intelligent dog breeds there is, but I've never seen the appeal. And those funky haircuts they make the poor dogs wear? It was too bizarre for my taste.

"Bark away, guys. I'm no fan of poodles, either."

Deciding I really didn't want any further distractions, I tip-toed out of the room, snuck back downstairs, and pulled out two worn (and thoroughly chewed) rubber treat dispensers. I stuffed each of them full of dog treats, added a smear of creamy peanut butter, and then carried them back upstairs.

Re-entering the dogs' room, I saw that neither of them had budged an inch. Then, in perfect unison, both noses lifted and I could hear each of them sniffing the air. I placed both of the treat-filled dispensers in front of them and hastily exited the room.

I didn't hear a peep out of them for nearly a half hour.

I was making significant progress on my book. I was about three-quarters of the way through and had just stopped to make an adjustment to one of my female character's clothes. My description of her Victorian era wardrobe didn't quite sound right, specifically her leggings, so I decided to do a few last-minute re-writes.

Wanting to be sure I had placed appropriate attire on my Victorian-era character, I made the mistake of looking up tights and fishnets on the Internet, and I can only assume Google's logic went something like this:

Search query for fishnets detected. Considering acceptable results.

1st suggestion: women in fishnets?
2nd suggestion: women out of fishnets?
3rd suggestion: women sans attire?

Would anyone like to guess which one Google ended up choosing? Needless to say, I got an eyeful. Damn suggestive searches. I miss the good old days where I could do a simple search for something, and that's all I'd get. Now, these search engines are scrambling to predict what you want to see and have it pre-loaded for you. Before you've even finished typing it.

It's a pain.

After I hastily cleared out my browsing history, purged the temporary data from my computer, and scheduled an immediate virus scan of every square inch of my hard drive, I finally felt like I could relax again. Sometimes the Internet was more trouble than its worth. Most of the time, however, it...

My cell phone buzzed angrily. I got the distinct impression it didn't like being muted. Well, who was calling this time?

"Zack? It's Vance."

"Hey, buddy. What's up?"

"Remember when you offered your help just a little while ago?"

"Mm-hmm. What's the matter? Why do you sound so spooked?"

"I need your help, pal. Badly."

"Of course. What do you need us to do?"

"Meet me at the park on Oregon Street."

"What? The park where I called you from earlier?"

"Yes, that's the one. Put a rush on it, Zack."

"Why? What's the matter? What's happened?"

"They took my dog, Zack. Anubis has been stolen!"

THREE

A large crowd had gathered by the time the dogs and I returned to the same park we had visited earlier in the day. Sherlock and Watson were both whining with anticipation, seeing how each of them had recognized our present location. Sherlock looked over at me, barked exasperatedly, and whined again. He pawed the door.

"I'm working on it," I grumbled. "Give me a minute, okay?"

Once the dogs had been placed on the ground, they immediately pulled me over toward the throngs of people. I couldn't help but notice it was the same area where we had played ball earlier. Coincidence? You tell me.

I heard several excited whispers as we navigated our way through the mass of onlookers. I heard several people say something about the appearance of Pomme Valley's cutest crime-fighting duo, and how quickly they'd solve the case. I had to laugh. They sure weren't talking about me. Then I saw something that had me rushing to intervene: several people were reaching out to the dogs, expecting to be able to give them a friendly pat on the back. Now, ordinarily, I wouldn't mind if someone wanted to pet the dogs, and I knew that neither of them would mind. However, that was if you approached from the front, where they could see you. I wasn't too sure how they'd respond to being surprised by a stranger touching their rear.

"Make sure they're watching you," I warned, as I saw the outstretched hands. "Sherlock and Watson are friendly, but as a courtesy, I always make sure that they are never surprised. They... Hey, Tori!"

Tori came hurrying out of the crowd, with her two young daughters in tow. Victoria and Tiffany, Vance and Tori's girls, eleven and nine respectively, were puffy-eyed, had tear-streaked faces, and were both sniffling. Tori looked as though she had been crying, too.

"Zack! I'm so glad to see you. Did my husband ... have you spoken with Vance?"

"I know about Anubis," I quietly confirmed as I cast a quick look at the two young girls. Tori's daughters were already upset. The last thing I needed—or wanted—was to further aggravate the situation. "What happened? Where did you last see him?"

Tori turned to point back at the way they had come.

"We were just throwing the ball around, like we've always done. When Victoria threw the ball, it..." Tori hesitated as she heard her oldest daughter sniff loudly. Her voice lowered. "Please excuse us. You're not catching us at our best. As I was saying, the ball went into the trees just over there. Anubis went in after it. We gave him a few moments and then called him back."

"He never returned," I guessed.

Tori nodded miserably.

"Can you show me the exact point where Anubis went into the trees?"

Tori wiped the corners of her eyes and slowly nodded. Right about then, she looked down and noticed the corgis, both of which were staring up at her. She smiled and instantly squatted down to their level. Sherlock and Watson swarmed all over her. Both of the dogs could sense that something wasn't right, and both were doing their best to offer comfort to an extended member of their pack.

"Look!" Victoria cried as she spied Sherlock. "It's Mr. Anderson's dogs!"

Tiffany shyly approached, patted Watson once on her back, and when the timid corgi gave the friendly gesture a lick in return, Tiffany wrapped her arms around the corgi in a full-on bear hug. Within moments, the young girl was rocking in place, with the corgi swaying in place with her.

"Who would have taken our dog, Zack?" Tori quietly asked. "Why would they take him? He's our dog. We have to get him back. The girls are devastated!"

"I wish I had an answer for you," I slowly

began. "What I can promise you is..."

"I'm so sorry!" Victoria practically wailed, startling everyone within a twenty-foot radius. "It's all my fault!"

"No, it isn't," Tori said as she wiped her eyes again. She turned to her eldest daughter and took her hands in her own. "Someone took Anubis from us. You aren't responsible for that."

"But I am!" the young girl insisted. "I'm the one who threw the ball too hard. If it wasn't for me, Anubis would still be here."

"Nonsense," I argued. "You can't blame yourself for this. You didn't force Anubis to run away, did you?"

"Well, no," the girl reluctantly admitted.

"You didn't go up to some stranger and say, 'Hi there. Here. This is my dog. I don't want him anymore. Take him please,' did you?"

The girl's eyes widened. "No!"

"Well, then, you have nothing to worry about."

"Exactly," Tori agreed. "No one is blaming you, sweetheart. Daddy will catch whoever did this."

"Unless we get them first," I quietly mumbled under my breath.

Tori, overhearing, managed a sly grin.

"Daddy!" Victoria all but shouted. The young girl sprinted across the crowded park and threw herself into her father's arms, just as Vance was exiting his vehicle.

"It's okay, Vick," Vance was telling his eldest daughter. "We'll get Anubis back. That's a promise, baby girl."

"I'm not a baby anymore," Victoria complained, but refused to release her grip of her father's neck.

"I don't suppose you've seen Zack or the corgis, have you?" I heard Vance ask. Victoria still had her arms wrapped around her father, and together, they started my way. Vance's irregular gait reminded me of a clumsy three-legged sack race, since Victoria refused to let go of her father's waist, and he was forced to carry her weight every time he took a step.

Victoria nodded. "Yes. Mr. Anderson is here. He was talking with Mom."

"I'm over here, pal," I called out to my friend as he slowly approached.

Victoria continued to act as dead weight, causing Vance to stumble a few times. My friend gently pried his daughter's arms off and smiled affectionately at her.

"Daddy has to go to work. Zack and I are gonna find out who did this. When we do, I'm... Tiffany? What's the matter? Are you okay?"

Vance's youngest daughter was still cradling Watson and gently rocking in place. I took one look at the pair of them and silently handed Watson's leash to Tori. I nudged Sherlock to get his attention.

"Watson can stay here. Tiffany, will you take

care of her for me?"

The girl looked briefly up at me and gave me a barely perceptible nod.

"Thank you. We'll be right back. Sherlock? Ready to go to work?"

As we headed toward the woods, I sidled closer to Vance and saw that he had a look of grim determination on his face. I can only imagine what type of phone call he must have had with Tori after being told that Anubis was missing, and quite possibly, the latest victim of this notorious dognapper. I looked down at Sherlock and shuddered. How would I feel if someone took one of my dogs from me? If I had to, I'd spend every cent in the bank to get them back.

"We'll find him, pal," I quietly vowed.

"I sure hope so," Vance muttered. "Anubis is a momma's boy. There are times when I think that dog only tolerates my presence because Tori makes him. His loyalty is definitely to her and the girls, not to me."

"Has he ever run off like this before?" I asked as we stepped foot inside the woods. We navigated around a few trees as we checked the area for clues. "Victoria said she thought she was to blame, having thrown the ball too hard. I mean, what in the world happened? How on earth did those dognappers manage to make off with a dog the size of Anubis? I mean, he's a German Shepherd, and a highly intimidating one at that. I would have thought he'd bite anyone who tried to lay a finger on him that he didn't personally know."

Vance nodded. "True story. He's very protective of us, and a simple growl is all it typically takes to make anyone head in the other direction."

I felt a tug on my leash. Sherlock was pulling me over to a huge tree with thick green bushes growing completely around the trunk. Sherlock stopped at the closest bush and lowered his nose to the ground, sniffing cautiously. I glanced over at Vance. He had stopped walking and was studying the corgi intently.

"Did you find something, boy?" Vance hopefully asked. "Is there something there?"

Sherlock woofed softly. He promptly sat, sniffed again at the base of the bush, and turned back to us. He woofed again.

"I'll take that as a big 10-4," Vance muttered. He knelt down on the ground so he could lower his head to look under the bush. With a grunt of surprise, he pulled out a brand new, nearly drool-free yellow tennis ball.

"That couldn't have been under there for too long," I mused. "Look at this thing. It looks brand new. Do you think it's the ball Anubis was chasing?"

Vance studied the fuzzy yellow tennis ball for a few moments.

"I'm not sure. I'll ask when we go back. If it is, is there anything else in the area? Foot prints?

Dog tracks? Sherlock, do you see anything else?"

Sherlock had been watching Vance hold the ball. When it became apparent that he wouldn't be given the toy, his nose dropped back to the ground. He sniffed the base of the bush, snorted, and then tugged on the leash. It looked as if he wanted to check the rest of the bushes.

"There's nothing else here, Sherlock," I told the corgi, once we had made a complete circuit of the tree. "What else would you like to check out?"

We canvassed the surrounding area. Nothing attracted Sherlock's interest. He didn't even pause to sniff the air. Quite the contrary, it looked as though he thought I was simply taking him for a walk. As we returned to the same bush that had the ball under it, Sherlock suddenly turned to look back toward the park. His hackles raised and he started woofing.

"What's he doing?" Vance asked. Curious, he turned to look back the way they had come. "Is there something back that way?"

"The park is back that way, right?"

Vance turned to stare incredulously at me.

"Seriously? Are you asking me what I think you're asking? Come on, man. Your sense of direction can't be that bad."

"It is, and I am."

"Right. Well, yes. That's the way we came in. Why?"

"That's the way Sherlock wants to go," I

pointed out. "Let's go see what's gotten him so riled up."

When we made it back to the park, we were shocked to see nearly three times the number of people present. Apparently, word had gone out that there had been yet another dognapping, and the people of Pomme Valley were appearing in droves in order to help search. The moment we arrived back on the scene, however, was the point in which pandemonium broke out.

"Look! It's a corgi! That must be Sherlock!"

"Isn't he cute?"

"He must be looking for the missing dog! He must be friends with the missing dog!"

"He helps solve crimes, you nincompoop. Of course he's looking for the missing dog."

As it happens, Sherlock was friends with … make that, *is* friends with Anubis. I'd better not let Vance or Tori hear me talking in the past tense like that. They're already stressed out enough as it is.

A surge of people pressed forward, intent on meeting Sherlock in person. I managed to look down at my dog just as I watched his ears slowly fold flat against his head. Anyone who owns a dog will know that when their ears drop like that, it's typically not a good thing. Sherlock started growling.

Ever the observant officer, Vance hurriedly stepped in front of me and Sherlock, held out a hand, and signaled everyone to stop.

"Please keep your distance, people. We're on official business. We ... hey! What the--? Zack, check it out! I can see Watson, only I don't see Tiffany anywhere."

Surprised, I looked up, "She must have gotten away from her. What do you want to bet she heard Sherlock growl? Grab her leash, would you?"

There wasn't any need. Watson came bounding over to us, took her place by Sherlock's side, and added her own growls to that of her packmate's. Concerned, I looked down at the two of them before lifting my eyes to study the crowd of people. What was spooking them?

There were faces in the crowd that I recognized. The big dude from the antique store was present. I think his name was Burt. He caught my eye and nodded in my direction. Then there was Woody and his daughter, Zoe. They both looked distressed. I could see teenagers, men and women in business attire, young mothers with children, and even a group of senior citizens all standing nervously about.

Watson whined, and started fidgeting in place. If I didn't know any better, I'd say she was nervous about something. A loud clamor had me looking up. The cause of her discomfort was easy enough to figure out. There were too many people present. All were jostling with each other, having arguments, and giving opinions, even though no one was asking for them. It was too much to bear.

"I'm getting them out of here," I told Vance. "I think they're on overload at the moment."

"Agreed. Let me go find Tori and the girls. I need to ask about this ball. It's the only piece of evidence we've got."

As if by magic, Tori appeared next to Vance. She quickly spotted me, noticed I was holding two leashes, and breathed a visible sigh of relief.

"Tiffany? She's over here! Watson found her daddy! It's okay, sweetheart!"

Two very sullen girls appeared. Vicki was still sniffling and now Tiffany had a crestfallen look on her face. More so than she had fifteen minutes ago, that is. I squatted down next to Tiffany and smiled at the girl.

"Hey, it's okay. Were you worried about Watson? The little booger does that all the time to me, too. If she can get away from me, she can certainly get away from you. She must have heard Sherlock."

"I'm sorry she got away from me," her timid voice said.

"No harm done. Vance? Do you have something you need to ask Victoria?"

Curious, Victoria looked at her father and waited. Vance pulled out the tennis ball and held it out to her. I waited with bated breath to see what the girl's reaction would be.

"Is this the ball you were throwing for Anubis?" Vance asked his daughter.

Victoria took one look at the ball and burst into tears. Vance sighed and immediately thrust the ball back into his jacket pocket. He pulled his daughter in for a hug.

"Well, that answers that," I quietly said.

"Did you find anything else?" Tori asked, lowering her voice so neither of the girls could hear. "Tell me Sherlock found something."

I nodded. "He did, yes. He found that ball."

"But nothing else?" Tori pressed.

"Nothing, I'm afraid," I admitted. "I took him all around the area where we found the ball, but nothing attracted his interest."

"That's so very disappointing," Tori sadly said. She stifled a sob. "Do you think he's okay?"

"Knowing Anubis, I'm sure he's fine," I assured her. "I can only hope he took a chunk out of who-ever snatched him."

"You and me both," Tori agreed. "Do you want to know what really concerns me?"

I swallowed nervously. Did I want to know this?

"Uh, sure."

"What if Anubis is lost in there? What if … what if he's become hurt and can't find his way out? This park is right up against forest land. There are any number of places for a dog to get lost."

"You can't think that way, Tor," Vance said as he released his daughter and turned to face his wife. "We checked the area where the ball was found. There were no tracks, no footprints, no nothing."

Tori stopped in mid-sob and stared at Vance. She shook her head, sending her long red tresses tumbling about.

"No tracks? That doesn't make any sense. There should have been something there. Are you sure you looked everywhere?"

"You said that the ball was thrown into the woods just over there," I reminded Tori as I pointed at the beginning of a path. "That's where we went into the trees, and that's where Sherlock found the ball. He never hesitated. He went straight over to a bush and found it."

"That's not where I said to go," a small voice piped up. Vance, Tori, and I turned to look. Victoria had her hands on her hips and was frowning at us. The girl turned to point at a spot nearly thirty feet away. "The ball bounced over there."

"Then why did we find the ball over here?" I asked.

"You most certainly did not," Tori argued, at the same time as she stared at her oldest daughter. "I was here, young lady. I watched where you pointed. They went into the trees at the exact spot you had indicated."

"Well, maybe I did, and maybe I didn't," Victoria pouted. "What I meant was, the ball went in over there."

"Like father, like daughter," I quietly mumbled.

Vance frowned at me while Tori looked away with the beginnings of a smile. I gave the dogs' leashes a gentle tug and pointed them toward the second spot. Sherlock was already headed in that direction. After a few moments of hesitation, Watson followed suit.

"We'll be right back," Vance promised. "We're going to check it out. We can't leave any stone unturned."

"We'll be here," Tori assured us.

"Listen, pal," Vance told me in a hushed tone, just as soon as we were out of earshot, "I am so sorry about that. Victoria can be a little scatter-brained at times."

"What, are you talking about Watson? Don't sweat it. She gets away from me all the time. So does Sherlock, for that matter."

"I was referring to Victoria sending us off on a wild goose chase. Tiffany was the one who was holding onto Watson."

I shrugged. "No worries. Sherlock found the ball, didn't he? It wasn't a total loss."

"True. I can only hope that he … Zack, look. What's Sherlock looking at now?"

Sherlock had dropped his nose back to the ground and was cautiously sniffing the dirt, as though he had picked up a peculiar scent.

"I'm not sure. Sherlock? Whatcha got there, buddy?"

Sherlock woofed once, turned to look up at me, and then returned his gaze to the ground.

Vance brushed by me to squat down low, next to Sherlock. He gently ran a hand along the ground.

"Well, well. What have we here? Good job, buddy."

Sherlock's nub of a tail threatened to wiggle right off his derriere.

"What is it?" I asked, as I squatted down next to my friend.

"We have ourselves what looks like a tire mark."

I studied the single tire impression that had been pressed into the soft earth. I turned my head to follow the track backward, intent on seeing its origination. The tire track terminated at a huge fern.

"What only leaves one tire mark?" I quizzically asked. "A bicycle? How do you steal a dog with a bike?"

"You don't," Vance said. "Look at this track, Zack. There's only one. It's narrow enough to be a bike tire, but the track is so very shallow."

"So?"

"That suggests a couple of possibilities. First, the bike that made this mark was incredibly light, or two, the person riding it was small, like a kid. Plus, have you ever tried to ride a bike in a straight line for an extended period of time? It's almost impossible. There'd be variances in the impression which would indicate two tires. Look around, pal. The ground is uneven. It's nowhere close to being level. Besides, I think this mark did not come from a bike."

"Then what's it from?" I asked. "A unicycle?"

"I'm thinking we're looking for a wheelbarrow."

I groaned. Of course. What else would you use if you had a 70-80 pound dog to move? I really ought to stick to making wine. And, truth be told, I wasn't even good at that. Caden was.

A wheelbarrow. That meant that someone had to be holding the handles, which meant that there should be footprints on the ground. I glanced over at Vance, but he was already squatting low and scanning the earth. Clearly, he arrived at that conclusion long before I did.

"See anything?" I hopefully asked. "Any footprints?"

"Well, this strip of dirt is too narrow," Vance said, as he ran his hands lightly across the breadth of the dirt trail. "I can see some depressions in the grass on either side, which suggests that someone had walked through here fairly recently."

"But no discernible tracks," I guessed.

Vance nodded. "Unfortunately not, damn it."

"Well, let's see where the tracks go. Sherlock, lead the way."

Sherlock sniffed the ground, turned to look up at me, shook his collar, and then proceeded to head off down the path, away from the park. As Vance and I walked deeper into the forest, we couldn't help but notice the popularity of the path we were on. It seemed as though we were passed by joggers every couple of minutes or so. The last person to pass by was pushing one of those three-wheeled jogging strollers. As soon as the woman had disappeared down the trail, Vance shook his head.

"I know what you're thinking. Don't bother. Those tires were way too skinny. We're still looking for a wheelbarrow."

"Do you really think we'll find it?" I asked.

Vance shook his head. "No, but I am hoping this trail will shine some light on how some creep managed to steal my dog and get away with it."

Two more joggers passed by us, talking animatedly between themselves as though they were sitting in a coffee shop. I shook my head with amazement. I can pretty much guaran-damn-tee you that if I were jogging, there would be no way I could carry on a conversation. Not without sounding like a chain-smoking asthmatic.

A nagging thought occurred.

"Shouldn't we have someone blocking the trail so the people will stop using it? How are we supposed to follow the wheelbarrow track if we can't see it?"

"We lost the track several hundred feet back," Vance nonchalantly informed me. "Right now, we're following Sherlock. I'm willing to give it a few more minutes, but I'm starting to get a bad feeling about this. I don't think we're going to find anything else out here. I think we would have by now."

"You may be right. I get the impression Sherlock thinks I'm taking him on a walk. I haven't seen him sniff the ground in a while."

We heard the sound of approaching footsteps from behind us. Vance immediately turned and held out a hand, indicating he wanted the person to stop. A woman in her early twenties appeared around the bend, saw the two of us, and came to a stop. She pulled a set of earbuds from her ears and looked expectantly at us.

"Yes? Can I help you?"

"Do you know where this trail goes?" Vance asked her.

The woman nodded. "Of course. This trail is one of the more popular hiking trails. My pedometer says it's nearly three miles long."

"Where's the other end of this thing?" I asked. In case I hadn't properly demonstrated how much of a lardball I was, I yawned.

The girl briefly smiled. "This is the trail that will eventually end up just north of the Community Center."

"I'm not walking that far," I groaned.

"Are there any roads anywhere along the way?" Vance hopefully asked.

"Not that I can recall."

"Thank you. You've been very helpful."

The girl replaced her earbuds and resumed

her jog.

"I'm not really up for a three-mile walk," I told my friend. "If you'd like to give it a try, I can give you Sherlock's leash."

Vance shook his head. "No, there's no point. Look over there. Do you see that? Through the trees? That's G Street up there. We're close to a road. It would be fairly easy to park a car out of sight, use the wheelbarrow to move the dog, and then escape without anyone seeing them. Damn. This doesn't bode well."

"What do we do now?"

"Back to the park. I want to see if any of those people saw anything."

We had just stepped foot outside the trees and back into the park when both dogs started growling again. The crowds were still there, but the number of people was considerably less. What were they growling at? Had they noticed something? Should I mention it to Vance?

Deciding I should tell him, regardless of how foolish it sounded, I tapped my detective friend on the shoulder.

"What?"

"There's something you ought to know."

"What's that?"

"This is the second time we've returned to the park and Sherlock has started growling."

Surprised, Vance turned to regard the people milling about.

"Is that so? Do you think he suspects something?"

"How should I know? I don't speak dog."

Vance pulled out his notebook and eyed the citizens of PV who were still loitering in the area.

"I'm gonna go talk to them. Someone might have witnessed something, regardless of whether or not it's pertinent."

"What should we do?" I asked as I looked down at the dogs.

"Go home. I need to stay here and keep searching. I have to be able to tell the girls that I did all that I could to try and find Anubis."

"Then I'll stay with you."

"While I'm interviewing potential witnesses? I don't need the dogs for that. Zack, do me a favor? Go home."

FOUR

There was something about this case that wasn't sitting well with me. PV was a very small town, yet this marked the second (that I am aware of) case of a missing dog in the last week. There must be something I was missing. Practically all the dognapping cases I had ever read about involved some punk taking the dog and then waiting until a cash reward was offered, thereby allowing the perpetrator to simply stroll up and collect the money. It made me wonder if that's what was happening here. Who in their right frame of mind would steal a dog with the sole intent on collecting a reward?

Damn punks. But, I digress. Back to the business at hand.

I picked up the copy of the Medford file and began to read. The first owner had offered a reward. In fact, the Labrador's owner was so desperate to get his dog back that he had put up several collectible rifles valued at close to $10K. I know. I looked up their value. The townsfolk were gonna go ape once that news broke. Whether or not Vance will offer a reward for Anubis' return remains to be seen.

I felt that the chances of all this happening in a tiny town like Pomme Valley were remote. And I mean very remote. There had to be a reason this was happening. I do think it would be interesting to see if anyone tried to collect the collector's rifle offered by the first owner. However, I had a sneaking suspicion the reward would remain unclaimed, regardless of how many people would try to collect it.

Nevertheless, I wanted to do some research. I wanted to know if anyone else in the area had reported the theft of their beloved pets. In this day and age, everything seemed to be computerized. It was worth a shot, wasn't it?

Once I was back home, I headed upstairs to my office. Pulling up an Internet search engine, I entered my search parameter and crossed my fingers.

Missing dogs in Rascal River Valley Oregon

I know. It was a fairly generic search, but I was eager to see what came up. After a moment's hesitation, the web page returned a page full of results. After scrolling through the "sponsored results," which took up the top half of the page, I began to skim through the matches. My hopes fell as I saw links to various police departments, breeder pages, outdoor fishing, Pomme Valley wines, and a slew of others. Clearly the search engine couldn't find all my search terms in one location, so it gave me partial hits, only the returned results were nowhere close to what I needed.

One of the web pages caught my eye. The link in question was from a family's personal blog, and it was a plea to the general public to help the post go viral. The family was missing its dog.

Intrigued, I leaned forward and clicked on the link. What I read broke my heart. The family's beloved golden retriever, Sandy, had been reported missing after a scheduled two day stop in Medford. The family had evidently decided to stop by one of the city's parks to enjoy a picnic lunch and had let their dog out to run around. I'm sure you can guess the rest. After spending the rest of their vacation searching for their beloved dog, they ended up returning to their home in San Antonio, Texas, empty-handed. This was nearly three years ago.

My eyes skimmed through the details of the story. Hmmm. Just like the other dognappings, this one had happened during the daytime, too. Not only that, but according to the article, the park was packed with people. Medford, I was dismayed to learn, had more than twenty parks scattered across the city. This particular theft occurred in Prescott Park, their largest.

My eyebrows shot up as I found the details of the park online. Over 1,700 acres? For a park? Wow. That would be a lot of territory to cover. No wonder nothing turned up on the missing dog.

Curious to see if there were any other reported missing dogs in the Medford area, I tried a few more searches. Wouldn't you know it? I found evidence of five other missing dogs—all of them happening around three years ago—and all without any type of resolution.

I reached for my cell. Vance needed to hear about this. Why anyone else hadn't discovered this was beyond me.

"Hey, Zack. What's up?"

"You're not going to believe what I found online."

"You found something? And Sherlock wasn't involved?"

"Thanks a lot, pal."

"All right. Hit me with your best shot. Whatcha got?"

"On a hunch, I decided to see if there were any other cases involving missing dogs in the surrounding area. I started with Medford. I ..."

"We already know, buddy," Vance interrupted.

"You do?"

"Six cold cases where the perp was never caught. That's nearly half a dozen families who never got their dogs back, Zack."

I felt totally deflated.

"Oh."

"It's a good attempt. We might be able to get you to stop writing romance novels and start working on crime stories yet. Out of curiosity, did you look at any other areas besides Medford?"

"Umm, no. Should I have?"

"Well, a good detective would have ... I'm just messin' with you. As soon as the first dog was reported missing, we called our pals over at MPD and had them send over all cases that had anything to do with a missing dog."

"And you've got those files now?"

"I'm looking right at 'em."

"Cool. Have you found ... wait. Wait a moment. You said 'just under half a dozen families' yet you said there were six cases."

"Wow. That took you way too long to notice. You'd better stick with romance."

"Bite me, pal. Spill. What did you mean by that?"

"Of those six missing dogs, one of them was returned."

"What? Which one? How? Why?"

"That's what I was getting ready to find out. Wanna tag along?"

"Heck yeah! Umm, with or without the dogs?"

"You know what? Bring them along. Our dog owner might be more inclined to talk to us if he sees another dog owner. Bear in mind, we need to stop by the MPD station first."

"Why?"

"As you may or may not know, Medford is out of my jurisdiction, Zack. While I'm certain Chief Steingartner wouldn't mind me asking a few questions, after all, he is one of my father's golfing buddies, it is considered professional courtesy to ask permission first."

"Couldn't we just call him on the phone?"

"Who, the chief or the guy who got his dog back?"

"Either. Or both."

"Captain Nelson and Chief Steingartner are pretty good friends. I wouldn't want to do anything that'd make PV look bad. Plus, I have several buddies on the force there I haven't seen in a while. I wouldn't mind saying hello. Besides, I think he'd like to meet you, Zack."

"Oh, great. This isn't someone who thinks I'm guilty of murder and belongs in a cell, is it?"

"Nope. Well, not that I'm aware of. He is a fan of the dogs, though."

"Ah. Got it."

* * *

"So, would these two be the famous Sherlock and Watson I've heard so much about?"

I nodded. "Yes, they be. Are. They are. I mean, yes, they are."

Vance chuckled. "Switch to decaf, okay? Relax. You're fine."

We were standing in a conference room inside the MPD station house where every, and I do mean every, cop on duty in the Medford area looked to be present. I was able to count at least twenty different officers before the constant shuffling of people inside the room made me lose track. Every single one of them wanted to meet the dogs in person. Every single one of them received a friendly lick from each of the dogs. I later found out that Medford employed over fifty police officers, as opposed to the paltry eight who worked for PVPD. Chief Steingartner explained that, while Medford had a population that was over 75,000 strong, the Medford metro area had well over 200,000 people in it. An area that size needed a larger police force, and as such, had a larger budget.

The Chief of Medford Police was a robust man in his early fifties, at least 5'10" tall, and had a full head of thick black hair. I could see some type of tattoo on the chief's right arm, extending at least six inches below the sleeve of his short-sleeve uniform. I sidled closer to see if I could tell what the tattoo depicted.

It was a design I had seen before. Well, not this exact design, but the same elements were there. It was a dagger with an eagle clutching a globe in its claws. Wrapped helically around the two images was a ribbon, and on it were the words "Death ... Before ... Dishonor." It was a design commonly used by US Marines when getting tattooed on their arms, legs, backs, etc. Looks like the chief was a former Marine.

Chief Steingartner squatted down next to the dogs and patted both of the corgis on their heads. Doggie biscuits were produced and offered. Sherlock and Watson gently took the proffered treats and quietly crunched them up. Little snots. They still snap up any goodies I give them, threatening to take my fingers off at the second knuckle. One would think I starved them on a regular basis.

"No wonder the crime rate has been dropping in PV," one cop snickered. "Look at those two. I'm sure the crooks are shaking in their boots whenever they see those two coming."

The chief angrily stood and rounded on the one who had spoken.

"Is that so? Well, Mr. Mitchell, for your information, those dogs are responsible for solving three murder cases. One case kept their owner out of jail, another involved a missing pendant —which Sherlock there located—and the third case involved catching a serial burglar who had stepped up to murder and was wanted in multiple states. Tell me again, Mitchell, how many cases have you solved in the last year? What's that? None? These dogs have a better record than you, detective. I'd keep your comments to yourself."

Properly shamed, the detective dropped his eyes to the ground. "Yes, sir. I'm sorry, chief."

Chief Steingartner turned back to the two of us.

"Now, Detective Samuelson, Mr. Anderson. What can the Medford Police Department do for you?"

Vance stepped forward and held up a manila folder.

"We're checking out a series of missing dogs in PV," my friend began. "After we did some checking, we saw that a few years ago, Medford had a rash of similar cases. We were hoping we could compare notes, be allowed to talk to some of the people involved, that sort of thing."

"Who do you want to talk to?" Chief Steingartner inquired.

"Three years ago, over a span of seven or eight months, Medford had a number of missing dogs. However, one of them returned. I was hoping we'd be able to look at the original file and track the owner down."

The chief was silent for a few moments, but then his face broke out into a huge grin.

"Sure, why not? They're only dogs. I see no harm in that."

Only dogs? *Only dogs?* Obviously, the captain of the Medford PD had never been a dog owner. No self-respecting owner of a dog ever thinks of their beloved pet as a possession. Rather, they're companions. At least, that's what Sherlock and Watson are to me.

So, thanks to that little comment, I was now frowning. A quick glance at my friend confirmed he was, too. Vance noticed my scowl and quickly nudged me, shaking his head no. He managed to throw his face into neutral just before the chief looked his way.

"Thank you, Chief Steingartner. If you could just point out the way to your records room?"

"I'll do better than that," the chief told us. He glanced around the room, as if he were searching for someone. His eyes lit up as he saw a girl with her back to us, filing paperwork inside an open three-drawer filing cabinet. "Cindy, would you come over here for a moment?"

The girl threw a glance over her shoulder to see who was talking. Noticing that it was the chief, she hurriedly jammed a few folders inside the top drawer, closed the cabinet, and hurried over. She was short, around five feet tall, had shoulder length blonde hair that was tied into a pony tail, and was wearing a beige blouse with a matching skirt. A secretary, perhaps?

"This is Cindy, one of our interns. She handles a lot of the records. She'll show you to the records room and see to it that you get what you need."

The girl smiled brightly at us and nodded. Her gaze dropped to the floor and her eyes widened. She even let out a little gasp.

"Oh, aren't they cute! They're corgis, aren't they?"

I nodded. "Yes, ma'am. This is Sherlock, and the other is Watson."

The girl gasped again. "Sherlock and Watson? Ohmygosh, I've heard of these two. From Pomme Valley, right?"

"I told you everyone knows your dogs," Vance

laughed. He looked at the girl and smiled. "Detective Vance Samuelson, PVPD. This is Zack Anderson, owner of Lentari Cellars."

Chief Steingartner, in the process of sitting down in one of the chairs in the conference room, practically leapt to his feet.

"You own Lentari Cellars? Really? You make one fantastic bottle of wine, my friend."

I chuckled and shook my head. "I wish I could take the credit, but I can't. I will pass that on to my winemaster, though. He's the one who makes all the magic happen."

"Gentlemen, if you'll follow me."

We followed the intern down several indistinguishable hallways, stepped through a number of rooms, until we came to a large, heavy metal door. Before I could order myself not to react, I snorted, but quickly disguised it as a cough. Heavy metal. Jeez. What was I, a teenager?

"It's right through here. Can you tell me what you're looking for? I might be able to help you."

"Well, we already know we'd like to talk to the dog owner who had his dog stolen, but somehow managed to recover it."

"How long ago was this?" Cindy asked as she began flipping switches on a nearby panel, which had about six switches total. Overhead, large fluorescent lights flickered into life.

We were now in a large, cavernous room that was filled with aisles of metal shelving stacked high with boxes and plastic bins. What I was looking at reminded me of one of those warehouse stores, the kind where its damn-near impossible to find what you're looking for, and trying to find someone to help is even more difficult. Stacks of boxes and bins climbed all the way to the ceiling, nearly ten feet above my head. I sure hope someone had all this stuff catalogued and indexed.

"About three years ago," Vance told her. "You're an intern? I didn't think interns were required to dress up in business casual attire."

"We're not," Cindy assured us, with a smile. "I hope to find a job here someday, so I'd like to make a good impression."

"What type of job are you looking for?" I asked as we followed the girl inside the large room.

"One day I would love to become a detective. For now, anything that offers a paycheck would be nice."

"If I had any say in it, I would hire you," Vance assured the girl.

"Is PVPD hiring?" Cindy asked.

Vance shook his head, "Not that I'm aware of, I'm sorry."

"That's okay. Now, let me think. Missing dogs. I think I remember hearing about that. That should be in Number 3."

Cindy promptly approached a set of four huge filing cabinets, selected the top drawer of the third cabinet, and slid it out. She flipped through a few files before she shook her head, closed the drawer, and selected the next one down. After a few more moments of fruitless searching, she closed the second drawer and tried the third. Thankfully, the fourth drawer yielded what she was looking for, since she pulled out a huge armful of manila folders and slowly walked back to us. Then she noticed the large, dented metal table and changed course.

"Let's see," Cindy said, as she dropped the stack on the table and opened the first file, "we're looking for missing dogs. I've pulled every case that happened three years ago. It doesn't look like there's any rhyme or reason to the filing system here, except that the cases are in chronological order. I'll start with this stack. Detective, you start with that one. If these missing dogs were reported three years ago, then they'll be in here somewhere."

"Can I help?" I asked.

Cindy slid several dozen folders my way.

"Help yourself. The more the merrier."

Thirty minutes later, we found what we needed. I mean, come on. Medford might be bigger than PV, but it's still a small town as far as I was concerned. It wasn't that hard to find a specific type of case file.

Cindy smiled politely, returned the unneeded files to the cabinets, and excused herself. I opened the first folder in front of me and skimmed through the contents and immediately set it aside. An elderly woman's miniature schnauzer was stolen and, sadly, was never returned.

My next folder contained all the files for a missing boxer, owned by a single guy a few years younger than me. His dog, too, was also never recovered. I quietly placed the folder in my discard pile.

"One missing schnauzer, and one missing boxer so far," I glumly reported. "Here's a missing Chow. Whatcha got over there?"

"I've got a missing Australian Shepherd, and this one," Vance began, flipping open the newest folder, "has one Portuguese ... wow. I have no idea how to say that."

"A Portuguese Water Dog?" I slowly asked, confused about which word my friend could possibly be stumbling over.

"I've heard of Portuguese Water Dogs, smartguy," Vance grumped. "This one, though, is a Portuguese Podengo ... um, Pehqueeno."

"Say what?" I demanded, abandoning my file and standing up so I could lean over Vance's shoulder. "Say that again?"

Vance slid the file over to me, "No way. You say it."

I had taken one semester of remedial Spanish in high school. I could only hope I was doing my old teacher justice.

"Portuguese Podengo Pequeno. Wow. Never

heard of it."

Vance suddenly grunted with surprise and tapped the same page I was looking at, only farther down.

"Zack, this is our guy. Look. It says here that his dog was recovered."

"Got an address?" I asked as I gathered up my files and carefully put them on top of the filing cabinet in the tray provided.

"Yep, it's here. Come on. I want to see what kind of dog this Portuguese thingy is. I've never heard of them and yet there's one in town? Do you think it's a coincidence that the strangest sounding breed that we've ever heard of just happens to be nearby?"

"The AKC has some pretty crazy sounding breeds of dogs, pal," I argued. "Wanna hear the weirdest I've ever heard of? There's a breed of some Mexican hairless dog that I can never pronounce that starts with an 'x'. That one would have my vote."

"Hmmph."

"Look, there are pictures in here," I commented, as we paged through the file.

"Pictures are commonly found in a police file, Zack," Vance reminded me as he threw me an unsettling look.

"You know what I mean. Look at this one. Tire tracks. Do you think they're the same as the one we saw yesterday?"

Vance studied the picture for a few moments

before shaking his head, "Nope. Look. You can see two distinct marks in the dirt. Unless there were two reported dogs at the same time, and the perp made two trips, I'd say not."

"I'm surprised someone didn't run those treads through that database you're always bragging about."

Vance flipped a page in the report and tapped a yellow sheet of paper.

"They did. Here are the results."

Eager to hear more about the tires, I leaned forward.

"The tires are a generic 12" by 2.25" design found in many stores."

"What type of store would carry a tire that small?" I asked, bewildered.

"Off the top of my head, I'd say any store that sells baby supplies."

"Huh?'

"These are stroller tires, Zack. In fact, the report even goes one step further and says that these tires are typically found on jogging strollers. You know, the ones with the big, rubber tires?"

"Ah. Got it. That doesn't really help us, does it?"

Vance shook his head. "Nope."

"Now what?"

Vance closed the file and placed it in a tray with several others.

"Now we go talk to this guy and see if he

knows why his dog was returned to him."

* * *

"I'd like to help you guys, but I haven't a clue why my dog was returned to me."

We were sitting inside the home of Mark Cooper, owner of Rico, the Portuguese Podengo Pequeno. Vance actually had Mark repeat the name of Rico's breed several times to ensure he had the pronunciation down. I am proud to say that I actually got the pronunciation right. Rico's owner and Vance were sitting on a sectional couch that fit neatly in the corner of the living room while I chose to sit on a recliner opposite them. Sherlock and Watson took up their posts on either side of my chair, choosing to sit rather than lay down. It almost looked as though I had two guard dogs keeping an eye on me, only there was no way a corgi could pull off an intimidating look.

The dogs were silently staring at each other. Rico, being less than four years old, had his butt up in the air with his tail swinging wildly back and forth. He wanted to play and was hoping the corgis did, too. Both Sherlock and Watson continued to regard the newcomer without making a sound.

Oh. I guess you're probably curious about Rico. I'll pass on what I learned from some online research, since his owner, incredibly enough, didn't know too much about the breed. Rico is a Portuguese Podengo Pequeno. The breed was recognized by the AKC in 2013. The "Podengos," as their owners typically call them, are a member of the hound group. It is a primitive breed, being known for its small size. I'd have to agree. Rico couldn't be more than thirteen pounds. They have erect ears, like my corgis, have wedge-shaped heads, and come in two coat types: smooth and wire. Rico's coat is long and harsh, and has a bearded muzzle, making him a wire-coat Podengo.

"Look at the size of him," Vance was saying. "Anyone could walk up to him, pick him up, and slide him inside a jacket pocket. I've had cats that were bigger than him."

"Keep your voice down, dude," Mark crossly said. "You'll hurt his feelings."

Prior to becoming a dog owner, I would have laughed at that particular comment. I kid you not. Now, however, having experienced first-hand how sensitive my dogs can be, especially if —God forbid—I have to chastise them for something, I found myself siding with Mark. So, what did I end up doing? I frowned. At Vance. Thankfully, I managed to wipe the scowl off my face before he noticed.

"Podengos are becoming more and more popular," Mark was telling us. "They're the perfect dog. Small, playful, rarely barks, and are good with other dogs. See?" Mark was pointing at the corgis. I looked down in time to see Rico sniff noses with each of the corgis. Watson was giving me the impression that she might like to play. On the other hand, Sherlock was giving me the impression that he wouldn't give Rico the time of day.

Dogs.

"How is he around strangers?" I asked as I leaned down to hold my hand out.

Rico recognized the invitation and promptly trotted over, but was brought up short as Sherlock repositioned himself. He sat in front of my outstretched hand and dared Rico to venture closer. That was enough to send Rico back to Mark's side.

"He loves everyone," Mark was saying. "And that's the problem. It wouldn't take much to get him to go with you."

"Give him a piece of food and he'll follow you anywhere?" Vance guessed.

Mark shook his head. "All you'd have to do is pat him on the head and you're his new best friend."

"Any ideas how Rico got away?" Vance asked as he continued to scribble in his notebook.

Mark shrugged. "Sure, that's the easy part."

Vance's head snapped up at the same time mine did. Mark knew how Rico had escaped? What a break!

"Okay, I'm all ears," Vance said. His pen was hovering just above his pad of paper. "Why would the dognappers let your dog go and no one else's?"

"Oh, they didn't let him go," Mark assured us.

Vance looked as baffled as I felt. He shared a look with me before turning back to continue the interview. He cleared his throat and tried again.

"You told me just a little bit ago that you had an idea why they—namely the dognappers—would let Rico go. Now you say they didn't?"

Mark pointed an accusatory finger at Rico and chuckled, "You'd have to know him. His name may be Rico, but I really should have called him Houdini. He's been escaping from pens ever since I got him at ten weeks old."

"You're suggesting that Rico escaped from his captors by finding a way out of his pen?" I slowly asked.

Mark nodded. "Yes. That's exactly what I'm saying. He's escaped out of every pen I've ever put him in."

"Do you have any idea who'd want to take Rico?" Vance continued.

Mark shrugged again. "Not really. I mean, look at him. He makes friends easily. He gets along with other dogs. People will stop me on the street and tell me how cute he is. On more than one occasion, I've had people tell me they remember meeting Rico before. Do they remember me? Nope. Nada. Nothing."

"I can totally sympathize with you, pal," I murmured. "Been there, done that."

Mark heard me, threw me a grin, and returned his attention to his canine best friend. Rico had reared up on his hind legs and was waiting for his owner to pick him up. It was right about then that I noticed the couch.

The only way I recognized this particular model of couch was because I ended up doing a little bit of research on the model when I introduced several new characters for my latest book. This was a Sloane leather sectional, built by a company called American Leather. This particular model, I knew, typically retailed for around $6,800 in average stores.

My eyebrows shot up. This was an expensive couch for a single man. A quick glance at my friend confirmed that Vance and Mark were now going over a list of potential suspects. I decided to take this time to glance around the living room of the house we were in.

On the wall, a seventy-inch LED TV had been professionally mounted. There, housed in a recessed cabinet set into the wall on the left of the television, I could see the makings of a sophisticated home theater setup. I casually glanced up and confirmed that I saw not one set of surround speakers but two, making the receiver in the cabinet a 7.1 channel electronic miracle I would love to have in my own home.

I inched closer to see if I could get a model name and number. Just then, Sherlock woofed. I immediately glanced down. Much to my delight, Rico's continued perseverance was finally melting Sherlock's cold exterior. It looked like my tri-colored corgi wanted to play.

Returning my attention to the wall cabinet, I noticed several open video game cases scattered on the floor in front of the TV, indicating he had not one, nor two, but three different high-end game systems. Through the hallway on my right, I could see a mountain bike resting against the wall near the door leading into what I assume was the garage.

Then I remembered the car in the driveway as we pulled up. It was a Toyota Highlander, which is already pricey to begin with, but I remembered seeing the 'hybrid' decal below the model name. Those things had to be at least 30K or greater.

Everywhere I looked, I saw something that had a comma in its price tag. This guy was either loaded, or had a family who was loaded. A quick check of the guy's attire and appearance had me leaning toward the latter. He was wearing a faded t-shirt and ripped jeans. No shoes or socks.

"Tell us about the day Rico was taken," Vance instructed.

"I've already been through this," Mark complained.

"I know you have," Vance said as he tried to soften his voice as much as possible. "Anything you can tell us could be helpful."

"You're a cop, right? Can't you just read my

statement from the files?"

"What happened to you has been happening to other dog owners in Pomme Valley," I said, drawing Mark's attention. "Do you remember how bad you felt when you lost Rico? It's happened twice recently. We don't want it to happen to anyone else. Come on, buddy. Just walk us through it, okay?"

"Fine. We went to Prescott Park. It's Rico's favorite park. He loves to run, you see, and he'll typically run circles around any other dog he sees."

"Was he off leash?" Vance asked. His attention was back on his notebook and he was once more taking notes.

"Obviously," Mark snorted. "Anyway, I was throwing a tennis ball for Rico—one of his favorite pastimes—when the damn ball bounced into the trees. Now, since this has happened many times before, I wasn't worried. Rico has always brought the ball back, but not that time."

"What happened?" I asked, as gently as I could.

"Well, whoever it was that took him must've been hiding just inside the trees, because as soon as Rico went after the ball, I heard him yip."

"He yipped," Vance repeated as he wrote in his notebook.

"Was it a yip like you'd hear if you accidentally stepped on him?" I asked.

Mark looked at me with a look of horror on

his face.

"I've never stepped on my dog, thank you very much. But yeah, if something, or someone, surprises him, he'll make a noise like that."

"But no barking?" Vance asked as he continued to look down.

Mark shook his head. "No. No barking."

"The original police report said that Rico was found in the same park a week later?"

Mark nodded. "That's right."

"How did he seem?" I asked.

Both Mark and Vance looked over at me.

"What was that?" Vance asked.

"What do you mean?" Mark asked, at the same time.

"Was he tired, hungry, thirsty, stressed, or scared?"

Mark was silent as he considered the question.

"The people who found him in the park said he didn't seem agitated, or scared. They offered him some water, which he drank a little, but not much. He didn't even act like he was hungry."

Now Vance was nodding, "Which suggested someone was caring for him."

"My thoughts exactly," I confirmed. "But, in the same area?"

Vance looked up. "Hmm?"

"Mr. Cooper said that Rico was found in the same park. Wouldn't that suggest that he was being held somewhere in the vicinity?"

Vance slowly nodded and hastily added more notes to his notebook, "It would. Well, at least, it would in my book."

"Mine, too," Mark added.

"Thank you for your time," Vance formally announced as he rose to his feet and held out a hand. "You've been a big help, Mr. Cooper."

I promptly got to my feet, too. Mark slowly stood and, with a shrug, shook both of our hands.

"I'm not sure how that was helpful, but if it was, you're welcome."

On the way home, Vance and I compared notes.

"Did you see the stuff in the house?" I began. "I'm pretty sure that guy's family is loaded. Huge TV, game systems, home theater system…"

Vance pulled out his notebook, flipped to the first page of notes, and showed it to me.

Affluent dog owner

"That was the first thing I noticed, after the SUV hybrid in the driveway."

"I saw that, too."

"He said that his dog's abduction happened during daytime hours," Vance recalled.

"With people present," I added.

"Right. Another common denominator is the ball. That's precisely what happened with Anubis. What is this guy doing, hanging out in the trees and waiting for an errant ball to bounce inside? That makes no sense whatsoever."

"It happened to that guy with the three chocolate Labs, too," I reminded him. "I just don't know how that could help us."

"Neither do I," Vance admitted.

I checked the back seat of my Jeep and saw that both Sherlock and Watson were snoozing on the seats.

"Talk about an interesting dog breed. I didn't even know that one existed."

Vance nodded. "We've been hit with a wide variety, that's for sure. What have we seen so far?"

"Are you talking about dog breeds? Well, in Medford alone, there was the Miniature Schnauzer, the Boxer, and the Chow."

"I had the Australian Shepherd and the Pachinko," Vance added.

I fought to keep a straight face.

"Er, the Pachinko? Isn't that a Japanese pinball machine? I'm pretty sure they weren't called that."

"Oh, yeah?" Vance countered. "You don't remember any better than I do what that little dog was called."

"Sure I do," I argued. "They were called 'Pankos'."

Vance stared at me as a smile spread across his face, "Pankos, huh? Named after seasoned bread crumbs? Let's face it. Neither of us remember."

I checked the status of the corgis in the rear mirror. Both were still asleep. In fact, both had their mouths cracked open and had their tongues sticking out. Corgis. You gotta love 'em. Thank goodness there hadn't been any other corgis involved. I could only imagine the hell their owners must be going through while...

Wait a minute.

Schnauzers, Boxers, Chow Chows, Australian Shepherds, and Pankos, or whatever they're called. All different breeds. No repeats. I didn't know off the top of my head which breeds had disappeared from PV, other than the chocolate Lab, but I had a sneaking suspicion that the breeds were all different there, too. Was this significant? Could this be the first clue to help us crack this case and find Anubis?

FIVE

B ack! Get back, foul de-
mon! Go back to the pits of hell from
whence you came!"

Titters of laughter met my ears. Curious, I
leaned around Caden—and his blasted Suitcase
of Samples—to see who was laughing at me. Apparently, two kids—who looked to be around
sixteen or so—had snuck in behind my winemaster. Why Caden decided to bring two teenagers with him, I'm not sure.

The girl was slim, had brown shoulder-length
hair, hazel eyes, and was wearing a dark purple
shirt with (of all things!) gold shorts. The boy
was just as slim as the girl, had short brown
hair, and was a few inches taller. Oddly enough,
he was also wearing purple and gold clothing.
Were they making a fashion statement? Or, more
likely, were they students and these were their
school colors? Curious, I turned to Caden and
gave him a questioning look.

"Zack, meet Kimberly and Doug. They're high
school students who have each expressed an
interest in winemaking. I thought I'd give them
some invaluable experience by allowing them
to see the inner workings of a real working win-

ery. Guys, allow me to present Zachary Anderson, owner of Lentari Cellars."

"You're the guy who owns those two corgis, aren't you?" the girl asked, amazed. "Sherlock and Watson? I'd love to meet them someday."

Doug formally shook my hand, "It's good to meet you, sir."

Confused, I looked at the two teenagers, and then back at Caden, "So, you're just showing them around in here, is that it?"

Caden nodded. "That's right. They're both exceptional students…"

Kimberly blushed at this.

"…and on the principal's honor roll. The school actually reached out to me about this as a way to reward them for all their hard work. I didn't think you'd have a problem with it. In fact, both have expressed interest in volunteering here. Remember the conversation we had a few days ago?"

Bemused, I could only nod.

"They're willing to work for the experience."

"Like interns?" I asked.

Caden's face lit up. "Yes! Exactly. So, what do you say, Zack?"

I stepped forward and shook each of the kids' hands.

"Slave labor. Awesome. Kimberly, Doug, welcome aboard! The only thing I have to ask you is, how do you feel about being exposed to expletives?"

Surprised, the girl blinked a few times before turning to look at her fellow student, "Uh, okay, I guess. Why?"

I turned to look at the boy, who grinned and shrugged nonchalantly.

Satisfied, I looked back at the girl and nodded. "You'll see." Ignoring the kids, I then turned to Caden and pointed at the tiny glass of wine. "If you think I'm trying that without a can of soda here, pal, then you're full of doggie doo. There's no way I'm tasting that nasty-ass crap without some way to remove the taste."

Both kids were laughing at me by now.

"Zack isn't a fan of wine," Caden explained to the two students. "As such, he's the perfect guinea pig whenever I'm working on a new recipe."

By this time, my arms were across my chest, a scowl was plastered on my face, and I was grumbling. Not only had Caden lured me out of the house and up into the winery under false pretenses (couldn't get his key to unlock the front door), but then he wanted me to put on my guinea pig hat and try some new-fangled concoction he just revealed he'd been working on. I mentally vowed to install a hidden refrigerator and keep it well stocked with soda. This would mark the fourth time my winemaster had cornered me in my own winery.

I was also fairly certain that, for every time it happened, I promised to install a mini-fridge.

And yet, here we are. For the fourth time. Me … soda-less.

"For Pete's sake, Zack," Caden complained as he held a small taster glass with several ounces of a dark, ruby-colored liquid out in front of him. "I'm not trying to dupe you into thinking I'm giving you shark blood, okay? This is just a small sample of a pinot noir I've got in the works."

"There's no soda in here," I flatly pointed out. "If you think that I'm willingly taking a sip of that wine—any type of wine—then you're sorely mistaken."

"What's got you so worried?" Caden asked. I could hear the exasperation creeping into his voice.

"You," I answered. "Don't you remember what you said once I asked what it tasted like? Do you remember what you asked me?"

Caden's face broke out into a huge grin. "Er, something about country living?"

"Not even close. You know what you said. When I asked what it tasted like, you wanted to know if I had ever been to a farm. My answer, you will recall, was a very guarded 'yes.' Then I asked why, only you changed the subject on me."

"What smells do you associate with a farm?" Caden asked as he winked at the two kids.

"Smells? I always remember smelling hay. Animal poo. What's your point? What does that have to do with wine?"

"I think you'll know once you try the wine."

"You think I want to try something that reminds me of animal poo? Are you freakin' insane??"

"It doesn't taste like animal manure," Caden assured me. "It just has a rustic smell to it, and that it reminded me of a barn."

"Oh, no, no way."

"I'll try it," Doug volunteered, raising a hand.

Kimberly shrugged and raised her hand, too.

"How old are you two?" I asked.

"I'm seventeen," Kimberly answered.

"Same here," Doug added.

"Nice try," Caden told them, shaking his head. "You're both underage. You have at least four years to wait before you'll ever taste test the wine here. Besides, I know how much Zack loves the title of Official Test Subject. I'm constantly trying to find a recipe that he'll drink. Something besides a dessert wine, that is."

"You don't like wine?" Kimberly asked, amazed, as she turned to look at me. "Why would you buy a winery?"

"I can't stand wine," I confirmed as I looked at Kimberly, "and I didn't buy this winery. I inherited it. Thankfully, I don't have to like the wine, although Caden here sure does his damnedest to make me an oenophile. As such, he takes care of the place for me."

"A what?" Kimberly asked, confused.

Caden was grinning at me.

"Nice, Zack! You remembered the word. Even got the pronunciation right, too."

"Didn't believe me when I told you my other job is a writer, did you?" I joked. I turned to Kimberly. "An oenophile is a connoisseur of wine."

"You're a writer?" the girl asked, impressed. "Would I have read any of your books?"

Caden's smile threatened to split his face in two, "It's a distinct possibility, especially if you read romance novels."

Kimberly sighed wistfully. "I love romance novels. They're the only books worth reading."

"Psssht," Doug scoffed. "Horror novels are the best. No one can compare to Stephen King."

"Which books have you written?" Kimberly wanted to know.

I sighed. Ordinarily, I would have shied away from this particular topic. However, last Christmas, my mother let it slip to my friends here in PV just what type of books I write. Ever since, I've decided not to be ashamed of telling people that, when I'm not running a winery, I'm a romance writer. Still, it didn't stop my face from turning as red as a Coke can. Damn that Caden!

"The vast majority of the books I've released have been under a pseudonym. And that name is... hoo boy, you're gone love this. Do you want to know the name that you might know me as? It's Chastity Wadsworth."

Doug snickered, but Kimberly gasped aloud.

"Chastity Wadsworth? The Chastity Wadsworth? No way! I'm a huge fan of your books! I have copies of everything you've ever released!"

I grinned at the girl and gave a mock bow in her direction, "Why thank you, milady. Your patronage is greatly appreciated."

"I always thought Chastity Wadsworth was a woman," Kimberly continued. "Then again, I can understand why you'd want to keep your identity hidden. If I bring some of them here, would you sign them for me?"

I nodded. "Sure! I'd love to."

Kimberly beamed her appreciation at me and then fell silent. I also couldn't help but notice Doug's snickers died off the moment he saw how infatuated Kimberly had suddenly become with Yours Truly. In fact, I could see that he wanted to ask me something, but was hesitant to bring it up.

"What's on your mind, Doug?"

"You've written all these successful books. You must be making a ton of money with them. Why bother with this winery? I would have sold it and let someone else worry about it."

"How did you know the books were successful?" I asked. "I never mentioned that part."

It was Doug's turn to blush.

"Omigod!" Kimberly squealed. "You read romance novels, too!"

"Do not," Doug mumbled, clearly uncomfortable with the recent turn of events.

"Which ones have you read?" Kimberly

wanted to know. "Which series is your favorite? I absolutely love the Misty Plains series. Her latest book, Misty Moors, is fan-tabulous! Oh, I guess that'd be his latest book, not her. I'm sorry, Mr. Anderson."

"Call me Zack. And don't worry about it."

"I don't wanna talk about this anymore," Doug grumbled. He looked around the sparkling clean storefront we were standing in and walked over to the display case, showcasing a selection of Lentari Cellars' finest. "Talk about a sweet job," Doug continued, in what I recognized as a desperate ploy to change the subject, "I mean, you've got your own winery and can charge whatever you want for a bottle."

"It's not that easy," Caden began, as he pulled the two teenagers away. "You have to factor in cost of production, demand, and…"

As Caden led the two students into the heart of the winery, through the door marked Staff Only, I decided to make a break for the house. Sooner or later, Caden was going to realize I had managed to avoid trying his latest creation and would no doubt come looking for me. I had just unlocked my front door, and stepped inside, when my cell rang. The volume, unfortunately, was set loud enough to wake up both dogs on the couch. Sherlock was spooked enough to fire off a warning woof at me.

"Zack! I'm damn glad I caught you."

"I'm not going anywhere today, pal. It's Wednesday, which means it's a writing day. In fact, you couldn't have timed it better. Caden is currently here, and I'm trying my best to avoid him. He's got some new..."

"Zack!" Vance all but shouted into the phone. The detective had timed my pauses well, because as soon as I had taken a breath, he interrupted me. "I hope you're not busy, buddy."

The note of alarm in my friend's voice spooked me.

"No, not really. What is it? What's happened?"

"There's been another dognapping."

"Son of a biscuit eater!" I swore. "Just tell me it's not another kid's pet."

"I wish I could. Get down to the park. I'll fill you in once you're here."

"Which park? The one off of Oregon or the one on 8th?"

"Oregon. Make it quick, Zack. And bring the dogs."

"We're on our way."

* * *

"Whose pet do you suppose it is?" I quietly asked the dogs, as soon as I had stepped out of my Jeep and placed both of them on the ground.

Sherlock and Watson stared up at me, ears fully raised.

"Come on. Let's go see if we can help out."

I noticed Vance and several other cops the

moment we entered the park, so I had parked my car as close to him as possible. Upon hearing my Jeep, Vance had spun around and began moving toward me. Both Sherlock and Watson recognized the extended member of their pack and whined with anticipation.

"Hey, you two," Vance said, as he squatted down to pat the dogs on the head. "I sure do hope you can find something."

"So, what's going on?" I asked my detective friend. "Whose dog was stolen? You indicated you knew the owner?"

Vance nodded. "I did. This couldn't have happened to a worse person. Do you see Captain Nelson over there, next to the water fountains?"

I shielded my eyes from the sun and squinted. "Yes. You're telling me someone was stupid enough to steal Captain Nelson's dog?"

"No, although you're close. Do you see the woman and the girl he's standing next to?"

I looked where he indicated and noticed a woman with a protective arm around a young girl. The two of them were gently rocking back and forth.

"I do. Who are they?"

"The woman is Valerie, and the girl is Sydney. They're the captain's daughter and granddaughter."

"Oh, snap."

"It gets worse," Vance confided. "Sydney, who you can see is no more than nine or ten, is autistic. Her dog is a specially trained therapy dog."

I groaned. "That sick son of a bitch stole a kid's therapy dog? Man alive, how low can you go? Hey, what kind of dog are we looking for?"

"We're looking for a one-year-old beagle," Vance informed me. "Snoopy was just over a year old and was fresh out of obedience school that all therapy dogs in training are required to go through. From what the captain has told me, Sydney and Snoopy bonded almost instantly. The family *needs* to get this dog back, Zack. Words cannot express how important it is that we get this dog back."

"It's important we get all these dogs back," I countered, "not just the one. Don't worry, we'll see what we can find."

"Hold up. Let me finish taking these statements and I'll go with you."

While Vance interviewed several anxious-looking bystanders, I saw Captain Nelson suddenly glance my way. A look of grim resolve appeared on his face. He broke away from the group of people and started walking in my direction. I had to check behind me to see if there was someone else he might be angling for. Unfortunately, there wasn't.

"Mr. Anderson."

I nodded at him. "Captain."

My two dogs promptly sat in unison, as though they had been given a strict order. Sherlock whined as he looked upon the newcomer.

Captain Nelson squatted down next to the corgis and gave each of them an affectionate pat on the head. He silently regarded my dogs for a few moments and then slowly stood up. Then he cast a quick glance around us, as if checking for eavesdroppers.

"Mr. Anderson," the captain said again as he dropped his voice, "I'm hoping you've already talked to Detective Samuelson? I assume that's why you're here?"

"Unofficially," I assured the captain. "We'll try not to get in anyone's way."

Captain Nelson grit his teeth. "Well, let's make it official, and keep it quiet. I'd like you and your, uh, companions, on the case. Help Vance locate my granddaughter's dog. Will you do that for me?"

Surprised, I could only nod.

"Standard pay for police consultants is..."

"You don't need to worry about that," I interrupted. "I'm not worried about money."

"Standard pay for consultants," Captain Nelson continued, ignoring my protest, "is two hundred a day, plus any expenses incurred while on the case. Be sure to keep all your receipts and turn them in to Becky once this infernal dognapper has been located."

Becky—as you have probably guessed—handled all of the department's finances. She also helped Julie man the phones and handle all the department's media relations. I told you PV was a small town.

I nodded, still amazed that I was now on the payroll of the PVPD.

"Good. Find Sydney's dog. We need ... oh. I guess I should be talking to you two. Sherlock, Watson, find that beagle. I'm counting on you both. Don't let me down."

Both corgis were staring up at the captain, not moving a muscle. Sherlock snorted once, stood up, and gave himself a vigorous shake. After a few seconds, Watson mimicked her pack-mate.

"Do you have anything that belongs to Snoopy that might smell like him?" I asked, before the captain could walk away.

Captain Nelson stared at me for a few moments.

"Come on," I insisted. "I've seen the shows. I've got the dogs here. They may not be blood-hounds, but it might help them follow a trail if they know what scent they're looking for."

"Just a moment. Sydney was throwing a ball around. I'll see if she still has it."

A few minutes later, I was handed a purple tennis ball. The captain nodded once at me and then hurried back to his family. I saw him lay a sympathetic hand on his granddaughter's shoulder. I spotted Vance, nodded toward the open woods, and headed off. The detective met me at the wood's edge, and, without saying a word, I passed him Watson's leash. Together, the two of us headed toward the same path I had been on a few days ago.

"What was that all about?" Vance wanted to know, once we were inside the woods and away from prying eyes.

"The captain just hired me as a consultant."

Surprised, Vance turned to me and pulled me to a stop.

"Are you sure? He hasn't used a consultant in years, let alone offered to pay them."

"I tried to tell him not to worry about the money, but he ignored me. He wants us to find his granddaughter's dog as soon as possible."

Vance nodded glumly. "Understandable. From what I hear, that little beagle has worked miracles on his granddaughter. Having a pet is oftentimes the best therapy you can give an autistic child. I wasn't kidding when I said Snoopy was a therapy dog."

"We'll find him," I vowed. "Sherlock, Watson, go do your thing. We need to find this dog as quickly as possible, okay? Wait a moment. Here, you two. Take a whiff of this. This ... no, this isn't for you. It's not a toy."

Both corgis stared at me as though I was the dumbest thing on two legs.

"Well, okay, fine. This is a toy, but it's not for you. Can you smell the other dog on this thing? That's who we need to find."

Sherlock sniffed once, turned on his heel, and tugged on his leash. Encouraged, I gave him some slack and started to follow. Vance stepped aside to let us take the lead. I couldn't help but notice that his right hand was resting on the butt of his service revolver on his right hip. Here's hoping he wouldn't have to use it.

Just as we rounded the first bend, which consequently blocked all views of the park behind us, Vance and I paused as we heard voices chatting animatedly about something I couldn't make out. The voices grew louder, which prompted Sherlock to let out a warning woof. Watson's ears jumped straight up and she added her own soft growls to that of her packmate.

Nearly a dozen senior citizens, out for a walk in the park, appeared on the path. Every single one of them was wearing fanny packs with a bottle of water on each hip. Two of the women were pushing strollers. Also worth noting was each of the elderly ladies had on a big, floppy, purple hat. These women must've belonged to some type of club.

"Top of the morning," Vance offered, as he gave the women a smile. "Have any of you ladies noticed anything out of the ordinary today?"

All ten women looked up at Vance at the same time, as if they were just now noticing that they weren't alone. Conversations were abruptly silenced as the women stared at Vance, mouths agape. One by one, the small group of seniors looked over at me. The woman at the head of the group, who happened to be pushing a stroller, cleared her throat and approached Vance.

"Well, hello there, young man. Isn't it a glorious day? And what do you mean, out of the ordinary? This is Pomme Valley. We pride ourselves on good, clean living. You won't find anything amiss here."

Vance's face reddened. "Er, I wasn't insinuating that you were doing anything illegal, only that..."

My tongue-tied friend trailed off as he looked at me. I could see he was flustered. By a group of sweet old ladies? Come on, buddy. You're a cop. You shouldn't be intimidated.

"We're looking for a beagle," I told the women. "One was reported missing from around here. He was a little girl's companion and she desperately needs him back."

"You're looking for a missing dog?" another woman gasped as she placed a hand over her heart. "Oh, heavens no! Not another one! That poor little girl."

Nearly a half dozen different conversations immediately broke out. I noticed one woman, with what looked like a purple sombrero on her head, look around at her companions. She must have decided her group was taking a break, 'cause she pulled one of her water bottles out of its holster and practically drained it.

Apparently, that was all it took. Within moments, the entire group was reaching for their water bottles and were quickly draining them. Judging from the way these ladies were guzzling their water, you'd think we had just interrupted a twenty-mile marathon. I waited a few moments before I gave the women what I hoped was my most disarming smile.

"You ladies are obviously very observant," I continued, as I smiled at their spokeswoman, "so I'm hoping you might have seen something that could help us? Maybe you've seen a small dog wandering the area? Perhaps you've seen someone lurking in the trees? Have you seen any wheelbarrows? Although, in this case, beagles aren't that big. He might not have needed one."

"You're looking for a sea gull?" one of the women asked in a rather loud voice as she looked up. She clutched the brim of her purple mini top hat fearfully, as if expecting to get hit with an avian aerial bomb.

Another woman, wearing a large brim purple Kentucky Derby hat, groaned aloud. "No, Milly. They're looking for a beagle. For heaven's sake, check your batteries."

Milly frowned and then started fiddling with her hearing aid, presently visible resting on the upper part of her ear.

The group spokesman, er, spokeswoman, selected one of the women standing quietly nearby, and pulled the left-hand bottle free of the fanny pack. She took a small sip and immediately held it out behind her. There was a mad rush as the ladies all clamored to retrieve the bottle first. A few minutes later, after the bottle had passed through the hands of all the ladies present, it was returned to its owner. Completely empty.

Concerned that the women were dehydrated, and needed water, I pointed back toward the park. The last thing I wanted to do was perform CPR on an elderly woman.

"There are some vending machines back there," I helpfully suggested. "Several of them have bottled water. Would you like me to fetch a couple?"

One of the women giggled hysterically, while yet another snorted with laughter.

"Water? Heavens no. Edith filled her bottle with coconut rum. Didn't you, dearie?"

Edith blushed and stared at her feet. "Well, I did mix it with diet Coke. I used a ten-to-one ratio."

"Ten parts soda to one-part rum?" I chuckled. "That's not too bad, I suppose."

The women fell silent. I couldn't help it. I cracked a smile.

"Or would that be one-part soda to ten parts rum?"

Now there were affirmative nods from all around.

Vance shook his head and mumbled something under his breath. Right about then, Edith looked down and spotted my dogs. She clapped her hands together and squealed with excitement, which, if you recall, was corgi-speak for 'let's be friends.' Then I noticed a few disapproving frowns from several of her companions. They caught me giving them a quizzical look and before you can say 'Aren't they cute?' the friendly grandmother personas appeared once more. I'm not sure I've ever encountered anyone who didn't adore the corgis on first sight.

"Now, don't you worry about us," the first woman confided with a sheepish smile. She had noticed me staring at the women near the back of the group. "Between you and me, I think a few of the girls forgot to take their bran this morning."

I heard several grumbles coming from behind me.

"See what I mean?"

"You'd better not be talking about me," the same woman who thought we were looking for seagulls said.

"I'm not, Milly. Although, I should mention, I saw you had some of the rum. We all know you can't hold your liquor."

"I can drink you under the table any day of the week," Milly challenged, as she turned to regard her friend.

One of the women with a stroller pushed through to the front of the line.

"Ladies. There will be a time and place for everything. And, I will say for the record, Milliford has challenged Mary in front of everyone. So, that means that next week's meeting will be held at Red Barn Tavern. Drinks will be on the loser. All in favor?"

"Aye!" the women chorused.

"The motion is carried. Now, in the meantime, lieutenant…"

"Detective Vance Samuelson," Vance interrupted. "And you are?"

"Winnifred Silversmith. I am the president of ELLA. I trust you've heard of our noble organization."

Vance shook his head. "Nope, I'm sorry."

"We are the Esteemed Lavender Ladies Assemblage of Pomme Valley," Winnifred explained. "There will be chapters popping up all across the country, you mark my words. We'll be as popular as the BPO Elks."

"And the Lions," Edith proudly added.

"As I was saying, detective," Winnifred continued, "you can rest assured that if I, or any of my ladies, notice anything out of the ordinary, you will be the first to know."

"Ask him for a business card," one of the women whispered as she leaned close to the club president. "He's awfully cute!"

"Hush, Teri," a yet-to-be-named lady scolded. "He'll hear you."

My eyebrows shot up and I eyed my friend. It was Vance's turn to blush, and trust me, he did. I snickered, but managed to turn it into a cough.

"Bite me, pal," I heard Vance whisper.

Teri held a hand up to her mouth. "Oh, my! Did I say that too loud?"

The ELLA ladies giggled uncontrollably, thus proving that everyone had heard Teri's comment. Smiling at the two of us, they continued on their way. I looked down at the dogs. Already disinterested, Sherlock was ready to continue on. Giving the inquisitive corgi all the slack that I could on the leash, we moved off.

"That was something," I remarked, as soon as I was sure we were out of earshot. "Did you like those hats? And that one lady. Teri, was it? She liked you."

"Drop it, amigo," Vance warned, "or I'll bring up Clara Hanson again."

My face paled and I immediately touched three fingers to my brow.

"Consider it dropped. Scout's honor."

Allow me to shed a little context here. Clara Hanson is the owner of A Lazy Afternoon, PV's one and only bookstore. She is also the owner of a little African gray parrot named Ruby, who for some inexplicable reason, was infatuated with both me and Sherlock. And, unfortunately, so was Clara.

I fought to suppress a shudder.

"Moving on, do you really think there's still a trail to follow? There was, what, close to a dozen ladies in that purple hat group? I'm not sure what Sherlock is going to be able to find."

We both looked down at the dogs. Sherlock had his nose to the ground and was continuing to tug on his leash. For all intents and purposes, he looked as though he still had the scent.

The route we were following didn't appear to be a path, but it could have doubled as one. We were following a three-foot-wide discoloration of earth, which signified a shift in the natural vegetation. I knelt down to inspect our path, only to discover there was no point in looking for tracks. The discoloration was where the dirt had changed into solid rock.

"This is wide enough for a wheelbarrow," Vance observed as he knelt down beside me.

"Only it wouldn't be needed," I reminded him. "We're talking about a beagle. They aren't that big."

Vance nodded his head. "True."

I felt a tug on the leash. Sherlock wanted to keep going.

Ten minutes later, our luck held out. Or, I suppose you could say that Sherlock's reputation continued to remain untarnished. The natural rock line abruptly ended and the dirt resumed. The three-foot-wide path easily doubled in width and stretched away, to the south. I looked down at the ground and saw a very welcoming sign: soft dirt.

There, clearly discernible in the earth, were two thin tire tracks, which we followed for nearly twenty-five feet. Then we saw a very welcome sight: tire tracks! Someone had brought a car in here! How? Where the hell was the road?

"Whatcha got there?" Vance asked as he came up behind me.

I pointed at the ground. "Those thin tire tracks just switched to big ones. Either those skinny tires suddenly tripled in size, or else we're now looking at tire tracks!"

Vance let out a whoop and dropped down to a knee. He whipped his cell out and snapped a few pictures. I could see that he was bringing up his message app on his phone and sending the pictures off to someone.

"I've asked the boys at the lab to take a look at these," Vance told me. "I kinda think we might have an answer in remarkable time."

"Really? How can you be so sure?"

Vance shrugged. "Call it a hunch. In fact, I'll bet you lunch that we'll have a positive match for those tires in less than thirty minutes."

"Make it twenty minutes," I countered.

Vance thrust out a hand, "Deal."

Yep. I lost. It only took ten.

"How did you know you'd get a response so fast?"

Vance shot me a sidelong look, "'Cause I dropped Captain Nelson's name and said this is about his granddaughter's missing dog."

"Cheater."

"I'm thinking Casa de Joe's sounds good."

"Yeah, yeah. So, spill. What'd you find out?"

"They're 215/70R/15s. They even found the exact make and model."

I had to admit, I was impressed.

"Okay. What about those thin tracks?"

"Same generic track like the wheelbarrow from before, only narrower."

"Damn. Okay, so what about the tire tracks? Get anything good?"

"They're Nexen N'Priz AH5s. It's a standard touring tire."

"Standard? Oh. That sucks. That probably means they're fairly common, right?"

Vance clapped me on the shoulder. "Zack, are you kidding me? I can actually show my face before the captain 'cause I have something to report. We have a lead! Way to go, Sherlock! You, too, Watson! You saved my hide, little buddies."

SIX

Two days passed without any real progress in the investigation. Thanks to the techs at the crime lab, and the help of ye Almighty Internet, I learned that those Nexen N'Priz tires were just as standard as they sounded. Between Pomme Valley and Medford, there are fifteen different tire stores which carry the Nexen brand. I should also mention that Medford has two warehouse stores and they each have an automotive department that services cars and trucks. They carry the tires, too.

So much for that lead.

While Vance continued to pore through the backlog of case files from Medford, and at his express urging to leave him alone for the day, I decided to spend my free time catching up on all the paperwork around the winery. First on my To Do list required the use of my cell. Who was I calling? Well, let's just say that I was about to make Caden's day.

"Hello?"

"Is this the Parson residence? Could I speak to Tim, please?"

The person who had answered the phone sounded like he could've been my age. I had hoped it would be old man Parson himself, since he and I have a casual friendship. Being the neighborly type, I have passed him several bottles of wine from time to time. In return, he'd give me more apples and nectarines than I would know what to do with. Thankfully, Jillian knew all about canning and preserving fruit. My basement—and hers, for that matter—were filled with dozens of jars of various goodies.

Sorry, random thought: why do they call it 'canning' when you're filling up glass jars? I'll let that one slide for now.

Now, back to the issue at hand. If there was any chance that the Parson family was thinking about selling a piece of their farm off, then I had to at least try to put in a good offer. What harm was there in trying to broker a deal?

"Yes, this is the Parson residence. Who is this?"

"My name is Zachary Anderson. I own..."

"Mister Anderson!" the speaker all but shouted at me. "You're the owner of Lentari Cellars, aren't you?"

"Guilty," I confirmed with a chuckle.

"And ... and you are the owner of those two little dogs who solve crimes, aren't you?"

I felt my face go slack. Why did I continue to get surprised? It was a well-known fact that my dogs were more popular than I was.

"I, er, umm ... sorry. You caught me off guard. I do own two little dogs."

"Yes! I knew it! You're the owner of those two corgis!"

I wasn't too sure how to take this.

"Well, yeah. That's me. Sherlock and Watson are my dogs."

"I'm Jason Parson. I'm Tim's son. I'm the one who just took over the family farm. Pleased to meet you, Zachary!"

"Call me Zack. It's nice to meet you, too, Jason. Listen, the reason I'm calling is that my winemaster mentioned to me that you might be interested in selling some of your acreage off. I thought it'd make a great investment in the winery."

"Are you looking to expand Lentari Cellars?"

"Not at the present moment. However, when we're ready to expand, it'd be nice to already have the land. What do you say? Are you interested in selling?"

"Not only am I interested in selling, but I think it's safe to say that my entire family would love to hear that Lentari Cellars is interested in buying it. In fact, I'll personally guarantee that I'll make you a deal so good that you won't be able to refuse it."

I laughed. I was really starting to like Jason. He had an easy-going, personable attitude. I had already decided to accept whatever offer he was willing to give me when he hit me with...

"How does thirty-five acres sound?"

"Thirty-five? Seriously? Wow. I thought

Caden said you were only interested in selling twenty acres."

"Twenty would be the number I'd be willing to sell a stranger. Now that I know you're interested in the land, I'd much rather you have it. I know my father would agree. He's always been fond of your wines."

"I'm not sure I was looking to purchase that many acres, Jason. I haven't even heard what you're asking for the lot of twenty acres, let alone thirty-five."

The number Jason gave me had both my eyebrows jumping straight up.

"Are you sure? I'm willing to bet that you could easily get five times that amount."

"I know I could. We don't need the money, Zack. When dad gave control of the farm to me, he literally told me I could do whatever I wanted with it. He and mom are buying a house in Florida right on Lake Okeechobee. You see, he loves to fish for big bass. What better way to do that by fishing right off your front porch?"

"With that said, you're probably looking at getting rid of the farm as quickly as possible."

"That's right. I have a second buyer interested in the fifty acre plot to the west. I'm sure I can get him to take the second fifty acre plot sitting adjacent to it."

"If you offer him a deal like mine, then I'm sure he won't be able to say no."

"That's what I'm counting on. What do you

say, Zack? Will you buy it?"

"Jason, it's a deal. Hey, I don't suppose you guys have any tractors for sale, do you?"

"We had several, only all three have been sold. Sorry, buddy."

"It's okay. It's probably for the best. Caden said something about a buying a specialty tractor, one that's made narrower than most so that it'll fit between rows of vines."

"That's right. I know exactly what you're talking about. My buddy runs the John Deere dealership in Medford. I've heard him mention the special orchard tractors once or twice. Want me to make a call and see if he has any available?"

I fought to suppress a smile. If I managed to pull off buying a tractor after sealing the deal for the thirty-five acres, then Caden was gonna positively have a cow. And yes, as morbid as it sounds, that was something I had to see.

"Jason, that'd be awesome. I don't need anything fancy, or too big. It's just for day-to-day use around here at the winery."

"What do you need it for? What type of work do you need to do? I'm sorry, I'm not trying to be nosy. I know Alan—my friend—will ask."

"You know what? I really don't have a clue. I don't know the first thing about farming, or growing plants. I let Caden handle all aspects of handling the grapes. What I can tell you is that, right now, Lentari Cellars has ten planted acres, with an additional five ready to go."

"You had fifteen acres set aside for grape production?"

"No, we *have* fifteen acres for grape production. No need to use the past tense there."

"No, you now have fifty acres for grape production."

A smile formed on my face.

"Yeah, I guess you're right. Wow. That'll take some getting used to."

"Let me make a call. Alan will contact you if there's anything he can do for you."

"Sounds great, Jason. Thanks again! For everything. I mean it."

"You're more than welcome. Just do me a favor?"

"Name it."

"Bring the dogs by before the end of the month, okay? That's when mom and dad will be officially moved out of the house."

"You got it, pal."

I ended the call and looked down at the dogs.

"You guys now have a lot more room to run around. What do you say to that?"

Both corgis were up on the couch in the living room. Watson rose to her feet, circled three times, and then sank into a Flying Squirrel. Now, an explanation may be required for you non-corgi owners. A flying squirrel—for a corgi—was where the dog would stretch out their two stumpy front legs in front of them and do the same for the back legs. It certainly didn't look comfortable to me, but it must've been perfectly satisfactory for a dog 'cause Watson always slept in that position.

Sherlock preferred Dead Roach. Hey, you can't make stuff like this up. Google it. As I was saying, Sherlock sleeps on his back with all four paws in the air, much like how you'd find a dead roach in your house—upside down with all its legs sticking straight up. On a whim, I searched online several months ago to find out why certain dogs preferred different sleeping positions. Flying Squirrel is considered a very restful position, but also allows the dog to resume movement should the need arise. As for Dead Roach ... well, this is where I'm quite proud. Only a confident, secure indoor dog would choose to sleep in such a supremely vulnerable position. Clearly, Sherlock trusted me and felt completely safe in his home environment.

I wouldn't have it any other way.

Seeing how the dogs were down for the count, I decided to tip-toe upstairs to my office. I wanted to check my email. I had sent my latest book to my editor and I was anxious to hear what she thought about it.

Nothing.

My inbox was empty. Sighing, I headed back downstairs and was quietly lacing my shoes to head up the hill to the winery when my cell rang. Sherlock rolled onto his stomach and opened both eyes to regard me coolly, as if he was accusing me of sneaking out of the house without him. Watson's eyes were open, too. Without moving a muscle, both dogs stared at me, unblinking.

"Hello?"

"Is this Zachary Anderson?"

"It is. Who is this?"

"Alan Matthews. I head up the sales department here at John Deere of Medford. How are you today?"

"I'm just fine, Alan. Jason told me to expect your call if you were able to do something for me. Am I right to understand that you can? Do something for me, that is?"

"You're looking for a tractor for Lentari Cellars, am I correct?"

"You are."

"And you just recently added an additional thirty-five acres of farmland to the winery?"

"Jason obviously clued you into our deal, yes. Whatcha got for me?"

"If you'd like to come down to the showroom, I'll show you which models I think would be a good match for you."

"Can you give me an idea how much these things run?"

"It really depends. The models with enclosed cabs typically run much higher than those without. Jason said that you were looking for a tractor that wasn't too fancy, is that right?"

"Correct."

"Do you have any idea what attachments it would need to run?"

"Attachments?"

"Yes. Sprayers? Tillers? Will you be doing much digging?"

"Jason asked me pretty much the same thing. I really don't know, Alan. I've got someone else who handles all of that. I get to handle all the finances. Yay for me, right?"

Alan let out a hearty laugh.

"So, how much do these things run?" I asked again.

"The narrow models start around $35K and they can go up to $65K."

"Sixty-five thousand dollars?? Holy cow. I had no idea those damn things were so expensive. Caden has been smoking the good stuff if he thinks I'm paying that much for a friggin' tractor."

"Take it easy, Mr. Anderson. I said they can go *up to* $65K, but that particular model wouldn't suit you."

"And what would?" I asked, sounding a teensy bit testier than I probably should have.

"The GV model is the smallest we have. It'd be perfect for a winery your size."

"Hey, I don't want something the size of a riding lawn mower, either."

Alan let out another laugh.

"I hear you, Mr. Anderson. The GV comes equipped with more than enough power to get the job done."

"And how much do they run?" I warily asked.

"The GVs start at $35K."

"That's better, but egad, that's still a lot of money."

"You know something, Mr. Anderson? I think I might have just the thing for you. We sold one of our older narrow tractors late last year to a farmer who, unfortunately, has since passed away. I'm fairly certain it was a 5GV. Anyway, his family asked us to see if we could find a buyer for it. I'm willing to wager they'd be interested in cutting you a deal."

"Provided they still have it, of course."

"Fair point. Let me give them a call. Good news or bad, I'll call you back, okay?"

"Sure thing, Alan."

The call ended, leaving a bad taste in my mouth. I hated dealing with car salesmen. Sure, this was a tractor we're talking about, but I still couldn't help but feel that I was dealing with a smarmy creep who was trying to hose me for everything I was worth. Thankfully, Alan was a friend of Jason's, and I'd like to think that Jason wouldn't deliberately steer me toward someone who was unscrupulous.

A quick glance at the couch confirmed both corgis had fallen asleep again. I decided to check my email a second time—still nothing—and then proceeded to check out YouTube for some videos of the 5GV. I wanted to see what I would be getting myself into.

Turns out the 5GV is a fairly robust tractor. I can also see why they're great for wineries. It's built narrow enough to squeeze through rows of vines without squishing anything.

Wanting to make certain that I wouldn't be cheated by whatever price this other family would be asking for the tractor, I checked some farming equipment want ads. Hey, don't laugh. It exists. See for yourself.

That's when I heard my cell phone ringing. Wouldn't you know it? I left it downstairs. I managed to take the call on the fourth ring, just before I'm sure my voice mail would've taken the call. It was my new friend from Medford.

"Mr. Anderson? Alan Mathers. We spoke on the phone earlier?"

As if I would've forgotten what transpired only thirty minutes ago.

"I remember you, Alan. What's up? Did they still have the tractor for sale?"

"About that tractor..."

I sighed. It was no longer for sale. Oh, well. It was worth a shot.

"It's sold, I get it. I appreciate the time and..."

"It's still for sale," Alan interrupted. "Only, it isn't the model I thought it was."

"Oh. It isn't one of those special narrow models? That's fine. Hey, we tried, right?"

"You didn't let me finish. It's a narrow model, only not the model I thought it was. It's a

5083EN. This particular model is a few years old."

"How old is a 'few years'?"

"It's a 2012 model."

"Ah. Well, I suppose that wouldn't be too bad. How much are they asking?"

"Fifteen thousand."

"Only 15K? Alrighty, what's wrong with it?"

"Nothing. I'm told it was barely used."

"Then why ask so little for it? I mean, if you were going to buy a house, and the owner accepted your lowball offer, wouldn't that entice you to seek out a home inspector?"

"I'll be honest with you, Mr. Anderson. I had no idea their asking price was so low. I could have sold this thing many times over had I known. I thought it was an older tractor and they wanted way too much for it."

"Let me guess. You're saying that either I buy it or else you will."

I was met with silence on the phone.

"Fine. Tell them I'll buy it, provided it passes a health inspection from a mechanic."

"Done."

I made the arrangements and then terminated the call. Well, I certainly hadn't planned on spending that much today. I had added thirty-five acres of land to the winery, as well as bought myself a genuine tractor. If this didn't prove to Caden that I was willing to invest in the winery, then nothing would.

My cell rang again.

"Son of a biscuit eater. Come on guys, leave me alone. I've got work to do."

Caden's number was on the screen. Someone's ears must've been burning. How should I break this to him?

"Hey, Caden. What's up?"

"Hi, Zack. Got a minute?"

"Sure. What's on your mind?"

"Kimberly and Doug are due back in to the winery tomorrow. I wanted to run by a list of tasks and activities the kids would be allowed to do that could give them more insight into a working winery."

"I trust you, Caden. Feel free to have them do whatever you..." I trailed off as I realized I had the perfect opportunity to spring my surprise on my winemaster. "Tell you what. You're right. Why don't you swing by the house and we can discuss it?"

I heard a knocking on my front door. Both corgis were on their feet in a flash. They jumped to the ground amidst a flurry of barks and made a beeline to the front door. A quick check out the window confirmed my suspicions. I laughed, told Caden to come on in, and disconnected the call. Caden poked his head through the front door.

"Is this a bad time?"

"Not at all. Come on in. No. Wait. Let's go outside."

"Are you okay?" Caden asked me. He was giving me a concerned look. "You're acting weird."

"I wanted to show you something."

"Oh, yeah? Really?"

"You don't have to act so surprised, smart guy. I do have ideas from time to time, you know."

Caden laughed and clapped a friendly hand on my shoulder.

"I know you do. Sorry. What is it you want to show me?"

"Well, it concerns that land you want me to add to the winery."

"It's a helluva investment," Caden insisted. "You really ought to consider it."

"Where's the land at?" I asked as we walked down the front porch steps.

Sherlock and Watson were waiting for us at the bottom of the stairs, having gone around the landscaping so they wouldn't have to tackle the unsurmountable obstacle the steps presented. Caden stooped to give each dog a pat on the head. Then he straightened, turned to the right, and made a sweeping gesture with his arm.

"Over there. See the Parson farm at the base of that small hill? The land he wants to sell us starts at the road on the eastern side of the property. All of their land which borders us on the north and west are up for grabs. This is really too good to pass up."

"Do you have any idea how many acres comprise the Parson farm?" I asked.

Caden was silent for a moment as he considered.

"Umm, over a hundred, I think. It's not too big as farms go, but it's still pretty significant. Why do you ask?"

"Because I just bought thirty-five of those acres to add to Lentari Cellars."

"You just ... what? What?! You bought how many acres??"

"Thirty-five. I told him I only wanted to buy twenty, but he gave me such a good offer that I couldn't refuse. Heck, he sold me the land for far less than I was expecting to pay for the original twenty."

"Holy crap. How do you get so lucky, Zack?"

I shrugged. "Maybe my charm? My good looks?"

Caden shook his head, "There's gotta be something more than that."

"Kiss my derriere, amigo."

Caden laughed. He turned back toward the Parson farm and shook his head in amazement. Then I saw him angle his head toward the winery, as if trying to guess how much of the visible land now belonged to me.

"You're not doing this just because I insinuated you'd be a fool not to invest in the winery, are you?"

I shook my head. "Nope. It wasn't a good idea, but a *great* idea. We've more than tripled our working acreage. I'll leave it up to you to fill those acres up."

Caden rocked back on the balls of his feet, "Oh, man. I have so many plans on what I'd like to do for this place."

I held out an arm and gave it a circular, sweeping motion.

"Have at it. I've trusted you this far, and you've proven time and time again that I haven't misplaced that trust. Go ahead. Let's see what you can do."

Caden chortled and rubbed his hands together gleefully.

"Okay, the first thing I'd like to do is … is … run for cover. I'm sorry, Zack, but I have to go. Like, now. I'll be in the house. I don't think I want to know what I'll do or say if I stay out here with you."

Puzzled, I looked at Caden as though he had lost in mind.

"What's the matter with you? Where are you going?"

By the time I had turned to my winemaster, the front door was already swinging shut. Then I heard it. A car was coming down the driveway. A black 1985 Cadillac Seville, if you want to get technical. In its prime, this particular car would've turned heads wherever it went. At the moment, it was turning heads, all right, only not for the right reason.

The car looked beat up, haggard. The paint

was faded and chipped, one wheel was missing its decorative chrome hubcap, and the sounds coming from the engine suggested the car was long overdue for a checkup. The car wheezed up to me and backfired several times after the engine was shut off. I groaned as I saw why Caden had beat a hasty retreat.

Abigail Lawson extricated herself from her car. She was wearing a dark blue blouse, a matching blue skirt, and once more had her hair pulled up into a severe bun. She slowly pulled her bulbous eyeglasses off her nose and fixed me with a cold stare. I was more than willing to return the gesture.

"Mr. Anderson."

"Ms. Lawson," I returned, with all the warmth of an Antarctic winter.

Abigail Lawson is the daughter of the late Bonnie Davies, former owner of Lentari Cellars. To this day, Abigail believes her mother should never have left the winery, or her house, to me and it pisses her off to no end. She's already tried to force me to sign over the estate several times, claiming her mother hadn't been in her right frame of mind. As you can imagine, it didn't go over well.

"I suppose you're wondering why I'm here. Well, it's to … call off your dogs, Mr. Anderson. We have business to discuss."

I looked down at the two corgis. Both had the hair on the back of their neck sticking straight up and Sherlock was giving Abigail a full-throated growl. Watson was growling, too, but she was drowned out by her packmate. I gave them each a pat on the head, and looked back up at Abigail.

"On the contrary, we don't have a single iota of business to conduct with one another."

Abigail held up a thick manila folder.

"Actually, we do."

"If you're once more trying to get me to sign over the house and winery, then save your breath. It's not going to happen. Not now, not tomorrow, nor ten years from now. Are we clear on that?"

"I'm not asking you to give the winery to me," Abigail contradicted.

"Well, *there's* a first," I muttered. I saw Abigail's nostrils flair in anger, which meant she must've heard me. I didn't care. I could say whatever I wanted on my own property. That wouldn't be changing any time soon. "What are you doing here? What's on your mind? You can't possibly tell me that this is a social call."

Abigail's lips thinned. "It isn't. Look, I know you don't know the first thing about running a winery. I do. I will take it off your hands."

"I'm not selling, lady," I reiterated. "I have no desire to move. As a matter of fact, I like it here."

"Then don't move. Keep the house. It doesn't matter. The winery will be moved to New York."

"So, that's your plan? You're going to sell Lentari Cellars to one of those huge corporations? I told you before, I'm not giving up the winery."

Abigail unfastened the envelope and pulled out a thick sheaf of papers.

"I already have a group of investors standing by. They've agreed to pay double the winery's current value right here, right now, if you're willing to sign. However, this offer will only happen once, Mr. Anderson. I do suggest you take it."

"You're trying to buy the winery now? What's with this sudden change of heart? Does it have anything to do with all the awards Lentari Cellars has been winning? Including last year's PiNWO Grand Championship?" At the look of surprise on Abigail's face, I had to laugh. "Why do you look so surprised? This is my winery. You had better believe I keep track of any and all awards Lentari Cellars has earned."

Not true, but she didn't know that. Instead, I was met with stony silence.

"Lentari Cellars is not for sale, Ms. Lawson," I formally announced, drawing up to my full height. "The winery will remain in PV. This place started out local and that's the way it's gonna stay. Besides, it's what your mother would have wanted."

Abigail's face purpled with rage.

"You have no right to bring up my mother's..."

I held up my phone and cleared my throat at

the same time I took a menacing step toward my uninvited guest. Both dogs took notice and immediately abandoned their growling for barking. Abigail, for her part, started to back away from me.

"You're about to be forcefully evicted," I told her, adding enough malice to my voice to make her believe it. "You can leave under your own power or you can leave with a couple of police escorts. It's your call."

"This isn't over, Mr. Anderson," Abigail spat, throwing as much venom into her voice as she could muster.

"On the contrary, it is. Go. Pester someone else for a change."

The Cadillac was coaxed back to life and it belched out a cloud of dark exhaust as Abigail stomped down on the accelerator. I could tell that the Caddy's tires wanted to spin, but the engine lacked enough horses to do it. It was pathetic, if you ask me. I waved the air in front of me as the noxious cloud of black fumes dissipated and looked down at the dogs.

"She was just as pleasant as the last time we saw her, wasn't she?"

The front door banged open.

"That crazy old witch tried to take control of the winery again, didn't she?" Caden guessed.

I nodded. "She came with financial backing this time. She said she had a group of investors who were willing to pay double what the winery is worth. Then she admitted she was going to move the winery to New York."

"Words cannot even begin to describe how much I loathe that woman," Caden began.

"Don't let her ruin your day. You just found out you have a lot more land to play with. You were about to tell me what some of those plans were, remember?"

Caden nodded. "That's right. So, I was thinking..."

My cell started ringing. Again. It was Vance.

"Hold that thought, Caden. Hey, Vance. You're not going to believe what I did today. I... what? Really? Are you serious? That's awesome! Where is he now? Yes. Absolutely. I'm on my way."

"What's going on?" Caden asked.

"That was Vance. You remember those dognappings? Well, one of the dogs was just found."

"Oh, yeah? That's gotta be good news, right? Which one was recovered?"

"The chocolate Lab."

Caden groaned. "Oh, man. I was really hoping to be able to join the search for that dog. Did you know, the owner was going to give away a collectible John Wayne rifle to anyone who returned his dog to him? Damn. I'm a huge John Wayne fan."

"Sorry, pal. Anyway, I have to go. We're going to talk to the owner."

Caden grinned and headed toward his car, "No

worries, Zack. I'll head back to my place. I'll start drawing up some plans. Dude, we're gonna have a lot of fun with this!"

SEVEN

Half an hour later, I was sitting inside PV's one and only police station, in interrogation room #1. Actually, I should clarify. I wasn't in the main part of the interrogation room—since I wasn't the one being interrogated—but the quiet, darkened room on the other side of the two-way mirror. There were two people presently occupying the main room: Vance and an older man I didn't know. Also in the room was one very energetic chocolate Lab, who apparently didn't like to be ignored since she would let out a loud piercing bark every ten seconds or so. The owner, naturally, would scold the dog and order her to be quiet. That, unfortunately, would only last a few moments before the Labrador would resume its barking.

Sensing a disturbance behind me, I turned to see the door to my room quietly opening. Captain Nelson appeared. He nodded once at me and sat down in a nearby chair.

"Did I miss anything?" the captain quietly inquired.

I shook my head no. "You've got great timing. Vance has been in there for about fifteen minutes, waiting for the owner and his dog to show up. They just did, maybe three or four minutes ago."

"Good."

Three loud, ear drum shattering barks pierced the air. I saw Vance cringe. The dog's owner immediately scolded the dog and again apologized for his pet's raucous behavior.

"I'm sorry about her. She likes to play. She thinks the only reason I've been put on this earth is to play ball with her."

Vance smiled. "It's okay. I have a German Shepherd myself. She has her own distinctive ways to get my attention, believe you me. So, who do we have here?"

"This is Chip," the elderly man responded as he gazed proudly at his dog.

Vance looked down at the dog and stretched out a hand in an open invitation. The Labrador practically leapt off the ground and couldn't hurry over to him fast enough. Chip's thick tail thumped loudly on the table legs as the dog sniffed Vance's hand.

"You're a pretty boy," Vance proclaimed as he gave the friendly dog a scratch on its head.

"Chip is actually a girl," the owner corrected.

Vance's hand paused in its scratching, "A girl? Umm, okay. Sorry. I thought Chip was a boy's name."

"It's short for KoChip."

"Ah. That's a nice name. Now, Mr., uh…"

"McGee."

"Mr. McGee. Please start from the beginning. How did you get your dog back earlier today?"

A look of surprise swept over my face as I turned to the captain. "He found his own dog? Really?"

Captain Nelson nodded. "Yes. As for the *how* of the matter, let's hear what he has to say, shall we?"

"Oh. Sorry."

"I've searched that park every day for hours," Mr. McGee was saying. "I took my two other girls with me, hoping they'd be able to pick up Chip's trail. However, not once did they ever act like they could smell her."

Vance began taking notes in his all too familiar tiny notebook, "Go on, Mr. McGee."

"I'll have you know that both of my girls were on leashes this time. I wasn't about to take any chances with them. They're all I've got left."

"I understand, Mr. McGee. Please continue."

"The three of us were headed to the same trail that we must have searched half a dozen times. Just before we stepped into the woods, I heard barking. My girls did, too, 'cause I could see 'em cocking their heads left and right, like they couldn't figure out what they were hearing. I called again, only this time, who do I see jumping out of the bushes, as though she's been hiding behind a tree this entire time, but Chip herself!"

"That must have been a relief," Vance said, although I thought he sounded a bit disappointed.

"What are you frowning for?" Captain Nelson quietly asked from right beside me. At some point he must've moved, only I hadn't noticed.

"It sounds like Vance is disappointed, like he was hoping Mr. McGee had gone into the woods and found his dog coming from a specific location."

"Astute observation. I'm thinking that, too."

"So, I'm not sure how else we may be of help," Mr. McGee continued. "I was going to search for my dog, but instead, she found me first. End of story."

I frowned again.

"How long had Chip been reported missing?" I quietly asked.

Captain Nelson reached for the antique-looking microphone on the desk facing the window. He punched the big black rectangular button on its base and cleared his throat.

"How long has the dog been officially missing?"

Vance glanced up briefly at the mirror before he repeated the question.

"Nearly a week," Chip's owner answered. "And it had to be the most miserable week of my life. Except being married to my second wife, of course. What a piece of work she turned out to be. What kind of a person would hide my mother's antique silverware from me in the hopes that she'd be able to sell it once I had given up trying to find it? And then there was the —"

"Let's table that for another time, Mr. McGee," Vance smoothly interrupted. "Back to Chip. Do you have any idea why your dog was returned to you?"

"Returned, ha. She escaped, plain and simple."

Vance's eyes widened with surprised, "Escaped, you say. What makes you say that?"

"Because I think that dog was an escape artist in another life. I've seen her get out of kennels, pens, collars, and even harnesses. I figured she worked her magic on whatever cage was holding her and as a result, she escaped. And you know what? I'm not going to complain."

Vance stroked his chin thoughtfully as he turned to look at the window. "Interesting."

"What is?" I asked as I turned to the captain.

"Nothing," Captain Nelson assured me. "Whenever Detective Samuelson looks at the mirror like that it means he wants to know if I have anything to add."

"Do you?"

The captain shrugged. "Not really, no. The owner found his dog at the park. I don't think we can learn anything more from that. I suppose we might be able to put a bloodhound on the trail to see if we can determine where the dog came from."

"It's gotta be close," I murmured, more to myself than to anyone.

"What was that?" the captain inquired.

"Oh, I was just talking to myself. I was saying that, wherever Chip escaped from, it must be close. Plus, look at his condition. A dog lover was clearly caring for her while she was gone."

"How can you tell?"

Captain Nelson was now staring straight at me and I could see that I had his full, undivided attention. I scooted my chair a little closer to the window, prompting the captain to do the same. I pointed at Chip, who was resting by her owner's feet.

"The answers are there, with Chip. Look at him. I mean, her."

"What about her?" the captain wanted to know.

"Look at her condition. We can rule out running wild in the woods for close to a week. If she had, then her coat would be scraggly, disheveled. Look at the food and water bowls Vance placed in the room. Chip has barely had anything to drink. Mr. McGee stated that he came straight here after he had her checked out at Harry's office. What does that tell you?"

In case you had forgotten, Harrison Watt was the name of my best friend and, coincidentally, PV's only veterinarian.

The captain grunted with surprise, "It tells me that someone has been taking care of that dog."

"Look at the way she's laying at her owner's feet," I continued. "I've seen traumatized dogs before. They shake, they cower, and they'll never go to sleep in a strange environment. If I didn't know better, then I'd say that Chip is only moments away from falling asleep. That tells me that she feels safe enough in her current surroundings to allow herself to become vulnerable. That's a dog who I think enjoyed her time away from home."

"Become vulnerable?" Captain Nelson repeated. He frowned as he looked through the glass at the snoozing dog. "Why do you say that?"

"Because, believe it or not, I just did some research on this very subject. Granted, Chip is not laying on her back with her legs sticking straight up, but I will point out she's not in a fetal position, either. Dogs who are scared, and unwilling to expose any vulnerable parts of their anatomy —which are most outdoor dogs, for that matter —will always sleep in the fetal position."

The captain rose abruptly to his feet and headed toward the door. He motioned for me to follow. Curious, I did as I was instructed. After all, I was still a paid consultant for the PVPD.

"Sir?" Vance asked, as the door into the interrogation room opened, admitting the captain and myself.

"Our consultant here has brought up some good points," Captain Nelson began. "I'd like Mr. McGee to hear them."

Vance shrugged and turned back to Mr.

McGee.

"That's Captain Nelson on your left, and Zachary Anderson, one of our consultants, on the right. He apparently has a few questions for you."

"Not questions," I contradicted, "but some observations. Mr. McGee, could you confirm that you haven't given your dog any food or water since you've found her in the park earlier today?"

The elderly owner nodded. "That's right."

"Has Harry? Er, I mean, Dr. Watt?"

"No."

"Do you find that suspicious?" I asked.

Mr. McGee shrugged. "Kinda. Usually Chip eats like a horse, and I haven't seen her touch a morsel out of that food bowl yet. And trust me, she ain't picky."

"Suggesting...?" Vance prompted as he gave me a questioning look.

"That someone was feeding the dog," I patiently explained. "Someone was making sure that he, er, she was getting plenty of water. Look at her coat. If I didn't know any better, then I'd say someone actually brushed it for her." I knelt down next to the dog and ran my fingers through her fur. "Yeah, that's exactly what happened. Feel this. The coat isn't coarse, but nice and soft. You achieve that by brushing. Do you brush your dogs, Mr. McGee?"

Mr. McGee was running a hand through his

dog's fur. Surprised, he looked up at me and then over at Vance.

"I'll be damned. He's right. Chip's fur is not usually this soft. Someone brushed her?"

Vance looked at me with a puzzled look, "Wouldn't that suggest that someone swiped the dog in the hopes that they were planning on keeping it for themselves? Maybe try to win the dog over? This may not have been a dognapping after all."

"Or, it could mean the dognapper, or the dognapper's apprentice, was an animal lover," I hypothesized. "Someone clearly wanted to make sure the dog was being well cared for."

Captain Nelson rose from his chair, walked around the table, and squatted down next to Chip. He held out an outstretched hand and waited for the Labrador to come to him. The captain stroked the silky brown fur.

"You're right. This dog had to have been held near the park. Well, I think it's clear what you two need to do."

I sighed. "Check that park again?"

Captain Nelson nodded. "Yes. Be sure to take your two, er, assistants, with you."

Once the captain left, Vance looked over at Mr. McGee, who had been watching us. Then we noticed Chip staring at us as though we each had a raw steak in our pocket. Vance grinned as he looked down at Chip.

"What do you say, girl? Want to go to the park

again? Do you think you could get your daddy to help us out by telling us where he found you?"

* * *

"He said it was over here."

"No, he didn't," Vance argued. "Jeez, Zack. Every time I think your lousy sense of direction couldn't get any worse, you prove me wrong. Do you know what I'm gonna do? I'm going to get you one of those handheld GPS gizmos for Christmas this year. If you remember correctly, Mr. McGee said he found his dog southeast of the picnic area, farthest from the last barbecue pit you can see."

"Right," I argued. "That means he was talking about this pit."

Vance pulled his phone out, tapped the screen a few times, and then showed me what was on the display.

"See? This is north, and that is south. That means southeast is thataway."

"What app is that?" I wanted to know. The phone had a great big picture of what looked like the face of a compass, and the needle was pointing just behind my left shoulder.

"Do you know how they say there's an app for everything? This is literally a compass app. It's nothing fancy. Look it up. I think it'd come in handy for you. Provided you could figure it out, of course."

"Bite me, amigo," I grumbled.

"Besides," Vance continued, "look at the dogs. Sherlock wants to go southeast, too. I couldn't have asked for a clearer reason than that to head in that direction. We're going the right way, Zack."

"Who are you going to believe? Me, or the dog?"

"Do I have to answer that?"

I sighed and contemplated flipping Vance the bird. However, seeing how I was now on the pay-roll of the PVPD, I probably shouldn't piss off one of their detectives. Besides, Vance wasn't wrong. My sense of direction sucked rocks. I just hoped I wouldn't forget to install that compass app on my phone later today. I absolutely hated getting lost.

"Where is Mr. McGee now?" I asked as I turned to look back toward the main part of the park. "Didn't he say he was going to help us search?"

"He went home to get his other two dogs. He'll be here in just a few minutes."

Standing on the outskirts of the city park, near the border of the woods, I couldn't help but notice we were starting to draw a crowd. People walked by, saw both Sherlock and Watson waiting patiently to be allowed inside the woods, and began chatting animatedly amongst themselves. Fingers were pointed, cell phones appeared, and pictures were snapped (and presumably shared).

By the time Mr. McGee and his three Labs arrived, there was a group of about twenty people milling about in the park, just waiting to see what we were going to do.

"What is going on?" Vance quietly complained. "This is starting to look like a circus."

"Why don't we use them?" I countered. "They're here because they've no doubt heard about the dognappings, right?"

"So?"

"And, more than likely, they're fans of Sherlock and Watson. What do you say we make their day? Let's see if they'd be willing to help us search."

I heard the flapping of wings and, before I knew what was happening, a small animal had perched itself on my shoulder. A soft, feathered head nuzzled the side of my face, cooing softly in my ear. I stifled a groan, which caused Vance to look my way.

"I remember your avian admirer," Vance chuckled. "Wouldn't that suggest your favorite fan is here?"

"Well, if it isn't two of my most handsome admirers!" a loud female voice said from somewhere nearby. "Hello there, big boys! How are you on this fine day?"

I groaned as I turned to look at my shoulder. A small African gray parrot was returning my gaze. As if sensing how much discomfort his owner would inevitably give me, the bird chortled, bobbed its head a few times, and then whistled.

"Give us a kiss, Precious. Give us a kiss!"

"Hello there, Ruby. How are you today?"

"Hot and bothered, Precious. Hot and bothered."

My eyebrows shot open and a look of incredulous surprise appeared on my face. I glanced over at Vance to see him with a similar look on his face. Together, we turned to look at the bird's owner, one Ms. Clara Hanson, owner of A Lazy Afternoon bookstore, hurrying over to us.

Clara was in her sixties, enjoyed dressing as though she were in her twenties, and acted like she was in her teens. She also had no qualms about telling everyone who would listen that she was single, and indeed, ready to mingle. Her fourth husband, from what Harry had told me months ago, had dropped dead of an apparent heart attack. I quickly told my friend that the less I heard about the cause of death, the better.

Today, Clara was dressed in a dark blue jogging suit that, unfortunately, was unzipped all the way down to her navel, displaying quite of bit of her sports-bra encased chest. I looked up, got way more of an eyeful than I needed, and promptly dropped my eyes to the ground. However, I also noticed that Clara's face was red. Beet red.

"Did you teach your bird to say that?" Vance asked.

If possible, Clara blushed even further, "No. Heavens no. I have no idea where Ruby picked that one up. We're just out here enjoying the weather." Clara turned beseechingly to me and leered at me much the same way a predator would when it located prey. "So, my darling Zachary, I can't help but notice you brought your two adorable dogs with you. Your detective friend is here. Does that mean you're working a case?"

"Umm…"

"Ms. Hanson," Vance interjected, as he stepped up beside me, "you know full well we're working on a case. I can still hear the police scanner you left on in your car back there."

"Well, it's not against the law to be curious, is it?" Clara returned, placing her hands on her hips.

"Of course not. I wish more of our citizens had them."

"You do?" I said as I turned to my friend, dumbfounded.

"You do?" Clara echoed.

"Of course. It means you care about what's going on. Now, I think I'll go with your suggestion, Zack. Perhaps if you could round those people up over there and I'll take … Ms. Hanson? Would you take your bird back? Zack and I have work to do."

"Is there something I can do?" Clara hopefully asked as she pulled a few sliced carrots from her pocket. She tapped them on her shoulder, which had Ruby abandoning her perch and flying to her owner.

Carrots. I had no idea parrots loved carrots. You learn something new every day.

"There is something you can do," Vance was telling Clara. "You can be in Zack's group. Wait here while we gather everyone around. We're going to be conducting a search of the park."

"Oh, honey. You just made my day! So, what are we looking for?"

"We'll tell everyone at the same time," Vance promised.

Once we had assembled all the curious on-lookers, which turned out to be every single one of them (perhaps two dozen in all), Vance lined them up and split them into two groups. Mr. McGee arrived moments later with over two hundred pounds of hyper dogs. I quickly indicated he should join Vance's group.

As Vance was explaining what we were doing, which was to try and ascertain where Chip had been held while she was missing, I noticed that there were several dogs in my group. Besides Sherlock and Watson, of course. Both corgis had their ears sticking straight up and were giving warning woofs at any of the dogs, should they wander too close.

One woman, probably around my age, had a beautiful golden retriever. The silky golden coat sparkled lustrously in the sunlight. That was one pampered pup, I thought. Then a middle-aged gentleman appeared at the back of the

group and I saw an Irish Setter sitting compla-
cently on the ground by the man's right heel.

Sherlock woofed at this dog, too.

I noticed a young family with two small children near the front of my group. The man met
my eyes and nodded. Both of his children, a girl
of five and a boy of eight, were staring—trans-
fixed—at the corgis. Then the mother came into
view and I saw that she was holding a small
white dog. Maybe a bichon frise? Or some type
of terrier? Then I was able to get a closer look.
It had to be the smallest damn dog I think I had
ever seen. All I could see was a tiny ball of fluffy
white fur. The woman saw me looking at her and
smiled.

"Isn't she cute? She's only eight weeks old."

"Umm, what is she, exactly?"

The husband looked at me and nodded.
"Thank you. See, honey? He didn't know what it
was, either."

"She's a toy poodle, and only a baby at that,"
the woman huffed out, lifting her nose. "Just because you lost the coin toss doesn't mean you
have to be rude. You'll love her, Brian. I know
you will."

I glanced at the husband, who rolled his eyes
and shook his head. I felt some movement on the
leashes, so I glanced down to see what my dogs
were doing. Sherlock had his neck craned all the
way back in an attempt to study the white fluff-
ball. The woman, thinking it'd make a great pic-

ture, started to lower the sleeping puppy down to corgi-level when I noticed Sherlock's ears were now lying flat against his head. Watson's, too.

"Better hold off on that," I warned the mom. "When I see his ears droop down like that, it tells me he's not happy with the situation. I'm actually surprised the two of them aren't barking their fool heads off."

The woman immediately straightened and sighed. "It's no bother. I'm used to it. Other dogs always seem to get so jealous of little Sonya. Anyway, I'm glad we decided to go for a walk. I would've been upset had I missed the chance to help search for those missing dogs."

The family moved off.

"Remember, people," Vance was saying, "you're looking for anything out of the ordinary. Like I said earlier, we have reason to believe that one of the dogs who was dognapped has been held somewhere nearby. This dog managed to escape, so I'd like to see if anyone can tell where this dog came from. Everyone with me?"

People were nodding their heads.

"All right. Everyone head out. Concentrate to the south and the east, and everything in between. If you see anything, find either myself or Zack, or any policeman, for that matter."

"Don't forget to tell them to not do anything stupid," I quietly added.

Vance snapped his fingers "A damn fine point.

People, if you come across anyone that appears shady, or doing something that they shouldn't be doing, you are to find me or Zack immediately. You will not try anything heroic, is that understood?"

"I'd definitely try him first," I joked, pointing at Vance. "He's got the gun."

That comment earned a round of laughter. Just like that, the ice was broken and people began chatting amongst themselves as they moved into the forest. I literally watched people head out in all directions. So much for following instructions.

"What was Sherlock's problem with that white dog?" Vance asked as we stepped into the woods.

"I'm really not sure," I admitted. "It was just a puppy, although I had no idea dogs could get that small."

"What kind of dog was it?"

"The woman identified it as a toy poodle. That's the smallest version of that dog, right? There couldn't possibly be anything smaller than that. That thing couldn't have been more than a pound or two."

Vance nodded. "I think you're right. There's toy, then miniature, and then the big-ass variety."

"Big-ass?" I snickered.

"Have you seen them?" Vance asked as we pushed deeper into the woods. "I saw one last year that had to be well over sixty pounds and looked to be bigger than Anubis."

"Did it have that funky haircut like many poodles have?" I asked.

"Yep. Half the dog's fur was long, the other half shaved, with…"

Just as Vance was launching into a diatribe of weird canine haircuts, his cell phone started ringing. Loudly. It was enough to make both of us jump.

"Detective Samuelson. I … Hey Jules, how's it going? Where am I? At the park. Captain Nelson suggested … No, the one on the east side of town. As I was saying, Captain Nelson suggested we should try to figure out where Mr. McGee's recovered dog had been held. We figured out that it has to be … what? Would you please repeat that?"

Curiosity piqued, I sidled closer, hoping to be able to hear what Julie Watt, or 'Jules' to her friends, was telling Vance. I should also mention that Julie was my best friend Harry's wife. However, I don't know whether Julie was talking in a low voice, or else I was too far away, but I couldn't make out anything.

"Okay. Thanks, Jules. You'd better send Jones and Peters out here. We have a group of civilians helping us search through the park and I can't even begin to imagine how bad that'd make the PVPD look if we abandoned them. They're gonna need some type of supervision. What? No, we're on our way right now."

"What's going on?" I asked, as soon as the call was terminated.

Vance took my arm and guided us toward the park.

"There's been another dognapping. This one happened less than ten minutes ago."

"What? Where??"

"At the other park."

EIGHT

We arrived at a surprising scene of utter calm, since there were fewer people in this park than the other one. With that being said, in the time it took us to park our cars, four more cars pulled in next to us. Each of the cars, I noted with dismay, was crammed with people and their dogs. They piled out of the cars in time to see nearly a half dozen more turn into the park's drive. All were filled to capacity.

"This is just great," I heard Vance grumble. "I'm gonna have to call for backup before these people decide to take matters into their own hands."

I was somewhat reluctant to bring Sherlock and Watson into the middle of this throng of people, but I really didn't have a choice. I was here to investigate the disappearance of another dog. I certainly couldn't do that while hiding in my Jeep, although it sure sounded like a great idea.

"Whose idea was it to become a police consultant?" I asked the dogs as I placed them on the ground. Both dogs turned to stare curiously at me, as though they couldn't believe their canine ears. "Okay, stop looking at me like that. I enjoy solving mysteries just as much as you two do. And yes, maybe you're better at it than I am."

Sherlock snorted and turned on his heel, leading us straight into the heart of the park. I followed the dogs, and Vance followed me. Conversations came to an abrupt halt as Vance and I pushed by the curious onlookers in order to keep up with the corgis. Being low to the ground, Sherlock and Watson had no trouble navigating their way around the boots and sneakers they found in their way.

"Now might be a good time for you to make that call, pal," I whispered over my shoulder.

A few seconds later, I heard Vance on his phone, requesting backup. Turns out we wouldn't have long to wait. Apparently, they were already on their way. As for me, I had my hands full keeping a tight grip on the leashes and trying not to piss people off as I pushed my way by.

"Excuse me. Sorry 'bout this. Yeah, I know. I'm a klutz. Look, I'm just following my dogs, okay? Whoops, pardon me. Sherlock, I hope you know where you're going."

Of course, the din of nearly a dozen conversations started up again the moment Sherlock and Watson were recognized. It was as if someone had unmuted the park itself. Before I knew what was happening, it was suddenly so noisy that I could barely hear anything, let alone my detective friend who was directly behind me.

"Oh, look! There are those adorable corgis," I heard one woman say to her companion.

"They must be on the case!" the second woman exclaimed.

"Perhaps I should tell them that they're looking for someone driving a white windowless van?" a man's voice said.

"He's looking for no such thing," another male voice contradicted. "It wasn't a cargo van, but a minivan. And it was red."

"You're both wrong," a third voice added. "They're looking for a silver van."

"I thought the guy got into a lifted pickup truck?" a tremulous voice said. "At least, that's what I saw."

My head jerked up. The possibility of interviewing a witness who could identify our suspect wasn't something I could ignore. Realizing that I had to act on this new information, I pulled the dogs to a stop and turned to see a young guy, probably early twenties, with thick glasses and a pale complexion. Truth be told, this guy looked like he'd be more comfortable in front of a computer. Still, I had to talk to him.

"You saw this guy? Could you describe him for me? What did he look like? Any distinguishing characteristics?"

Pale Dude nodded, pleased that someone was paying attention to him.

"Yeah. Several. Let's see, this guy was huge. I'd say he was at least six and a half feet tall. Probably weighed around 300 pounds, easy. He was ripped. Covered in tattoos."

"Was that the guy that had some type of bag slung over his shoulder?" a woman asked, frowning.

My informant nodded. "That's right. I had forgotten about the bag. Yeah, he had a big green duffel bag of some sort. I think it could have been military issue. I couldn't make out what was in it, only that it looked heavy."

"How heavy?" I wanted to know.

"Maybe forty or fifty pounds? It's hard to say. I don't think I would have been able to lift it."

Without a notebook handy, I had to resort to my phone. I started texting all the details to Vance, so that there'd be some type of written record in place. I looked back at my informant and nodded appreciatively.

"Do you, by chance, happen to know the make and model of his vehicle?"

Pale Dude didn't bat an eye, "It was a 2006 Chevy Silverado 2500HD, with what looked to be at least an eighteen-inch lift kit installed."

I was surprised that he had such a detailed answer. I texted the information just as fast as I could. I'm sure I could have done it faster, had I used two hands, but I'm sorry to say that I'm a single-finger texter. Once I finished, I glanced up and around at the people who were gathering around us.

"Did anyone catch the license plate?"

"It was a personalized plate," I heard someone say. "You're talking about that big brown truck, right?"

My informant nodded. "Right, only it was dark blue, not brown."

"I thought it was more of a charcoal color," one woman decided.

"Are we sure we're all talking about the same truck?" I asked, raising my voice so I could be heard over the chatter coming at me from all directions.

Heads were nodding. I felt a tug on the leash. Both of the dogs wanted to keep heading farther into the park.

"Just a sec, guys. We're almost done here."

I sent the text off to Vance, who then seemed to magically appear by my side.

"Backup's on the way," Vance quietly informed me. "I got your text. How reliable is the information?"

"Completely," my informant answered, overhearing the question.

"Only you guys can't be sure of the truck's color?" Vance asked as he looked around the group. "Did anyone agree on a color?"

"Only that it was dark," a different man—who up until this point hadn't said a word—added.

"What about those two dog walkers?" a woman's voice asked.

Both Vance and I shared a look. With a sigh, Vance pulled out his notebook. He jotted down the notes I had texted him and then—and only then—did he turn to see who had spoken.

It was a girl in her late twenties, holding a Starbuck's coffee cup in one hand and a neon purple leash in the other. I followed the leash down to the ground to see what kind of dog she had. I pegged her as maybe a yorkie or a chihuahua owner, but surprisingly enough, the dog on the other end of the leash was anything but. It was a Rottweiler, and a big one at that. This beast had to be 140 pounds of solid muscle.

The Rottie was sitting on its haunches and staring disconcertedly at me, as though it was trying to decide whether or not I should be considered 'crunchy' or 'original'.

"That's one big dog," I heard Vance mutter.

"Who, Samson?" the woman asked. "Oh, psssht. There's no need to worry about him. Samson wouldn't hurt a flea, would you, big boy? That is, unless I tell him to."

Those great jaws opened and a pink tongue flopped out. Samson panted contentedly as I gave the Rottie a friendly scratch on the top of his head. Right about then, I heard a warning woof. Together, both Samson and I looked down.

Sitting directly between the huge dog's front legs was Sherlock, who was staring up at the much larger dog, as though he was daring Samson to do something stupid. When the huge canine continued to stare curiously at him, Sherlock woofed again. Samson cocked his head, regarded Sherlock for a few more moments, and then dropped his head down to the ground. Then, much to his owner's chagrin, Samson flopped over onto his back to expose his belly to the world.

I'm sure my mouth fell open. Had Sherlock just stared down a huge Rottweiler? We're talking about a little dog that couldn't weigh more than thirty pounds, staring down a Rottweiler, which had to have over a hundred pounds on him, easy. Watson, on the other hand, was peeking out at the large stranger from behind my legs.

Sherlock approached Samson, raised one of his stumpy front legs, and reverently placed a paw on his nose.

I'll be honest. The first thing that went through my mind was, I was going to have to test Harry's skills as a vet and see if he could surgically reattach a leg. After he removed it from the stomach of a Rottweiler, that is.

Thankfully, I had nothing to worry about.

Samson yipped excitedly, like a puppy, and stared at Sherlock as though the little corgi was the Grand High Poobah of the Canine Universe.

"Samson? What are you doing? Get back up, you goofball! Hey, Mister! How did your dog make my dog do that? I've never seen Samson back down from anything. It was one of the reasons why I got him."

I looked down at the small (in comparison) corgi and shook my head. "Haven't a clue. I was ready to grab both Sherlock and Watson and run for the hills."

"Sherlock? *This* is Sherlock? And that's Watson? Oh my goodness! I've heard of your dogs! Oooo, they're so cute!"

A high-pitched voice, you may recall, was corgi-speak for immediate acceptance into the pack. Sherlock wiggled with delight and actually rose up onto his hind legs and bounced a few times. Samson slowly rolled to his feet.

"Sorry 'bout that," I apologized, as I pulled Sherlock down. "He knows he's not supposed to jump up on people, yet he does it anyway, just to spite me."

"You have the cutest dogs," the girl continued to gush. "Not like my pushover. I cannot believe Samson is such a wimp."

"So, what were you saying about a dog walker?" Vance asked.

The girl held up two fingers, "Two, actually. There were two dog walkers. One was an older lady, with about five tiny dogs, and the other was a man who was younger than you. Probably more my age, I'd say."

Wise-guy. Why does the younger generation always make age-related comments at my expense? Teeny boppers.

"Where'd they go?" I hastily asked. I heard how gruff my voice sounded and flinched. Jillian would definitely not approve. "How many dogs did the guy have with him?"

"Well, this park only has one parking lot," Samson's owner pointed out. "They both left that way. I'm sorry, I didn't see what they were driving. As for the number of dogs, I'd say he had three or four. Hey, can I take a picture?"

Surprised, I could only stare at the girl.

"Of your dogs," the girl clarified. "I think they are the cutest, most adorable corgis I've ever seen!"

My face reddened. For half a moment, I thought she was asking whether or not she could take my picture, as though she was a devoted fan of my books. Well, nothing like a brutal reality check to bring one back to one's senses.

"Why do you think the man was a dog walker?" Vance wanted to know. "Many people have three dogs or more. Couldn't they have all been his?"

The woman shook her head. "These dogs acted like they didn't like each other. Each one wanted to go in a different direction."

"Like this was the first time they had ever spent time together," I breathed. I looked over at Vance. "What do you think?"

Vance thanked the woman and sent her on her way. He pointed at a section of the park nearly twenty feet away that, for the time being, was devoid of people. Once we were there, Vance consulted his notebook.

"Do you know how many different stories I've heard about this dognapper?" he began. "It's like everyone saw something different."

"Did you find any tire tracks?" I asked.

Vance nodded. "I did, yes. Three."

"Three sets of tire tracks? Well, hopefully one of them is the right one."

"No, you don't understand. I found a nice long section of dirt, with a very clear impression of tracks. There were three of them, all running parallel with one another."

"How big?" I wanted to know.

Vance held up two fingers, indicating no more than an inch and a half thick.

"Just like the last one," I observed.

"First one track," Vance recalled, "Then two, and now three. I wonder what the chances of the next one having four is."

"Hopefully there won't be a next one," I remarked.

"A good point."

"With regard to all the different versions of our suspected dognapper, do you think the truth is somewhere in there?" I asked. "Then it'd just be a matter of narrowing down the suspects."

Vance shrugged. "I have no idea if any of these stories will pan out. I think the two most likely candidates are the guy with the duffel bag in the oversized truck and this male dog walker. He clearly didn't have control over his dogs, so it makes me wonder if it might be our sympathetic dog lover."

"Doing what?" I asked. "Giving the incarcerated dogs a chance to stretch their legs?"

"It might be just as simple as that, so yeah. That could be it."

"Well, if that's the case, how do we go about identifying these two guys?"

Vance gave the surrounding environment a sweeping gesture with his arm.

"I say we do this the old-fashioned way. I'll canvass the area and look for anyone who might have video surveillance of the park."

The look I gave Vance must have had skepticism written all over it.

"What? It's possible."

"No, it's not," I argued. "It's not like there are a lot of possibilities around here. "Where do you think you'll find cameras? I see one building over there, on the west side of the park, and there's that brown one back there, on the south side. However, that's it, as far as I can tell."

Vance had a smug look on his face, which instantly made me defensive. What did he know that I didn't? I crossed my arms over my chest and scowled.

"What? You think you know something that I don't? I ... Sherlock, what are you doing? What are you growling at?"

Interested, Vance joined me as we looked at the large, distant building on the western perimeter of the park.

"What's wrong? Why is he growling?"

I shrugged. "No clue. Sherlock, knock it off.

There's nothing that way, okay? Calm down. Watson, no. Don't you start, too. Now, what were you saying?"

"I was saying, one—or both—of those two places will have exterior cameras."

"Bull."

"Care to put your money where your mouth is?"

My lips thinned. "All right. What's the wager?"

"If either of those two buildings have exterior video surveillance, then you'll have to ... you'll have to ... hmm."

"This ought to be good," I said to the dogs. Both corgis were watching the interplay between the two of us, like they were watching a tennis match.

Vance suddenly snapped his fingers. "I've got it. If I win, you'll put my daughters in your next book."

"Dude, I write romance novels," I reminded my friend. "It'd be kinda awkward to throw a couple of underage girls in there, dontcha think?"

"Their names, you idiot. You'll name two characters in your next book after Tiffany and Victoria."

"And if I win?" I prompted.

"Then ... let's see. What could I ... oh, I know! You've been pestering me to see that damn Hobbit movie for some time now. I'll watch that with you."

I've been pushing Vance to see one of the Hobbit movies, or one of the Lord of the Rings movies for quite some time. Those six movies happen to take up six slots in my Top Ten Favorite Movies of All Time list, and I was determined Vance would see at least one of them. The question was, which one? A devious idea just formed.

"Alright, pal. You'll watch the Hobbit movies with me if you lose, agreed?"

"Wait, you threw an 's' in there. I only said one movie, not two."

"There are six total," I clarified, which earned me a groan from Vance. "You'll either watch the complete Hobbit trilogy or the complete Lord of the Rings trilogy. My choice."

"Fine. You win."

"Extended editions."

"You're insane, but that's okay. I still agree."

"What do you know that I don't?" I demanded. "That's over ten hours' of movies and you didn't bat an eye. Have I already lost?"

Vance nodded. "Yup. That building there, to the west, is the Community Center. That's where Tori teaches her dance classes. In fact, you've been there, I'm sure."

"Of course I have. I watched you dress up as Peter Pan last year, remember? Who do you think recorded that video?"

"That was you?" Vance sputtered as he turned to me. "Are you the one who posted that clip on

YouTube?"

I grinned. "Maybe."

"Zack, that damn thing went viral. I had people all over the planet leaving comments on that."

"How did you even know you were on You-Tube?" I asked.

"Because Victoria found it and played it for me. I damn near snotted my beer all over the dinner table, and we had the Nelsons over for dinner."

I fought to keep my voice from quavering.

"The police captain?"

"Yes."

"And, uh, what did Captain Nelson think about it?" I asked, as I nonchalantly wiped the corners of my eyes with the back of my hand.

"He thought it was hilarious, you jerk."

"At least he has a sense of humor," I pointed out. I turned to indicate the smaller building that was on the park's south side. "And that? What building is that?"

"That? The brownstone? That's the town hall. It's where the mayor's office is. You'd better believe they're going to have cameras there. In fact, there's probably half a dozen all pointed outside."

"You don't know that for sure," I protested. "Besides, there's no way you'd be able to use anything from them. They're much too far away."

"If the quality is good enough, then the boys

at the lab might be able to enlarge the video while keeping the image viable."

"If you can't use the image, then you can't say that you won," I grumped.

"We never agreed to that. The bet was whether or not there was video surveillance equipment at either of those two buildings."

"Which you already knew there were," I pointed out. "I was set up. You owe me at least this."

Vance was silent as he pondered.

"Very well. If there's nothing I can use, then I'll put on my pointed ears and watch those movies with you."

Satisfied, I nodded. Vance moved off, intent on preventing himself from watching ten plus hours of Middle Earth goodness. As for me, I continued to watch the people shuffling aimlessly about in the park. Should we organize a search party as we had done at the other park? Speaking of the other park, I wondered if anyone had found anything yet.

While waiting for confirmation that Vance was going to attend my next Middle Earth marathon, the dogs and I wandered around the perimeter of the park. Sherlock and Watson, unfortunately, didn't bark once. Well, that's not true. They did fire off several warning woofs as a plethora of people walked by with all kinds of various dogs.

Various dogs...

I looked down at the corgis and frowned. Now that I thought about it, I couldn't remember one instance of a duplicate breed being stolen. Every single one of them was different, from the chocolate Labrador that Mr. McGee lost, to Snoopy the beagle, belonging to Captain Nelson's granddaughter, and finally, Anubis, the German Shepherd, belonging to Vance and his family. Not one of them was a repeat.

I found the nearest bench and sat down. I needed to think about this. Thankfully, both corgis cooperated by plopping down in the soft grass next to me to watch the people walk by.

What about the Medford cases? Were there any repeats in there? I had to wrack my brain to come up with a partial list of breeds that had been reported missing. There had been a boxer, a chow-chow, and that Portuguese breed I didn't have a prayer in remembering. None of them were repeats, either.

Excited, I stood. What did you want to bet that, if we were to compare the list of missing dogs from Medford and the missing dogs from PV, that none of them would be the same? And further, hadn't the breeds been grouped together by the AKC into six or seven categories? Was that important?

I pulled out my phone and searched for the answer. Yep, there it was. There were seven groups of dogs that were recognized by the AKC: terrier, sporting, non-sporting, working, hound, toy, and herding. And there, thanks to the power of the Internet, was a list of breeds and which group they belonged to.

After spending a few minutes running through the various breeds I could remember, I knew I had to find Vance. He needed to hear about this. I was certain this was the big break we were looking for. I thought of the captain's granddaughter—I forgot her name—and how badly she needed her dog back, and my resolve strengthened.

We're going to return Snoopy to you, kiddo. Safe and sound. That's a promise. Hmm, I could remember the dog's name, but not the kid's? I wonder what that said about me.

I saw Vance slowly walking back to me with a smug look of assurance on his face. Dammit. Guess I'm creating two new female characters in my next book. Oh, well. His daughters will be thrilled to be included in a novel. I just had to be certain I kept those characters 'clean'. Anyone who reads romance novels will know what I mean by that.

"Told you, pal," Vance began, as he grinned at me. "Both buildings have security systems. Both have exterior cameras."

"Were any of them pointed this way?"

"Two from the Town Hall and one from the Community Center," Vance confirmed. "All three are high-def cameras with built-in infrared sensors. I've seen our boys pull up a license plate number from over a hundred yards away with worse cameras. Know what this means? I'm saved. There'll be no little people with furry toes in my future, thank you very much. Hey, you're taking this a lot better than I thought you would. Is there something you're not telling me?"

"I've got something to tell you. Something that I think will help us out. Are we done here? Can we go get some lunch? I'll run what I have by you then."

Vance nodded. "Sure. Let me finish up here and we can go."

Thirty minutes later, we were sitting on the pet-friendly terrace at Casa de Joe's. As soon as the waitress left with our orders, Vance looked at me and raised an eyebrow. He pulled out his notebook and clicked his pen open. He was ready to write.

"I think that whomever is stealing these dogs is deliberately choosing each breed."

A look of disgust appeared on Vance's face as he clicked his pen again, retracting the ink tip.

"What?" I demanded. "It's a promising theory! Don't you think so?"

"That's your big news? Zack, we already know this. In fact, we put two and two together after the second dognapping here in PV."

I released the breath I didn't know I had been holding and my feeling of euphoria rapidly evaporated.

"That took the wind out of your sails, didn't it?" Vance observed. "I'm sorry, buddy. It's a good theory. However, it didn't pan out."

"What did you guys learn?" I slowly asked. Damn! I really thought I was on to something.

The waitress came by to refill our drinks. She caught sight of the corgis, stooped to give each a pat on their heads, and quickly retreated inside the restaurant.

Vance flipped backwards through his note-book. After a few minutes, he paused on a page and began to read through his notes. A minute or so later, he tapped his finger on the page.

"How many of those things do you go through?" I suddenly asked, before he could start talking. I was pointing at the notebook.

"What? These notebooks? Typically two or three."

"A month?"

"A week."

"Oh. Wow."

"You wanted to know about all the different breeds? Here's what we have."

"Just a moment," I said, as I pulled out my phone. Thankfully, the AKC page was still loaded on my screen. I looked at Vance's tiny notebook and pointed a finger. "Got any more of those handy? I'm thinking I should be taking some notes here."

"No, sorry. They're all in my desk back at HQ. Here, use the napkin."

While not ideal, it would do. I absconded with Vance's pen and prepared to jot notes in my makeshift notebook.

"Ready. What's the first one?"

"From PV or Medford?"

"Let's do Medford first. What do you have?"

"Boxer."

I punched in my search and then stared at the results.

"Working group," I reported. Then I jotted it down on the napkin. "Next?"

"The Portuguese Podengo Pequeno."

"Good job pronouncing that one. Let's see. Hound group.

"Uh huh. How about the yellow Lab?"

I tapped away on my screen.

"Sporting."

"And the chow?" Vance continued.

"Non-sporting."

"What about the Australian Shepherd?" Vance continued.

"Herding," I reported.

"And last, but certainly not least, the miniature schnauzer."

"I think that one should be terrier," I said, after a few moments of searching had passed. "Yep. There he is. Wait, that's the last?"

Vance consulted his notes, "Yeah. Why?"

"Because there are seven groups, not six. Thus far, we have six of the seven represented."

"Which one are we missing?" Vance wanted

to know.

"The toy group."

"Hmph. I assume only tiny dogs are in that group? I don't remember seeing anything that falls into that category."

"Let's check the PV cases," I eagerly suggested. My theory was starting to sound better with each passing moment. The icing on the cake was that I could see Vance was thinking along those same lines, too.

"Okay, the first dog to be reported missing was Mr. McGee's Chocolate Labrador," Vance informed me.

"Which we now know as sporting. What else?"

"Next up is Anubis," Vance grimly reported.

"German Shepherd. They're in the herding group."

"And Snoopy, the beagle?"

"Hang on. I'm having trouble finding the ... oh, there he is. The beagle is part of the hound group."

It was at this point that I noticed Vance started taking some serious notes.

"Then we have the dog that was taken today," my friend said next.

I looked up, surprised.

"I had forgotten about him. What type of dog was he?"

"She," Vance corrected. He flipped his notebook back a page and skimmed through his notes. "There she is. A chocolate-colored cocker spaniel was taken. Answers to the name of Kona."

"Cocker spaniel," I repeated, as I punched the breed into my phone. "There they are. Vance, the cocker spaniels are part of the sporting group, too. We have our first repeat! Wait. I'm not sure I should be excited or bummed."

Right about then, I noticed my friend's face. Vance's eyes had lit up. He hurriedly flipped through his notes, read a page and a half, and then excitedly snapped his notebook closed.

"On the contrary, buddy, you should be very excited."

"Okay. Why?"

"Don't you get it? What's the one breed that managed to escape from his captors?"

"Do you mean Chip?" I asked. "Don't you mean, 'her'?"

"Yeah, yeah. You know what I mean. What group does Chip belong to?"

"Well, she's a Labrador," I recalled, "so they belong to the..." I trailed off as my eyes widened.

Vance clapped me on the back, "That's right, pal. Labradors belong in the sporting group. You just said so yourself. That's the same group as the cocker spaniels. You can't possibly tell me that this is a coincidence. A member of the sporting group is taken. The dog escapes. Whoever took the dog in the first place is pissed. Now they don't have a sporting dog anymore, so what do they do?"

I was nodding. "They take another one. To replace Chip! But why didn't they take any dog from the toy group?"

"Maybe because they're fans of the toy group and have strict orders to leave any dog which belongs in that group alone?"

I glanced down at my napkin and read through the different breed names and their respective groups. Yes, sure enough, there were no representatives from the smallest AKC group there. Nor had there been any dognappings from that particular group here in PV, either.

Sherlock yawned and then shook his collar. My eyes flicked over to the tri-color back of my male corgi and my eyes widened again. Vance, who had been watching me closely, stiffened with surprise.

"What? What is it?"

"Is this the part where I tell you that, for the last couple of days, Sherlock has been barking at teeny-tiny small dogs?"

NINE

Damn it, Zack! What's the rule? Hmm? Didn't I tell you that, whenever we're all working on a case, if Sherlock and Watson start exhibiting peculiar behaviors, you're to tell me? How long has this been going on?"

"Umm, let me think. It's been several days now, about the same time as..."

"Let me guess," Vance interrupted. "From the same time as the first dog was taken?"

I nodded. "That sounds about right."

"They've only barked at small dogs? The kind that belong in this toy group?"

I pondered a moment and eventually nodded. "Yep. They've only shown interest in small dogs. Are you gonna yell at me now?"

"If this pans out, you can count on it."

"I thought you said that the police have already investigated this whole AKC dog group thing."

Vance shook his head. "No, what I told you was that we've already checked out the different breeds angle. We didn't spot any correlations between what's happened in Medford and the string of thefts here in PV."

"And now?" I prompted.

Vance nodded. "Hey, I'll be the first to admit that our investigators were a little on the lax side, especially since I was one of 'em. Clearly, we didn't dig as deep as we should have."

"And what about Medford?"

Vance shrugged. "What about them? They launched their own investigation and came up with the same results we did. Let them deal with their own problems. We've got our own to contend with."

"So, what's the next step?" I wanted to know. Being a newly hired police consultant, I was eager to sound like I knew what I was doing.

Vance shrugged and held out a hand, indicating I should answer my own question.

"Well," I slowly began, "I would think we would need to find out if there are any type of small dog breed clubs here in Pomme Valley."

Vance was nodding. "That'd be a great place to start. So, how do you plan on accomplishing that? I doubt the dog clubs are in the phone book."

I hooked a thumb behind me as I looked up. "There's a café less than two blocks from here. I'm pretty sure they have a couple of public computers there we could use. It'd be easier than trying to tap everything into this damn phone."

"What's the matter, pal? Is your eyesight starting to fail you? It's what happens with age, ya know."

I scowled at Vance. "Bite me. Why is it everyone gets such a kick out of cracking age jokes at my expense?"

"Well, I can't speak for others, but seeing you pout always puts a grin on my face."

"Jerk," I grumbled.

"Plus, you're the oldest one in our group."

I gave a visible start at this.

"What? Oh, man. Say it ain't so."

"You, Harry, and Jules are all the same age. Harry's birthday is two months after yours, and Julie's is one month after that."

"And how do you know this?" I demanded.

"We figured it out the other day. Quiet. You'll make me lose my train of thought."

"Mm-hmm."

"Where was I?"

"You, me, and Harry. I'm the oldest. You were saying Harry is several months younger than me?"

Vance snapped his fingers. "Right. Okay, so if you, Harry, and Julie are all are 43, and I'm 39, Jillian is 36, and Tori is 35, that would make you...?"

"The oldest," I groaned. "But, you have to admit, it's not by much."

Vance grinned at me, just like the Cheshire cat would grin at Alice.

"Whatever," I crossly said as I pushed to my feet. "I'm going to take the dogs home and then head to Wired Coffee & Café. We'll meet there in, say, about twenty minutes?"

"Sounds good."

Half an hour later, the two of us were perched uncomfortably on small barstools, staring at the flickering screen of an ancient computer that needed to be put out of its misery. Badly. And don't get me started about the layers of sticky residue I found on the keyboard. I was really starting to regret my decision to use a public computer. I should have just had Vance follow me home. My laptop was there, as was my encrypted, ramped up high-speed Internet connection.

So, why would I choose to come here? Well, to be completely honest, it was because of the wonderful piece of technological sophistication located in the corner of the café. Those who know me will attest to the simple fact that I enjoy drinking soda. It was my preferred method of ingesting caffeine. Interestingly enough, I've never really considered myself a caffeine junkie, but when presented with the overwhelming fact that I always seem to have a soda in my hand, I'd have to agree. Whatever. As I was saying, when I found out this sleepy little town had one of those ultra-modern choose-your-own-flavor soda machines, I found myself stopping by this coffee shop way more than I probably should.

Therefore, while Vance was pecking away at the computer, I ordered myself a large soda from the pick-your-flavor machine on the opposite wall and—as a joke—I ordered him the biggest cup of coffee that they'd sell me. Interestingly, for you coffee lovers, this shop calls its humongo size TDS, which stands for tall, dark, and scary. The name alone made me laugh. Then I wrinkled my nose as I caught a whiff of the thirty-plus ounces of black coffee.

Vance glanced briefly at me as I set our two drinks down on the counter.

"Hey, cool! Thanks, Zack."

Wow. He didn't raise an eyebrow and he didn't seem surprised. I set my much larger soda down next to his drink and focused on the monitor.

"You drink too much soda," Vance accused, as he caught sight of my 64-ounce cup.

"You drink too much coffee," I returned, pointing at Vance's coffee. "Dude, I bought that for you as a joke, just to see if you'd notice that I gave you the biggest cup of coffee that they sell. You didn't even blink. Then again, I'm not one to talk. Mine is bigger than yours."

Vance's clickety-clacking on the keyboard froze.

"That came out wrong," I groaned. "I didn't mean ... forget it."

"Consider it forgotten."

After a few moments, the guy using the second computer rose to his feet and left. I waited a few minutes to see if there were any other takers, but when no one sat down in front of it, I slid over to begin my own research. I wanted to know if any small dog clubs called PV home. Several minutes later, we had our answers. Well, at least some of them. Plus, I found out that the clubs weren't segregated by breed but by AKC group. Between Medford and PV, every single AKC group was represented by some type of amateur dog club.

Here they are, in no particular order. The terrier group has a club in Medford; herding has clubs in both Medford and PV; sporting could only be found in Medford. The non-sporting group has clubs in Medford and PV; hound also has clubs in both cities; working was only in Medford, and toy could be found in both Medford and PV.

I noticed Vance had just checked the time on his cell phone, so I chose that moment to take a healthy swig of my soda.

"What do you think?" I asked, as I looked at the detective. "Think we should go check out these toy-breed clubs?"

Vance nodded. "Sounds like a plan. How many are there and where can we find 'em? Does it say?"

I went back to PV's listing for toy group clubs and clicked the link. Sadly, it didn't tell me much.

"There's two," I said. "One in PV and one in Medford. I don't see a permanent address for PV's club. I'm not even seeing a contact number."

"Then how are you supposed to join their

club?" Vance asked, frowning. "There's gotta be some way to contact them."

"Looks like they have bi-monthly meetings, but it doesn't specify where," I added, as I continued to skim through the meager data on the screen. "It only gives the dates. According to this, the most recent meeting happened just last week."

"And there's nothing in there about a contact person?"

"Nothing that I can see."

"What about the other clubs?" Vance asked. "Maybe one of them knows how to get in touch with the other groups."

I instantly singled out the PV herding club, since that's the group Pembroke Welsh Corgis belonged to, and checked for contact information. We were in luck. Not only did the herding club maintain accurate, up-to-date information on their website, but they also had a phone number listed. I nudged Vance and pointed at the screen.

"Bingo. Found a number for the guy this web site says is the president of the PV herding club."

Vance nodded. "Beautiful. Give me the number. I'll give them a call right now."

While Vance wandered off to conduct his call, I continued to peruse through all the various club pages. Practically all of them had professionally done web sites, complete with forums where guests and users could leave comments for one another. Let me tell you, it made for some interesting reading.

Surprisingly, almost every club forum had a complaints section, and those sections were far and away the most popular. Apparently, people loved to complain about anything and everything. The most recent one involved a person griping about a pile of dog poo in the park, as if they could tell by sight and smell what breed was responsible. Dumbasses. I mean, seriously? Was it even possible to tell what dog did their business by studying their droppings? Man alive, people had way too much time on their hands.

I should also point out that it seemed like just about every club was at odds with another club. I mean, what were we, back in grade school? These were legitimate clubs, run by adults. How petty could one get?

Based on these forums, the answer to that was *extremely*. The sporting group were natural rivals of the non-sporting members. Okay, I could get on board with that. Then the terrier club members were at odds with the hound group. I must've skimmed through their entire forum—both of them—and was unable to find out what the problem was, for either side.

Coming up next, we have the herding group versus the working group. And finally, not to be left out, the toy group always seemed to be poking fun at the terrier group. Unsurprisingly, the terrier group didn't like that one bit.

Vance walked up to me, finished with his call. "So, whatcha got?"

"One mother of a headache," I answered as I leaned back in my chair. I took a healthy swig of soda and scowled at the computer. "You wouldn't believe some of the petty things I've found. These dog owners must not have anything else to do, and as a result, they take their clubs seriously. Too seriously, if you ask me. Either that, or they're bat-crap crazy."

"Probably both," Vance agreed. "So, you say they're crazy? Can you give me a 'for instance'?"

I shrugged. "If you look at the local hound group's website, and just about every other club website for that matter, you'll find a forum where people can leave comments for other members. However, it looks like the only thing it's being used for is to allow people to vent their frustrations. Look, it says here that someone in the terrier group illegally obtained all the cell phone numbers from the hound group and signed them all up to receive X-rated text messages."

I could see Vance fighting valiantly to keep a straight face.

"That, er, type of thing could, uh, definitely be construed as ... ahem ... malicious. I wouldn't want to receive those types of messages on my cell, either. How do they know the terrier group was responsible?"

I shook my head. "They don't. They're assuming. That's all this is, nothing but assumptions. I'm starting to think these missing dogs were probably supposed to be harmless pranks, but I get the impression that someone has taken the pranks a little too far."

"You're suggesting one of these groups is responsible?" Vance asked. After a few moments he was vehemently shaking his head. "I'm not buying it, Zack. These are people who are active members in dog clubs. By definition, that means they love dogs. There's no way any of them would willingly hurt a dog."

"I didn't say they were *hurting* the dogs," I argued. "Quite the contrary, I think whoever has them is taking great care of them. However, I just don't know what they're doing with these dogs once they have them. I will say, however, that I think you're right. I don't think these dognappers mean any of the dogs harm."

"So what else is left?" Vance wanted to know.

"I don't know. Maybe finding homes for the dogs in other cities? Other states?"

"Are you suggesting PV is involved with a black-market dog smuggling ring?" Vance slowly asked. He shook his head again. "Maybe in a big city, Zack, but not here. Not in PV. No way."

"What other theory fits the facts?" I demanded.

Vance held up his cell. "Let's go see if we can find one. Will is expecting us. We can find him at the post office."

"And who is Will?" I curiously asked.

"Oh, sorry. Will Olson is the president of the Pomme Valley herding club. He works down at the PV Post Office. I actually got him on the phone. I had meant to check to see if he was working today, only he's the one who answered the phone. Turns out he's the postmaster. Then I got to listen to a lecture about how, as a post-master, he's there whenever the post office is open."

"You were on the phone a long time," I re-called. "I just figured you must've had another call."

"That's how many times Will put me on hold," Vance muttered. "Every time I tried to ask him how long he was planning on being there today, someone would come up to the counter to ask a question. Before I could get the question out, he'd simply put the phone down, without notice. There's someone who takes his job very seriously."

"Will Olson," I mumbled incoherently. "The name sounds familiar."

"Do you know him?" Vance asked.

I shrugged. "I know I've seen the name some-where before. Damned if I can remember where. Oh, well. Maybe it'll come to me."

The Pomme Valley Post Office was located on 4th Street, adjacent to Traveler's Inn and across the street from Jackson's Gym, PV's only exercise facility. The post office building was a converted

Tudor-style house the city had been bequeathed after the owner had passed away. I remember Jillian telling me the house had been in such poor condition that the town had raised funds to have the building restored to its former glory. Well, let me just say, the town got its money's worth.

The sidewalk leading up to the single front door had been done using bright red bricks set out in a herringbone pattern. A gable-shaped canopy—painted dark green—was covering the front door. The front of the house had three six-pane windows overlooking the street, while a set of French doors—also painted the same shade of dark green—were on the left, leading into who-knows-where. A hand-painted sign, which stated that the monthly meeting of the PV branch of the American Philatelic Society had to be postponed this month, was displayed in the front window closest to the door.

I followed Vance inside and, this being the first time I've ever stepped foot in a small-town post office, looked around. Right off the bat, I noticed the house's original living room had been turned into the lobby. To the left, the dining room (I'm guessing here) had been divided into two smaller cubicle-type enclosures with customer post office boxes lining every square inch of the walls. Directly ahead of us was the counter, where presumably the cashier sat. There was also a closed door to the right of the counter. A manager's office, perhaps? Was that where we were supposed to meet Will, the postmaster?

Turns out the PV Post Office was predominantly a one-man operation. Will himself was behind the counter and, without any customers in the building, had been staring blankly out into the lobby. The postmaster looked to be in his mid-sixties, was as skinny as a beanpole, and had to be wearing one of the worst toupees I have ever seen. Nobody that old could have a head of hair that thick or luxurious without some type of help. To make matters worse, the toupee and the natural hair were nowhere close to being a match. The rug stood out like a sore thumb.

As we stepped inside the building, I noticed Will had slightly tilted his head our way as he tracked our movements with his eyes. Other than that, we elicited no other response from the old man. I got the distinct impression he wouldn't move or say a thing until we were standing directly in front of his counter. I gave Vance a 'this-is-your-idea, you-take-the-reins' look and took two deliberate steps backwards. Vance nodded, whipped out his badge, and held it up for the postmaster to see.

"You're Will Olson, right? I'm Detective Vance Samuelson, PVPD. I don't know if you remember me or not, but we've actually met a few times before. We spoke on the phone just a little while ago."

The postmaster finally stirred. He blinked a few times, as if awakening from a trance, and turned his head to look directly at Vance. After a few moments, Will slowly walked around the counter and entered the lobby through a Staff Only door. He held out a hand.

"I am Willard Olson, Detective Samuelson. What can I do for you?"

Vance shook the outstretched hand.

"You're president of the PV herding club, aren't you?"

Willard Olson nodded. "That's right. Besides postmaster, I'm also president of the Northwest Nippers."

Vance and I waited a few moments to see if Willard was going to offer anything else. When it became apparent that he had shared all he was going to, Vance and I gave each other another look. Trying to get information out of this guy was like pulling teeth. Bemused, I watched my detective friend to see how he'd handle the situation.

"Excellent. Mr. Olson, what do you know about the other dog clubs here in Pomme Valley?"

"What do you want to know about them?" the postmaster returned. "And please call me Willard."

Vance shook his head, "Not when I'm on duty, Mr. Olson. Now, are you familiar with any of them? Can you tell us who runs them?"

Willard nodded. "Of course."

After a prolonged moment of silence, I

sighed, as did Vance. We both were waiting to see if Willard was merely collecting his thoughts or else was painfully shy. Once it became obvious he was done talking, Vance scowled. Right away, however, I recognized what the uncommunicative postmaster was doing. He was behaving just like a computer. He wasn't going to do (or say) a damn thing until he was asked. I wrote a character just like that into my last book.

I laid a hand on Vance's shoulder, "Relax, pal. I've got this. Mr. Willard, is it?"

"I am Willard Olson, postmaster of Pomme Valley."

Leave it to me and my memory to goof the name.

"I'm sorry, Mr. Olson, er, Willard. Listen, this is a small town, right? You obviously know everyone in it, correct?"

Willard nodded.

"Therefore, if we were to ask you about the different dog clubs you're aware of, you'd be able to tell us all about them, right?"

Willard nodded again, looking bored.

"Okay, Mr. Olson. Er, Willard. Sorry, force of habit. Please tell us what you know about any Pomme Valley dog clubs, including who runs them. Provided you know, of course."

Willard began to speak, as if reciting lines of text on a teleprompter.

"Four dog clubs call Pomme Valley home," he

began. "Each of the four clubs belong to a separate AKC-recognized group. Those groups are as follows: non-sporting, hound, toy, and herding. The first on the list, the non-sporting group, is officiated by Ruth Reezen."

"Reezen," I repeated, as Willard took a breath. I looked at Vance. "That name sounds familiar. Why?"

"You're thinking of Don Reezen," Vance answered. "He's the principal of the high school. Ruth is his wife."

"Ah. Got it."

"They call themselves Paws & Effects," Willard added.

"Clever," Vance admitted.

"The hound group, otherwise known as the Savvy Sniffers, is presided over by Darryl Peniweather."

Vance shook his head, "I'm not familiar with him."

"He's a registered nurse who works at Apple of My Eye Clinic," Willard explained. "Would you mind telling me something, Lieutenant?"

"Detective," Vance gently corrected. "And certainly. What would you like to know?"

Willard nodded his head in my direction, "I would like to know if you were planning on introducing me to your companion. I am not overly fond of a lack of proper formalities."

I grinned sheepishly and stepped forward, at the same time Vance turned to me and waved me over.

"I'm sorry, Mr. Olson. Zack here has been quieter than normal for some reason. Almost forgot he was there."

My smile vanished in the blink of an eye. "Bite me, dude. And I haven't been quiet."

Thankfully, I saw a smile briefly appear on the elderly post-master's face.

"Mr. Olson, meet Zachary Anderson, owner of the finest winery this side of the Rascal River, Lentari Cellars."

Willard's eyes widened with surprise. I stepped forward and extended a hand. After a few moments of awkward silence, Willard shook it.

"Are you a fan of the winery?" I asked, hoping to get the old man talking.

Willard shook his head. "I've never cared for your wine, I'm sorry to say. However, I am a fan of your dogs. You are the owner of two corgis, are you not?"

I nodded. "That's right. Sherlock and Watson. You've heard of them?"

"This whole town has heard of them," Willard acknowledged. "I do believe I've extended the invitation to you several times to join the Nippers. However, I have yet to receive a response. As you may or may not be aware, Pembroke Welsh Corgis belong in the herding group."

So that's why I knew the name. He was right. I had seen several flyers appear in my mailbox, talking about enrolling the dogs in a local club. Truth be told, I thought they were advertisements for some type of dog show, and I had tossed them in trash. They were invitations to join a dog club? Good grief, I don't have time for that. In addition, now that I've met the club president, I wasn't convinced that it was something I wanted to participate in. The dogs were well loved, sure enough. As for me? Even though I'm certain Sherlock and Watson were better known than I will ever be, I still see an occasional finger point in my direction as I pass by. It's an inevitable side effect of being charged with murder. It tends to make people remember you. So, for now, I'd just as soon keep to myself.

Besides, if I wanted to hang out with other dog owners, then there are easier ways to do it. Harry & Julie recently became new puppy parents when they picked up an eight week old Australian Shepherd puppy. And, of course, Vance & Tori have a German Shepherd. Anubis was currently missing, but somehow I got the impression we would have the Samuelson family dog back safe and sound in just a few days. I finally felt as though we were making progress on the case. Now, with regards to Willard here, I think I was in trouble. Something was telling me that he wasn't going to let me off the hook. So, how do I play this? Feign ignorance?

"Umm, sorry? I didn't realize what they were."

"Did you even bother to read the flyer?" Willard asked me matter-of-factly, unwilling to let the matter drop.

"Er, no."

"We, at the Nippers, are quite fond of Sherlock and Watson. Everyone talks about their exploits. I personally think those two would make a great addition to the club. What do you say, Mr. Anderson? Can we count on your support? May I enroll you and your dogs in the club?"

I walked right into that one. This dude had the bull by its horns and wasn't about to let go until he got what he wanted. What was I supposed to do?

"Fine," I sighed. "You can enroll Sherlock and Watson, provided…" I trailed off, hoping the insinuation was clear.

"Provided what?" Willard suspiciously asked.

"Provided you tell us what you can about the other dog clubs. It's important, Mr. Olson."

Willard shrugged. "Very well. Seeing as how I'm already doing that, I will gladly accept the terms of your deal. You know about three of the four clubs, since we've covered Paws & Effects, Savvy Sniffers, and our own Northwest Nippers. The fourth is the Mini Me's."

"Let me guess," Vance interjected. "The toy group. Now we're talking. What can you tell us about them?"

Willard blinked his eyes a few times as a

confused expression appeared on his face, "Why would you say that? What do you have against the Mini Me's?"

I took a breath, intent on telling Willard that they were people of interest in an investigation. However, before I could say anything, Vance thumped me in the gut. He cast me a scornful look and very subtly shook his head no. Apparently now was not the time to divulge any facts from the case.

"We're investigating the recent string of dognappings," Vance said, as he turned to look at Willard. "We need to make contact with all the dog clubs, 'cause we want to make certain everyone is on high alert. We don't want to have any more missing dogs."

"Nice," I murmured.

Willard was nodding, "Ah. That makes perfect sense. Such a dreadful occurrence, taking someone's dog. I do hope you get to the bottom of these shenanigans as quickly as possible."

"We will," Vance promised. "Now, who runs the Mini Me's?"

"That would be one Mrs. Asta Johansson. She owns Treasure Chest, off the corner of Oregon and Main."

"I've been there," Vance admitted.

"So have I," I added. "I've bought Jillian a few things from there. I will admit it's not my favorite place to go, but Jillian seems to like it."

"Ditto," Vance mumbled.

"May I make a suggestion?" Willard asked.

Vance shrugged. "Sure."

"Talk with the Sniffers first. I would be willing to point the finger at them before I'd point it at any of the lovely ladies in the Mini Me's."

"Okay, I'll bite," I said. "Why?"

"Mrs. Johansson is quite possibly the most intimidating woman you will ever meet. No member of that club would dare cross her, unless they have a very good reason to."

"And if Asta is the one responsible?" I asked. "They could be following orders and are too scared to say no."

Willard waved a dismissive hand. "Pish posh. I still maintain this is nothing more than friendly rivalry."

Both Vance and I had turned around and were ready to leave when we both froze in mid step. Vance turned around first.

"Would you care to run that by me again? Rivalry? What rivalry?"

Warming up to the two of us, Willard actually smiled.

"Oh, I'm sure it's just friendly banter, although I must admit the sabotaging of Paws & Effects' company van was a bit much."

"Someone sabotaged a van?" I asked, incredulous. "One would've thought that you'd open with something like that and not offer it as an afterthought."

"I agree," Vance added, as his face grew grim.

"I knew if I said something up front, then you'd instantly jump to the wrong conclusions," Willard quickly explained. "And it would seem that's exactly what you've done."

"What other friendly banter do you know about?" I asked.

You could have heard a pin drop inside PV's Post Office as Willard nervously looked toward the door. Thinking there was a customer walking up behind us, I moved to intercept, only no one was there. I do believe our town postmaster was a wee bit nervous.

"Spill, Mr. Olson," Vance ordered. His voice had taken on a decidedly stern tone.

"All right, all right. Listen, we're all dog owners here. No one wants to see anyone get into any trouble."

Vance crossed his arms over his chest, "Out with it."

"Well, one of the biggest rivalries is between the sporting and non-sporting clubs. Each club will do anything they can to make the other look as bad as possible. Now, you didn't hear this from me, but I know for a fact that one of the most common pranks they pull on one another is to sign the other up for false donations."

Vance had whipped out his notebook and was scribbling furiously. "Go on, Mr. Olson."

"We, uh, that is to say, the Nippers might have been known to, uh..."

"Just spill the beans," Vance ordered. "I'm not

interested in arresting anyone for petty offenses. I want to know about these dog clubs. What did your club do, Mr. Olson?"

"I would prefer if you'd call me Willard," the postmaster quietly said. "It's less formal."

"I'm afraid not. Answer the question, please."

"The Nippers might've misplaced, er, taken some of the equipment from the park when Savvy Sniffers were practicing for this year's Cider Fest dog obstacle course."

"What did you take?" Vance asked as he continued to write down notes in his notebook.

"Oh, er, nothing much. Cones, pipes, and, um, PVC fittings."

I laughed out loud. "Wait. Just wait a minute. Were they practicing for those canine obstacle courses that I've seen on television?"

Willard nodded guiltily.

"You took their equipment so they couldn't practice?" Vance demanded.

"Everyone knows the herding group always wins," Willard all but whined. "It was all done in harmless fun. I still have their gear. It's safe and sound."

"Did this other group retaliate?" I asked.

Willard nodded. "Of course. They learned how to disconnect the battery in my Prius. Not an easy task for a hybrid vehicle, mind you. I've also caught them changing the Post Office's Hours Open sign to all times of day. Did I file a complaint? Of course not. It's all in good fun."

"Until someone's dog is stolen," Vance snapped.

"Is that what you think is happening?" Willard asked, appalled. "None of us would ever willingly steal another person's dog. Dog owners simply don't do that."

"Yet someone did," I added.

"Stay close to your phone," Vance ordered the postmaster as we headed for the door. "Chances are, we'll have more questions."

"I'm not going anywhere," Willard promised.

"Do you believe him?" I asked, once we were outside.

Vance nodded. "For now. Don't let Mr. Olson's age or demeanor fool you. He's a very active person. In fact, he has several acres of land he maintains, along with a large flock of sheep. He lets people rent out his sheep so their dogs can have fun herding them. You ought to try it with Sherlock and Watson."

"Actually, I think I will," I decided. "I'd love to see what the two of them would do in an actual herding situation. So, where to now?"

"Well, there are three groups we need to check out. I say we split up."

"Why don't we just go talk to this Mini-Me club? We need to talk to owners of small dogs. I don't see why we need to talk to the other clubs here in town."

"Ordinarily, I agree. However, you heard Mr. Olson back there. There's open acknowledgment of one group sabotaging the other. What if one group is deliberately doing this to point the finger at another? Before we can make any accusations, we need to know the whole picture."

"Fine. Do you want to split up?"

"Yeah, we'll cover more ground that way. Listen, I know the Reezens better than you, so I'll take the non-sporting group. The clinic that male nurse works at is less than a block from the high school, so I'll stop by there, too."

My eyebrows rose.

"You want me to talk to the Mini Me's? What if they're the ones responsible for the missing dogs? What then?"

"First and foremost, I don't think you have anything to worry about, but I'll tell you what. If you suspect anything, or if you feel your life is in danger, get your rear out of there and call me. Run, if you have to. I know Mrs. Johansson. I think she's in her sixties. You should be able to outrun her."

"Smart aleck. What if she sics a dog on me? She runs a dog club, after all."

"What is she gonna do?" Vance demanded as he rounded on me. "Order her group of five-pound fluffballs to bite your ankles? Are you kidding me?"

"Are you sure you don't want to switch? I'll take the clinic."

"I would have thought you'd want to take on the Mini Me's."

Perplexed, I could only stare at my friend. "Why?"

"Because I thought you had a thing for older women, what with your experience with Clara Hanson."

"Oh, bite me, amigo. I'm not afraid of an old lady."

"You know what? I've changed my mind. I think I'd like to be there to help interrogate the members of Mini Me's. Let's do this. You take Ruth Reezen and I'll go talk to the nurse. We'll meet up later to compare notes and then we'll go see the Mini Me's."

"Fine. Where do you want to meet?"

"I know Jillian is still out of town. Come over to my place for dinner tonight. We'll hit the toy group first thing tomorrow. Bring your dogs. I think it'd help the girls feel better. Vicki and Tiffany haven't smiled once since Anubis was taken, and it's killing me. What do you say? I might even see if Harry and Julie can come over."

About to protest, I agreed. Vance's daughters had to be heartbroken over the loss of Anubis. My dogs would most certainly cheer them up.

"You're on."

Thankfully, the Fates were on my side and I didn't have to interview Mrs. Johansson. Turns out Ruth Reezen was out of town, and the closest we would come to interviewing her was to talk to her husband, Don. Therefore, Vance decided to postpone talking with the Mini Me's until we could both be present.

Vance headed to the clinic while I drove to the high school.

* * *

"Thanks for agreeing to meet with me on such short notice. I hope you don't mind talking to me about these dog clubs. I've heard they can be a little eccentric."

"They're a bunch of crackpots," Don Reezen, principal of Pomme Valley High School, corrected. "Every single one of them. You wouldn't believe some of the stories Ruthie has told me. If she was here, I'm sure she'd could tell you stories that'd make you think twice about joining any dog club here in PV. But, seeing how my wife is visiting her sister in Portland for a few days, you'll have to settle with me and what I've overheard."

"Willard Olson, down at the post office, says all this stuff that's been happening is only friendly rivalry. He called it banter. Would you agree?"

"I most certainly would not. Has he told you some of the shit that they've pulled? Oh. Pardon me. I really shouldn't use language like that, especially when I'm at school."

"I've heard a lot worse, Mr. Reezen," I assured him.

"Call me Don. Okay, where do I start? Last month, Ruthie comes home from her latest club meeting, practically in tears. She said someone —she suspected somebody in one of the other clubs—keyed her car."

"Where was she at?" I asked, growing angry. "Was she home?"

Don shook his head. "No. She was at the library. Several of the dog clubs meet there."

"Really? I didn't realize the library would allow dogs inside."

"Only in the main lobby," Don clarified. "This is an incredibly pet friendly town."

I scribbled some notes into the small notebook Vance had given me. "Did this happen to anyone else in the Paws & Effects club?"

"I know of only one other," Don confirmed. "There may be more, but if so, Ruth hasn't told me about it."

"Keying someone's car—intentionally—is about as low as you can go."

Don nodded. "Agreed. Then, a few months ago, the members of one club suddenly discovered pornographic messages on their cell phones. Someone had obtained the list of phone numbers and signed them up on all manner of adult-oriented websites."

"Sounds like a juvenile thing to do," I decided. "Are you sure rival clubs are at fault? This sounds like something—and I'm sorry to say this —school kids would do."

"Doesn't it? However, kids are not responsible for this, adults are. What else can I tell you?

I know. How about this? Nearly a dozen members of that hound group reported their credit cards were all confiscated and destroyed when they tried to use them. What do you think about that?"

"I think someone clearly knows their way around a computer," I said.

"Exactly. Now, your hypothesis is that a rival group is responsible for all this trouble? Including the missing dogs?"

"Yes. Is there anything about the four clubs I ought to know? Has anything suspicious happened that we should be aware of?"

"Aside from the cars being keyed, no," Don said. "Not really. Oh. Wait. Just last month, Medford hosted its own canine competition. You know about that, right?"

I shook my head. "This is the first I've heard of it. What about it?"

"Well, you probably don't know that the reigning champion had been dethroned?"

"It's news to me," I admitted. "Who was the champion?"

"A black poodle. A small one."

I grunted once by way of acknowledgement.

"And the dog who dethroned him? A Basenji."

I made a circular motion with my finger. "Those are the dogs with the little curlicue tail, right? Okay, I'm familiar with the breed. What about it?"

"Do you know what group they belong to?"

"Herding?" I guessed.

"Hound," Don corrected.

"Interesting," I admitted. "And that helps me how?"

"Because the owner of the dethroned poodle just so happens to be the president of the Mini Me's."

TEN

Loud piercing barks echoed throughout the large, ranch-style home in the northern part of town. Two sleek corgis raced through the long hallway connecting the kitchen to the playroom, going at least Mach 2. Two young girls, ages nine and eleven, were in hot pursuit. I glanced over at the girls' parents and was rewarded with a welcoming smile. Just then, the two girls zipped by us again, going in the opposite direction, giggling hysterically. Two corgis streaked by, barking maniacally, as they attempted to catch up to their human targets.

"They needed this," Tori was saying. "Vance and I haven't seen or heard the girls laugh since Anubis was taken. Zachary, this means the world to us. Thank you."

"Don't worry about your dog," I replied as I glanced at Vance. "We're gonna get him back. That's a promise."

Suddenly, there was a knock at the front door. Vance's oldest girl, Victoria, made it there first. Without bothering to check to see who it was, she pulled open the door.

"Hey there, short stuff!" I heard a familiar voice say. "How're you doing, princess?"

"Hello, Doctor Watt," Victoria primly said. "Please, come in."

"I told you, you can call me Harry, kiddo."

I then heard a high-pitched yip that could have only been made by a...

"Oooo!" Victoria squealed. "You have a puppy!"

Like magic, Tiffany appeared next to her sister's side and gawked appropriately.

Harry, Julie, and their two kids stepped inside, arms laden with gifts. Instead of holding his customary six-pack of beer—as was the norm whenever Harry visited my house—he was instead carrying a twelve-pack in his left hand while holding a squirming puppy in his right. Julie was carrying a large, iconic, red and white bucket of chicken. Their son, Hardy, a stout lad of thirteen, smiled politely as he handed the bag containing mashed potatoes, coleslaw, macaroni and cheese, and biscuits to the closest adult, who happened to be Tori. Hardy's little sister, Drew, a tiny girl of six, stuck close to her father and only had eyes for the new puppy.

I glanced over at Vance's youngest daughter, Tiffany. She remained rooted to the spot as she watched Harry gently set the puppy down. The eight-week old Australian Shepherd yipped excitedly and took a few hesitant steps toward the girls. Right about this time, I heard doggie toe nails clicking on tiled floor as Sherlock and Watson approached. Both corgis were silent as they studied the new visitors, having completely missed the young puppy standing stock still near Harry's ankles.

The puppy yipped enthusiastically at the appearance of my two corgis. Sherlock's nose immediately dropped down and zeroed in on the tiny ball of fur. His ears jumped straight up and he cocked his head in perfect 'what's this?' canine fashion. He let out a soft woof, which alerted Watson, since she had missed hearing the tiny puppy's bark. As soon as Watson noticed the puppy, she let out a high-pitched bark as a greeting and bounded like a gazelle over to the small stranger. Watson lowered her head, kept her rear up high, and wiggled her short nub of a tail.

"That's encouraging," Harry observed. "I'm not sure about Sherlock, though. I remember him being somewhat standoffish when I had him in the kennel at my office."

"I'd expect any dog at a kennel to be standoffish," I remarked. "Think about it. The poor fellow would probably wonder what he did to end up on the shit list."

All four kids turned to give me a scandalous look.

"Pardon my French," I automatically murmured.

"You said a bad word," Victoria admonished as she shook a finger at me. "Mommy says we shouldn't talk like that."

Properly chastised, I could only nod, "You're absolutely right. I don't know what came over me. If I should happen to utter an abhorrence like that again, then you have my permission to … to … wash my mouth out with soap."

That statement garnered me a grin from the young girl. She waggled her finger at me again.

"Don't think I won't hold you to it."

I glanced over at Vance to see him grinning at me and holding up his cell phone. I groaned aloud.

"You recorded that, didn't you?"

"I've been on the receiving end of Vicki's scolding before. I can't tell you how glad I am to see someone else get into trouble beside me."

"So why are you recording this?"

"Why wouldn't I? I still have to find some way to get back at you."

I was taken aback. "At me? For what?"

"You're the one who made me put on that damn Peter Pan costume last year."

"Daddy!" Victoria scolded. "Language!"

Tiffany suddenly ran out of the room, only to return moments later holding a large, clear Mason jar sealed with a slitted metal lid. She held it up to her father, who immediately frowned. Visible inside the jar were numerous dollar bills and loose coins. Looks like the Samuelson family had a swear jar! I was also willing to bet that Vance alone was responsible for all the contributions that jar has seen.

Frowning at his daughter, Vance pulled out his wallet, extracted a single dollar, and held it out. My friend noticed I was smiling at his misfortune and immediately held the jar out to me. Knowing full well what he was trying to get me to do, the Samuelson girls turned their cherubic faces to me.

"Daddy's right," Victoria confirmed. "You said a bad word, too. You need to pay the jar."

Tiffany immediately handed the jar to her sister.

"I don't have a one-dollar bill," I reported, as I check the contents of my wallet. "I only have a ten and a twenty."

Victoria's face beamed brightly. "Oh, a ten-dollar bill will do!"

Her face was too eager. What was I supposed to do? Say no to the girl? Reluctantly, I held out my ten. Victoria snatched it out of my hand, as though she thought for certain I'd change my mind, and fed it to the jar.

"Tell me something, kiddo," I began, as Victoria finished shoving the bill into the jar. "Who benefits from all that money in there?"

"Why, we do!" Victoria exclaimed. "Tiffany and I get to purchase gift cards for our phones, so we can buy music, ringtones, and games."

I shook my head with bewilderment. "Phones? You use the money to buy stuff for your phones? Whatever happened to buying normal toys?"

"Those *are* toys to them," Vance grumbled under his breath. "All the kids have them. If they want to buy something, then they have to use their own money. Those phones will only run on gift cards."

"Yet, you seem to be the major contributor," I pointed out.

Vance held the jar up so that I could see the contents.

"Not any more. Look at that pretty ten in there. You now have the highest bill in there."

"And we greatly appreciate it," Victoria announced, snatching the jar from her father's hands. "We'll be listening. Whenever someone uses a bad word in this house, we pull out the jar. So, feel free to use whatever language you'd like! The stronger the word, the more you have to pay. Isn't that right, daddy?"

Vance grumbled something, but I couldn't make it out.

"There's this new game that I'd like to get for my phone," Victoria continued. "Between you and daddy, we should probably be able to get it before the week is over."

"Clever little entrepreneurs," I observed, as I watched two corgis and one mini Australian Shepherd follow the girls out of the room.

"Tell me about it," Vance grumped.

"That's actually a great idea," Hardy decided, speaking his first words since entering the house. He gave his parents a hopeful look. "Do you think we could do something like that at our house? I could use the money to buy stuff for my own phone."

"Hell no," Harry automatically answered.

The gaggle of kids was back, including the three dogs. Victoria held up the jar and jiggled it. Harry groaned as he handed over a dollar. Smiling profusely, Victoria skipped away.

"That can get old real quick," Harry observed. "That wasn't even a proper swear word. Trust me, I can come up with a few doozies."

"Something like that would help you clean up your language," Julie observed. "Tell you what, Hardy. Your father and I will think about it."

Satisfied, Hardy turned to follow the rest of the kids as they headed out of the room. Sherlock and Watson were leading the way, with the little puppy following as best he could. Directly behind him were the three girls. Hardy brought up the rear.

"So, what are you going to call that cute fluff ball?" I asked, as I looked over at Harry.

PV's only practicing veterinarian cracked a beer open, handed a bottle to me, and then another to Vance.

"Festus."

"Festus?" I repeated. "How'd you come up with that one?"

"Jules. She said she wanted to give the pup a suitable name. You saw him. He's always happy, and is a royal kick in the pants to watch. So, she came up with Festus. Jules says it's a biblical name, which I'm not crazy about, but as long as she's happy, I'm happy."

Vance nodded. "Smart man."

Inspiration struck. I took a pull from my beer and turned to Harry. I only had to wait a few moments until he looked my way.

"You're the town vet. You must have treated most of the dogs here in PV, right?"

Harry nodded, polished off his beer, and reached for another.

"Have you ever noticed anyone complaining about other dogs or their owners?"

Vance clapped me on the back. "And the winery owner comes up with the play of the day. Harry, what do you know about the different dog groups?"

"Are you talking 'bout the AKC groups? I am a vet, you know. What did you want to know about them?"

"Do you know anything about the four dog clubs here in PV?"

Harry tipped back his bottle, drained half of it, and let out a belch so loud that he could have broken the glass out of a window, had he been facing one.

"Harrison Stanton Watt," a woman's sharp voice snapped from down the hall, in the kitchen, "if you do that again, you're going to be personally donating so much money into that swear jar that Vance's girls won't need to worry about their college tuition. Is that understood?"

Harry's face reddened and he looked sheepish, "Sorry, Jules."

"Don't apologize to me, buddy," came Julie's harsh reply. "Apologize to our hosts."

"Okay, okay. Umm, whoops, my bad?"

"Is that how you apologize?" Julie's voice demanded. "What are you supposed to say?"

"That definitely tasted better going down than it did coming back up," Harry chuckled.

"Three strikes and you're out," Julie said, using an eerily calm voice.

"My sincerest apologies," Harry hastily blurted out. "I wasn't thinking, and if I had been properly thinking, I would never have allowed myself to release so much internal pressure at the same time. Indoors. It will never happen again."

"Hey, no harm done," Vance assured him. "In fact, feel free to do it again. You're going to pay for the girls' tuition? Be my guest!"

"You'd like that, wouldn't you?" Harry grumped.

"So, back to those dog clubs," I hastily interjected. "Have they been known to bicker amongst themselves?"

Harry choked on his beer, "Have they been known to bicker? Oh, man. Where the hell do I start? How about ... those people are bat-shit crazy?"

Victoria came skipping by, holding the swear jar out as though she was collecting donations on behalf of a street musician. I swear that kid must have been waiting just around the corner, out of sight. Both Vance and I had a smirk on our face as we turned to Harry. With a shrug, Harry pulled out a twenty and handed it to Victoria.

"Run a tab for me, kiddo. Something tells me that I'll use that up before the night is over."

Victoria snatched the bill from Harry and jammed it into the jar before her father could protest. She then skipped merrily down the hall, disappearing from view.

"As I was saying," Harry continued, "those people are out-of-their-minds crazy. Did you know that I was thiiiis close to breaking up a fist fight between several customers at my clinic? Three times, man. People are weird."

Vance's notebook found its way into his hand.

"Do you remember any details?" Vance asked, slipping into detective mode. "Who was involved, what they were arguing over, and so on?"

"It was over nothing but trivial stuff, man. The last one I broke up, which happened last month, was over which AKC group was best. And do you know what? Each time it happened, one —or both—of the owners wanted me to side with them, as if I'd side with either one of those mixed bag of nuts."

"Who?" Vance asked. "Who was involved?"

"Mrs. Barterson," Harry recalled, as he stroked his beard. "She has a Cavalier King Charles Spaniel. She actually started an argument with Mr. Kirkman, who was waiting to get vaccines for his Jack Russell Terrier. I swear they were moments away from a bare knuckle fist fight when I intervened."

"What were they arguing about?" I asked.

"Which breed has more energy, which is better with kids, and so on. Seriously, man. It's always over some petty thing that no one really cares about."

"Is this Mrs. Barterson as unpleasant as she sounds?" Vance inquired, as he scribbled notes.

Harry shook his head. "Actually, no. That's the weird part, man. If you were to see Mrs. Barterson on the street, you'd think, there goes a harmless grandmotherly-type lady who loves to bake cookies. If you were to look up the word 'grandmother' in the dictionary, then you'd see a picture of her."

"I wonder what set her off," I mused, as I finished my second beer. "Little old ladies usually don't get that angry unless you rub them the wrong way."

"The only thing I remembered was that it was about some type of event that had just happened, and apparently it didn't go the way Mrs. Barterson had hoped, or expected. She must have been talking to herself—or her dog—and was overheard by Mr. Kirkman. Now, I can tell you that Mr. Kirkman is a jerk, and has no qualms about admitting that. He probably said something contradictory, just to push her buttons, I'm sure."

"What about the other two altercations?" Vance asked.

Harry shrugged. "One was a Pomeranian versus a Newfoundland. They were arguing about which one made a better lap dog."

"Isn't a Newfoundland like, one of the biggest breeds there is?" I asked, puzzled.

Harry nodded. "Yep. Males can easily hit 150 pounds."

"That's no lap dog," I remarked.

"Tell that to the dog," Harry returned. "If the puppy is allowed to jump on the owner's lap while it's growing up, then it's going to expect to be able to do just that when it reaches adult size."

"I think I'd have to side with the Pomeranian on this one," I decided.

"Not if you're the Newfoundland owner," Vance argued. "No one breed is better than the other. It's all subjective."

"I disagree," I stated. "Corgis are the best."

"Hardly," Vance scoffed. "German Shepherds, all the way."

Harry made the time-out gesture with his hands.

"Guys? This isn't getting us anywhere. You two need to figure out what to do next."

"I think we need to talk to this Mrs. Barterson," I suggested to Vance. "I'd like to find out what made her so angry."

"It's getting late. We'll hit her up first thing tomorrow morning," Vance promised.

"What about that male nurse?" I asked. "Anything going on with the hound group?"

Vance nodded. "More of this same petty shit. Crap. Damn it!"

Victoria was back, in less than two seconds. Vance checked his wallet, groaned, and pulled out a five. Victoria snatched the bill out of her father's hand with a giggle, and disappeared down the hall.

"Anything else we should know about?" I asked.

"I suspect they're just as guilty as the rest of these clubs," Vance grumbled as he slid his wallet in his jeans pocket. "Nothing stood out, though."

I shrugged. "All right. Hopefully we can get something useful from the Mini Me's tomorrow morning."

"Did I say *we*?" Vance mischievously asked. "I meant, *you*. It's going to be just you tomorrow. I have to be in Medford until at least noon."

"Swell," I grumbled.

"Just try to contain yourself around her," Harry chuckled and he gave Vance a wink. "Everyone knows how much Zack favors older women."

"Dude, kiss my a-, er, butt."

* * *

"There really isn't much to say," Mrs. Gertrude Barterson was saying, as she set a plate of warm chocolate chip cookies on the coffee table before Vance and me.

Thankfully, Vance's meeting in Medford had been rescheduled. He had glumly admitted that he'd be able to accompany me to interview our argument instigator. I personally think the schmuck wanted me to talk to Mrs. Barterson all by myself. I knew within five seconds of walking inside her home that I wasn't going to have any problems with her. She was calm, reserved, and didn't try to dress like she was half a century younger. In fact, she did remind me of a stereotypical grandmother. I couldn't even begin to imagine this sweet old lady picking a fight.

Mrs. Barterson gave Sherlock and Watson an affectionate pat on the head and then set down a bowl of water for the two of them.

"I really don't know why I lost my temper like that. I can only assume it's because Mr. Kirkman is such an irritating man."

"What did he say that set you off?" I asked. I kept an eye on Sherlock, who had a propensity of dunking his entire snout into the water dish just to take a drink of water. And, just as I had predicted, a tri-colored nose surreptitiously dipped itself into the water. "That's far enough,

239

pal. This is not our house. No making any messes in here."

"Oh, it's quite all right," our gracious hostess informed us. "I love dogs. I would never chastise a dog just because they wanted to have a little fun."

Both Sherlock and Watson turned to look at me as if to say, 'There? You see? At least someone out there loves us.'

"You two had better behave yourselves," I warned again, dropping my voice so that Mrs. Barterson wouldn't overhear. I caught a nervous fluttering of hands out of my peripheral vision and looked over at our hostess. "Mrs. Barterson, do I know you from somewhere? Have we met before? You seem awfully familiar to me."

I had seen her before from somewhere, I just didn't know where. It was bugging me, and if I didn't figure it out soon, then it was probably going to drive me insane. Mrs. Barterson simply shrugged off the query.

"I've lived in this town for many years, Mr. Anderson. I'm always out and about, doing something. I refuse to be one of those fuddy-dud-dies who never leave their house. I detest bore-dom, so I volunteer at a lot of events."

I nodded. That had to be it. I had been going to a lot of events myself. With Jillian. She always loved to do things outside and interact with other people. As a result, I usually accompanied her and had met more people than I was ever going to remember.

"To answer your first question, Mr. Anderson," Gertrude began, "Mr. Kirkman insinuated I was a poor mommy for my little Carlos. I can take a lot of criticism, and have been known to turn my cheek about a great many things, but one thing I won't stand for is anyone trying to tell me I'm a poor mother for my little baby. Especially when the poor excuse of a dog he had with him was misbehaving just as badly as his owner."

"Good," I quietly muttered. "So we are talking about dogs."

Vance nudged my arm, indicating I needed to shut up.

"So, if you're looking for an unscrupulous character who, in my opinion, is capable of absconding with someone else's dog, then I'd be looking at him, not me."

"I would think a dog owner would refrain from wanting to harm another dog," I said, as I looked at Vance. A quick nod from my friend confirmed he agreed with me. "We're under the assumption that whoever is responsible for these dog thefts must not be a dog owner. At least, that's the general consensus."

"And you think I might have something to do with this?" Mrs. Barterson asked. A frown slowly spread across her sweet, wrinkled face. "Is that why you're here? I hate to disappoint you, but I am a dog owner myself, as you may recall."

"We're here because we want to find out why one dog owner would shamelessly pick a fight with another," Vance coolly clarified. "We know you had an altercation last month, so we're asking a few questions. We also know of several other small breed owners that were, shall we say, picking fights with other dog owners. So, all we were looking to do is to find out why one owner would think their dog is better than another."

Mrs. Barterson's nose lifted.

"Well, everyone knows that dogs in the toy group make the best pets."

Vance and I shared a glance.

"And why's that?" he asked.

"Isn't it obvious? You two said you were dog owners, correct?"

Vance and I both nodded.

"Then you'll know that people in general, who own pets, lead longer, fuller lives?" Gertrude asked. When no one said anything, she continued. "Single people—especially widowers—find much needed companionship with small pets. The smaller breed dogs are perfect for this. We seniors don't have a lot of strength in our hands. Therefore, it's easier for us to control a small dog than a larger one."

I shrugged. "Makes sense."

"Plus, small dogs have the best temperaments. They're perfect for houses with small children."

I frowned and held up a hand.

"Umm, excuse me? That isn't necessarily true."

Gertrude immediately frowned at me "Of course it is."

"No, it isn't," I argued. "I had an aunt who had one of those small little Chihuahuas. That was the meanest dog I think I had ever seen. He only allowed his owner to hold him. Everyone else ran the risk of being bitten if we so much as tried to touch him."

"There are always extremes in every situation," Gertrude said with a sigh.

"I had a cousin whose Yorkie yapped constantly and peed on everything," Vance added.

"And my father had a Dalmatian who liked to chew up anything that was leather," Gertrude snapped, allowing her matronly demeanor to slip. "What's your point?"

My eyebrows shot up. This woman, who could be easily mistaken for anyone's grandmother, had just rolled her eyes like a petulant teenager. I glanced over at Vance to see him frowning at Mrs. Barterson, too.

"Let's forget about that for now," I interjected, hoping to take the chill out of the air. "Can I ask you something? Are all the Mini Me's senior citizens?"

The firm lines set into the corners of Gertrude's mouth softened somewhat. "Most are, but not all."

"How many aren't?" Zack asked. "In fact, how many members are there in the Mini Me's?"

Mrs. Barterson sank down into an old-fashioned wooden rocking chair and picked up a half-done knitted blanket. Within moments, we heard the clickety-clack of knitting needles clicking together. She was silent for a few moments as she considered.

"Goodness, let me think. There's Mary and Bridget, who are in their late fifties. Don't ever tell them I talked with you about their ages. They would never forgive me. Oh! There's also Amanda. She's under sixty. The rest of us, as I'm sure you've already noticed, are old farts."

The crude, vulgar language was so unexpected that I burst out laughing, earning myself a scowl from Vance. Thankfully, Gertrude was laughing, too. She shook her head and clucked her tongue, like a disapproving mother.

"You want to know how many of us there are. Well, the answer to that is thirty-seven. The Mini Me's are the largest club here in PV. That can only mean small dogs are the most popular, correct?"

I looked at Vance, who shrugged. Neither one of us cared to turn her back into a bitter old woman. Therefore, we each let the matter drop.

"You say the club you belong to has over thirty-five members," Vance was saying, as he flipped through his notebook. "Why is that important?"

"Well, as you already know, there are four clubs here in PV. I will admit there is a competitive streak amongst the four to see who can lay claim to having the most members."

I nodded as I recalled Willard Olson's insistence that Sherlock and Watson join his club.

"All of our members are fine, upstanding citizens in Pomme Valley," Gertrude was saying. "These women hold places of honor. Former—"

"Excuse me," I interrupted as I held up a hand. "Did you say all your members are women? There are no male Mini Me's?"

Gertrude nodded. "That's correct."

"Why are there no men?" Vance asked as he looked up from his notebook.

When it looked as though Mrs. Barterson was taking a few moments to collect her thoughts, I added another question.

"Have there been no men who have applied to join your club?"

Mrs. Barterson fidgeted uncomfortably on her chair. Her knitting needles slipped out of her hands and fell onto her lap. It was a sight not lost to either Vance or myself.

"No, there are no male members. That's because no men have ever expressed interest in joining."

Vance nodded. "That reminds me about something. Speaking of applying for your club, how do you recruit new members? Zack and I found your webpage, only there was no contact information on it."

Mrs. Barterson proudly lifted her chin and stared directly at Vance.

"That's because only existing members can nominate prospective candidates."

"That sounds an awful lot like a fraternity," I decided. "Or a sorority, as it would be in this case."

Surprisingly, Gertrude nodded encouragingly, "Yes! Exactly! Our club has become so popular that we need to take steps to ensure only the right people are invited to join the Mini Me's."

"The right people?" Vance slowly asked as a frown appeared on his face.

Gertrude nodded. "Precisely."

"Do the other dog clubs take such measures when trying to get new people to sign up?" I asked. This meeting had taken a definite turn for the worse, and now all I wanted to do was get Sherlock and Watson away from this screwball.

"No. We're the only club to have enacted such measures to protect our club."

"Do you know which club is the smallest?" Vance asked. He looked at me and shrugged. "I might as well ask, right?"

"The Nippers are the smallest," Gertrude promptly answered. "Would you like to know why? It's because their president, one Mr. Willard Olson, is too eccentric, too weird."

I snorted with laughter, which drew a smile

from the old woman.

"You've met him, haven't you?"

I pointed down at the corgis. "He's trying to get me to enroll those two in his club."

Gertrude laid a motherly hand over my own, "By all means, don't do it, young man. Mr. Olson is several sandwiches short of a picnic, if you catch my meaning."

"Let's go back to your new members," Vance decided as he gave me a neutral look. "You said that new recruits need sponsors? Where do they meet?"

"The library," Gertrude answered. "Many clubs meet there."

"Uh huh."

"This month's meeting was actually the last one to be held there," Gertrude confided with a smile.

"Why's that?" Vance wanted to know.

"Our club has grown too large for the library to accommodate our recruiting parties. We have one every time we're ready to induct new members."

"How often is that?" I asked. I glanced down to check on the dogs. Both Sherlock and Watson were resting their heads on their front paws. They each had their eyes closed, yet both sets of ears were aimed directly at us.

"Once we have enough recruits, we'll—and forgive me for saying this—get the party started. We typically only hold one recruiting party a year."

"And you're saying that this year's party will be happening next month?"

"We've reserved the rec center three weeks from today," Gertrude confirmed.

Vance rose to his feet. The corgis were on their feet in a flash. Correctly guessing that it was time to go, I rose to mine, somewhat irked that my dogs hadn't waited for me to get to my feet first.

"Mrs. Barterson, I think we have all we need to know for now," Vance formally announced. "If something comes up, may we contact you again?"

Gertrude nodded. "Of course. Feel free to stop by anytime. Let me know in advance and I'll make you a fresh batch of cookies, Detective."

Vance nodded. "You can count on it, ma'am. Zack? It's time to go."

Mrs. Barterson led us toward the kitchen and a side door, which would put us closer to our parked car. Just as we reached the door, I noticed an old-fashioned chalkboard sitting next to the kitchen table. It was situated on a bamboo A-frame and had a small shelf under the board which connected all four legs together. Visible on the shelf was a wide variety of colored chalk, along with one black marker.

A glance at the board had me hesitating. I gently pulled the dogs to a stop. Sherlock immediately turned to see what the holdup was.

When he noticed I was no longer walking, he looked up at Vance, then at Watson, and then proceeded to give an exasperated snort as he slid to the ground.

Vance noticed I had stopped and turned to see what I was staring at.

"It's a blackboard, pal. Nothing more. Now, shall we?"

"Look at the equation," I said, as I pointed at the formula written on the board.

Vance looked at the board and shrugged. "What about it?"

In case you're wondering, written in elegant handwriting across the top of the board was the following equation:

$$x = (-b \pm \sqrt{(b^2 - 4ac)})/2a$$

Vance shuddered. "Does that ever bring back nightmares. I hated math in school."

I looked over at Mrs. Barterson with admiration written all over my face.

"You know about quadratic equations?" I asked, with unfeigned surprise.

The septuagenarian returned my surprised look.

"You knew what it was? Good for you, Mr. Anderson."

"Would someone care to translate?" Vance requested. "What's so significant about that gibberish?"

"It's not gibberish," Mrs. Barterson clucked.

"It's a higher form of algebraic equation. I was a high school math teacher for years in California. Several of my friends let it slip to their grandchildren that I was a math major, and now I tutor them in math. Really, I can't believe what passes for arithmetic nowadays. It would never have been deemed acceptable back when I was teaching. That's why I end up spending most of my time trying to translate the kids' math problems into something they can understand."

A look of disbelief spread over Vance's features as he hooked a thumb at the chalkboard.

"One of the students asked me if I knew anything about quadratic equations," Mrs. Barterson explained. Then she gave each of us a coy smile. "I don't suppose either of you could tell me what the root equation of that formula is, could you?"

I glanced over at Vance to see if he knew. Based on his previous outbursts, I was pretty sure I already knew the answer. Vance looked helplessly at me and shook his head. As for me, I had seen that particular equation before and knew what she was looking for.

"It's 'ax^2+bx+c=0'," I immediately answered, which earned me an incredulous stare from Vance. I shrugged. "Hey, what can I say? I enjoyed math in school. I took math all four years in high school and throughout college as well."

Vance shoved his hands in his pocket and approached the board. He whistled with amazement.

"You understand all this, huh? Wow. Are you taking more students? I have a daughter who has taken after me in the math department."

Gertrude shook her head. "I have all I can handle at the moment, thank you."

Being this close to the board, I was able to see all the different colors of chalk Mrs. Barterson had at her disposal when she was tutoring the kids. My eye then caught sight of the one and only marker on the tray. I frowned at it. It looked like a black permanent marker, only it had a neon yellow cap. What was that doing there? She wasn't using that on her board, was she?

Gertrude saw me staring at the marker and instantly rushed over to push the chalkboard out of the way. With each of the wooden legs resting on casters, the board smoothly sailed across the kitchen and bumped into the counter just in front of the sink. Then I noticed something that really made me sit up and take notice. However, my instinct was screaming at me not to say anything until we were well away from the house.

Only when we were headed back to the police station did I let out the breath I hadn't realized I had been holding.

"There's definitely something odd about her," Vance decided as he pulled his cell phone out of his pocket. He punched in a number and waited for the call to connect.

"Who are you calling?" I asked.

"Captain Nelson. I want a search warrant. There's something fishy going on in that house."

Surprised, I gave Vance an affirmative nod. "So, you noticed it, too?"

Vance looked questioningly at me. "Noticed what?"

"The reflection."

"What reflection? Oh, hi, Jules. I need to speak with the captain. Is he there? No problem. I'll hold."

"When she pushed that chalkboard across her kitchen," I continued, "it ended up by her sink. She has a window there. Sunlight hit the back of that chalkboard and made a large reflection on the ceiling. I'm glad Sherlock didn't notice it. He usually barks at them back home."

"So, you saw some reflected light. What about it?"

"Have you ever seen light bounce off a chalkboard before?"

"Well, no," Vance admitted. "Maybe that board came with glass on the other side?"

"And that marker?" I insisted.

"I saw you looking at that marker," Vance recalled. "I was going to ask you about ... captain? Yes, hello. I didn't realize you were on the line. Sorry. Anyway, I need a search warrant. Well, because we need to look around inside Mrs. Barterson's house. The marker? You heard that? Okay, hold on. I'll put you on speaker. All right, Zack.

What about that marker?"

"Well, it was a black marker with a yellow cap," I began. "Have you ever seen one of those before? Wouldn't that cap suggest the ink is yellow?"

"It is," Captain Nelson confirmed over the speaker. "I know what that pen is, and I'm surprised you found it inside a senior citizen's house."

"Wait a minute," Vance sputtered. "What are you guys suggesting? That a little old lady, who could be my grandmother, is using an invisible ink pen to write things on a piece of glass?"

I nodded. "Exactly. She got really nervous when she spotted me looking at it."

Vance perked up. "She did?"

"She did?" the captain echoed.

"That's why she pushed it across the kitchen. She wanted to get it away from me once she saw I had noticed that marker. Vance, I think we need to get back in there and look at that board."

"Getting a search warrant will take a minimum of five hours, and that's contingent on me being able to write it without any interruptions. Then it'll have to be reviewed, then probably reviewed again, and then placed before a judge. If he deems there is good probable cause, then he'll sign it."

"Detective, are you sure about this?"

Vance was nodding. "Absolutely, sir. In addition, I caught her in a lie."

Puzzled, I turned to my friend.

"You did? What lie?"

Vance leveled a gaze at me.

"Zack, she's no teacher. She's a former bus driver from Portland."

ELEVEN

A bus driver? She's a bus driver? Vance, how in the world could you possibly know that? Are you from California, too?"

"That's the lie I'm referring to," Vance matter-of-factly stated. "And no, I'm not from California. Neither is she, for that matter. Captain, are you still with us?"

"Yes."

"Mrs. Gertrude Barterson used to be a school bus driver for the Beavertowne School District in Portland for many, many years. Trust me on this."

"You realize that we'll need to verify this before we place that warrant in front of Judge Masterson, don't you?"

"I know, Captain. I know I'm right, but to cover our bases, could you have someone give that school district a call, just to back me up?"

"I'll take care of it, Detective. Just promise me you'll find Sydney's dog."

"You can count on it, Captain," Vance vowed.

The captain dropped off the line.

"How long do you think it'll take to get the warrant?" I asked.

"It all depends on how quickly we can convince Judge Masterson that we have probable cause," Vance explained. "He usually doesn't give us any trouble."

"So how do you know Mrs. Barterson?" I wanted to know.

"I saw her drive several times. You see, growing up, my mother was a single parent. She and another lady, who was also a single mother, made an agreement to watch each other's kids. Her son, Dale, and I became best friends in school. So, during the school week, I rode two different buses. Mrs. Barterson was Dale's school bus driver. She may have aged, but I knew I had seen her somewhere. By the way, good job on noticing that marker."

"It stood out on a tray full of chalk," I commented, feeling rather pleased with myself. "I just thought it was odd that there'd be a marker on a chalkboard. I hadn't really considered what was on the other side of the board until the sun hit it. That's what tipped it off for me."

"Stay by your phone," Vance ordered, as we pulled into the police station. Vance hopped out of my Jeep and turned to look back at me through the window. "I'll let you know as soon as the warrant is ready."

Once the dogs and I arrived home, I decided to research what was involved in writing—and obtaining—a signed search warrant. I was dismayed to learn that it could take anywhere from three hours, at the very earliest, to oftentimes more than several days. It all depended on the judge and whether or not he/she thought there was suitable probable cause. I was about ready to try my hand at looking up past cases of this Judge Masterson when my cell rang.

"Hello?"

"Mr. Anderson?"

"That's me. Who's this?"

"This is Alan Mathers, with John Deere of Medford. Do you remember me, Mr. Anderson?"

"Of course," I laughed. "I typically remember people that take 15K of my money."

Now I had the salesman laughing.

"That's definitely one way to look at it. Anyway, the reason I'm calling is that your tractor has arrived at our dealership. Our mechanics have gone over it and have given it the green light. Would you like to pick it up or would you like for us to deliver it to you?"

"Hmm. I don't have any way to get that thing out here. How much would it cost to deliver it to the winery?"

"I was really hoping you'd say that. I've been authorized to charge you one case of Syrah."

I started to laugh and was ready to agree with the simple demand when the teeny tiny part of my brain responsible for my math skills woke up.

"Let's see. That'd be twelve bottles of wine, at close to $80 per bottle, would make it almost $1,000." You could've heard crickets chirping on the phone. "I would imagine," I continued, "that your dealership already has a truck and a flatbed trailer, so the only expense you'd be out would be time and fuel. Does that sound about right?"

"I, er, see where you're going with this, Mr. Anderson. I apologize. I was simply hoping that..."

"You didn't let me finish, Alan," I interrupted. "As I was saying, the most your dealership would be out would probably be in the neighborhood of a couple hundred. So, let's do this. You throw in some type of extended warranty, which would cover the engine, hydraulics, and any other mechanical contraption which could break on that thing, and I'll agree to a case of wine a year for as long as you guys service my tractor. Deal?"

"Holy shit! I ... um, pardon my language. I'm almost positive the owner will go for that deal, but I will check, just in case. Tell you what. Unless you hear otherwise from me, consider it a done deal. When would you like this delivered?"

"Could you make it out here tomorrow? That'd work best for me."

"Absolutely. We'll be there tomorrow, around noon. Thank you very much, Mr. Anderson. I look forward to working with you in the future."

I'll bet you do, I thought, as I hung up the phone. Well, that's one less thing I have to worry about. A single case of wine a year was a price I was more than willing to pay, provided I didn't have to worry about the health of that tractor.

I had to admit, I was looking forward to seeing what my fifteen thousand dollars had purchased. Alan had mentioned what model my new tractor was, so perhaps a new search on Google wasn't out of the question? Before I could bring up the search engine, however, my phone rang for what had to be the umpteenth time today.

"Zack? It's Vance. I've got it."

"You've got what?"

"The warrant. I'm heading back to Mrs. Barterson's house. Meet me there, on the double."

"You already have it? What's it been, less than two hours?"

"Once Judge Masterson learned Captain Nelson's granddaughter lost her dog, he couldn't sign that thing fast enough. I don't have to remind you how important it is that we're right, do I?"

"Do you think we're wrong?"

"No."

"Good. I'll meet you there."

Being closer to my side of town, I arrived at Mrs. Barterson's house first. I arrived just in time to see three elderly women walk out the front door. Contrary to what Vance would say, my memory really wasn't that bad. I recognized two of the three women right off the bat. They were part of that group Vance and I had encountered in the woods while looking for that beagle. Coincidence?

Vance's Oldsmobile sedan pulled up beside my Jeep Wrangler and parked.

"How long have you been here?" Vance asked as he stepped out of his car.

"I just got here myself. Quick, do you see those three ladies? Two are getting in that minivan and the third is getting into that Prius?"

Vance squinted his eyes as he gazed at the nearby parking lot.

"Yeah. What about them?"

"I just watched them leave Mrs. Barterson's house."

"Okay. And? Maybe they're part of her knitting club."

"Except I saw two of the three in the woods with you a few days ago."

Intrigued, Vance whipped out his notebook and surreptitiously jotted down the license plate numbers of the two vehicles as they drove away. Then he checked his watch and slowly started pacing along the sidewalk.

"What are you doing?" I asked, confused. "Mrs. Barterson is right over there. Come on!"

"We're not going to serve a search warrant without backup, Zack. It's procedure."

"What's she gonna do to us?" I scoffed. "You saw her. She's a little old lady. I doubt very much that she'll be a problem."

"I don't know. I really shouldn't."

"It'll be fine, buddy. Trust me."

"What are you doing back here?" Mrs. Barterson nervously asked, once we knocked on the door.

"We need to take a look at your kitchen," Vance formally announced. "More specifically, we need to check out that chalkboard of yours."

Mrs. Barterson gasped loudly. After a few moments, she composed herself, crossed her arms over her chest, and frowned at us.

"I'm sorry, Detective. I think I've been more than accommodating today. The only way you'll be able to step foot inside my door is if you have a warrant. Until such time, you have yourself a good day."

Gertrude Barterson made a move to close the door, only Vance stepped forward and jammed his foot in between the door and frame in order to prevent it from closing. He casually reached into his jacket pocket, pulled out a somewhat ruffled piece of paper and smoothed out the creases that had appeared. Without preamble, he presented it to the elderly woman.

"Do you mean one of these? Lucky for me I happen to have one. Look. Do you see that? There's your name, and there's the address of this house. Do you know what that means?"

Mrs. Barterson gasped again, dropped the warrant, and sprinted for the chalkboard, which was still resting up against the counter where we had seen it several hours earlier. I should mention, though, that Gertrude's 'sprint' was nothing more than a slightly fast walk. Being in her late seventies, the elderly woman had the walking speed of a tortoise, along with the dexterity of a hippo. In her haste, she bumped into practically everything that stood in her way, spilling it onto the ground in the process. Then I realized she was doing that deliberately as she tried to prevent us from reaching the counter first. As she passed her sink, she quickly reached in to retrieve the frying pan that was currently drying on a dish rack.

"I guess that means we're in pursuit, right?" I snickered, as we both moved to follow Gertrude Barterson.

Trying valiantly to remain professional, Vance refrained from commenting and easily caught up with Mrs. Barterson. She was a full ten feet from the counter and the board. Vance started reaching for the fleeing form of the home owner when Gertrude turned to see him directly behind her.

"Don't touch me, you brute! Don't make me use this!"

"Mrs. Barterson, don't make it any harder on yourself," Vance soothingly told the woman. "Drop the frying pan, okay? Whether you like it or not, we have to take a look at that board. We suspect there might be some important information we need to see on the other side."

"I will smash that board before I let you people have a chance to see it," Gertrude vowed, giving Vance the fiercest snarl she was probably capable of. What we both saw—and heard—was Mrs. Barterson grunt and then frown at us.

Vance drew to a stop. Satisfied, and with her frown morphing into a smirk, Gertrude came to a stop, too. She was now about five feet from the counter, only she had her back turned to it so she could keep an eye on Vance.

"That really won't be necessary," the detective began. "You see, we already…"

"One more step and I'll destroy the board!" Mrs. Barterson ordered, her voice becoming shrill. She was now wielding the frying pan as though it was a club.

Vance pointed over at me. While Gertrude had been confronting Vance, I had simply walked around the two of them and placed myself in front of the board. Gertrude turned, saw me next to her prized board, and shrieked with dismay. Then, and this next part gets weird, she did the only thing she must've thought she was capable of doing.

She started throwing things.

Have you ever been in an old person's house? There are *things* everywhere. Suddenly, there was so much stuff flying through the air that you would've thought there was a poltergeist in the house. Figurines, commemorative plates, dolls, books, and anything else within reach was launched through the air. Oh, and the frying pan? That was the first to sail by my head. She might not have been able to run that fast, but boy howdy, she had an arm on her.

Once the small ammo was exhausted, Gertrude moved on to larger shells, namely small appliances, dishes, and so on. Ever get hit with a blender? For that matter, have you ever seen the movie *Scrooged*? Like Bill Murray, I can now say the line, 'The bitch hit me with a toaster' and keep a straight face.

"See?" Vance asked, as he turned to me. "This is why we always have backup when executing a search warrant."

"How was I supposed to know that she'd go bat-crazy?" I demanded, as I ducked to avoid getting creamed by an electric can opener.

"Mrs. Barterson," Vance tried again. "This is not going to end well for you if you don't stop resisting."

We both ducked as a waffle iron sailed over our heads.

"Mrs. Barterson, I'm going to have to ask you to stop trying to cause us harm or else you're going to end up wearing a shiny new set of bracelets, if you get my meaning. Do you understand?"

"Do you have one with you?" I hastily whispered.

"What, handcuffs?" Vance whispered. "Of course. I have two, actually."

We both ducked again as the glass decanter

from Gertrude's coffee pot smashed against the cabinets, spraying us both with glass and coffee.

"You give that board back to me right now," Gertrude screeched.

I was holding on to the board with my left hand and was dragging it along with me as both Vance and I continued to dodge airborne projectiles.

"I can't do that," I told the elderly woman. I spun the board around and confirmed my suspicions. On the flip side of the chalkboard was a cork board, only it had been covered by a sheet of glass. I couldn't see any writing on the glass, but that wasn't surprising, as I would need an ultraviolet light to be able to see anything that marker would've written. I pointed at the marker, which was still on the tray. "I know full well what that's used for. There's something written on this glass. We need to see what it is."

Gertrude was approaching a knife block when Vance finally reached her. With a practiced move, Gertrude's arm was twisted behind her back and she was gently—but firmly— pushed down until her face was resting on the counter. I heard the metallic clicking of cuffs being locked into place.

"I tried to warn you," Vance was telling the crying old woman.

"Please," Gertrude sobbed. "You can't. You mustn't! So many women will suffer if you don't let me break the glass. Or else wipe it clean.

What do you say? Will you help an old lady out?"

A look of utter resolve appeared on Vance's face. "Absolutely not, Mrs. Barterson. A lot of people are relying on us to return their beloved pets to them. If this board will help us locate those responsible, and I'm sensing you're somehow tied up in this, then it must stay intact. Zack? Would you watch her? I'm gonna find out what happened to our backup."

Vance had only been gone for a few moments before Gertrude Barterson, the cookie-loving grandmother to most kids in the neighborhood, freaked the eff out. With a high-pitched scream, the old woman frantically pushed herself away from the counter and rushed at me in what I suspected was a last-ditch effort to destroy the board. However, do you remember me mentioning that she had a top speed which rivaled a slow-moving tortoise? Well, all I had to do was walk in circles around the island in the middle of her kitchen.

"What is going on in here?" Vance demanded as he hurried back inside.

He saw a look of fury on Gertrude's face and slid to a stop. His right hand dropped to land on a gun holster strapped to his belt. I heard the snap of the buckle as Vance prepared to draw his weapon.

Right about then, the first of Vance's backup arrived. The black and white unit must have been nearby, because within thirty seconds of

Vance's call, two uniformed policemen were rushing inside the house.

"Restrain her," Vance ordered, as he pointed at Gertrude. "She's already in cuffs. Keep her away from that wheeled chalkboard. And I don't suppose either of you has an ultraviolet light handy, do you?"

Both cops shook their heads no. Ten minutes later, Mrs. Barterson sat, handcuffed, at her dinner table and glared at the two of us. Vance was pacing inside the house as we waited for the PVPD's one and only crime scene team to arrive. We knew that each of the two techs would have a UV light in their kits.

"Look," I began, as I caught Vance's eye, "she's got the marker, she's got the board. Wouldn't that suggest she would have some way to be able to see what she's doing?"

Vance stopped his pacing and stared at me. A smile formed on his face. He nodded.

"A valid point. We have the warrant. We should look for it. Guys? Split up. Search the house. Look for some type of UV light, okay? It'll probably look like an ordinary flashlight. If you find one, turn it on. You'll know you've found the right one when the only light you'll see will be a dark purple."

The two policemen nodded and disappeared into the house. I rose to my feet and made a move to follow when Vance stopped me.

"You're just a consultant. Stay put. Keep an

eye on her. If she has one of those special lights, we'll find it."

I shrugged and sank down into a seat across the table. Gertrude was now directing her angry glare at me. However, a piteous look of misery quickly appeared on her hardened face. I frowned. Was she playing me for a fool?

"Please, Mr. Anderson. You have to destroy that board. If you don't want to do it, then release me, so I can do it."

Growing angry, I crossed my arms over my chest and glared at the elderly woman.

"Mrs. Barterson, do you have any idea of the misery you've caused by stealing all those dogs?"

"I didn't steal all of them," Gertrude sniffed.

"But you did help, right?"

Gertrude remained quiet.

"Do you remember the beagle?"

Gertrude's red-rimmed eyes found mine. She gave a slight nod.

"Do you have any idea who it belonged to?"

I didn't figure Gertrude would favor me with an answer, so I kept pressing on. I wanted her to feel bad as I'm sure that little girl felt. And why shouldn't I? She took the service dog from Captain Nelson's granddaughter. She deserved to feel horrible.

"That beagle," I continued, "belonged to a little girl by the name of Sydney. The girl has autism, Mrs. Barterson. That dog helps keep her calm and focused."

Mrs. Barterson gasped aloud and then groaned miserably.

"Feeling like crap? Good. You should. You stole a service dog from a little girl. Live with that."

"I had no idea," Gertrude whispered. After a few moments, she sighed heavily. "It's up there."

"What is up where?" I asked, puzzled.

"You wanted to know where the dark light was. Well, it's up there."

Confused, I looked up at the white acrylic lighting panels on the kitchen's ceiling. The lights were on, but I didn't see any evidence of a black bulb up there. More confused than ever, I turned back to Gertrude.

"It's there," Mrs. Barterson insisted. "You can't see it while the others are on. You need to turn off all the lights and then use the dimmer next to the switches there."

"Why are you suddenly helping me?" I wanted to know. "Do you really think I believe this sudden change of heart?"

"I had no idea about that little girl. I'm trying to make things right."

I wordlessly walked over to the bank of switches and began flicking them off. Once all the lights were off, I twisted the dimming dial and waited to see what would happen. For the record, not a damn thing.

"You need to push it first to turn the fixture

on," Gertrude instructed. "Then twist the dial clockwise until you see the light."

I did as I was told. A quick check of the ceiling gave me my answer. One of the acrylic panels now had a long, thin black line running the length of the panel.

"Hey, Vance? You'd better come in here to see this."

Vance appeared in the doorway to the living room.

"What is it? Why'd you turn out the lights?"

I pointed at the panel. Vance stared, and then dropped his gaze until he locked eyes with Gertrude.

"I knew it, lady. I knew you were in on this."

"Go easy on her," I whispered to my friend. "She told me what to do in order to turn it on."

"She did? Why?"

"Because I made her feel guilty as hell about what she did with Sydney's dog."

Vance pointed at the board. "Bring that thing over here. Let's see what it says."

Once the wheeled board was situated under the dark light, Vance gently rotated it until we could see the glass. Lines of eerie yellow writing had appeared. No wonder Gertrude had wanted to get rid of this thing.

It was a checklist.

The closest approximation I can come up with to describe what I was looking at would be a scavenger hunt, only instead of locating obscure objects, I saw six different abbreviations. Each one was short for the name of one of the AKC dog groups, that much was clear. I shook my head as I looked at what was written on the glass. Six lines, when there were seven dog groups? Any guesses as to which one was missing? Yep, you guessed it. Toy Group was nowhere on the board.

Sprt: Labrador C Spaniel RL ✓
Herd: G Shepherd MM ✓
Hnd: Beagle EH ✓
Terr: J Russell HP
N-Sprt:
Wrk:

"Well, well, well," Vance mused aloud. "What have we here? Kinda looks like a shopping list, doesn't it?"

I tapped the scratched-out Labrador entry.

"Looks like this is where they lost the Labrador and had to get another dog to take its place," I said, as I tapped the scratched out Labrador. "What do you think this 'RL' is for?"

Vance was silent as he studied the text. He whipped out his cell, took a picture of the glass, and sent it off to who knows where. Then he turned to look at the sullen woman sitting—immobilized—at the dinner table.

"What does the 'RL' signify?" Vance asked. "It has something to do with a name, doesn't it?"

Gertrude sobbed harder and refused to meet

his eyes.

"I'm sure once we compare the initials here to the members of this club, then we'll have our answer," I told Vance.

"They're not members."

The voice was so quiet we almost missed it. In response, Vance and I turned to Gertrude. She was still staring at the surface of the table, refusing to look up, but at least she was no longer sobbing.

"What was that, ma'am?" Vance asked.

"Those aren't members. At least, not yet. They're recruits."

TWELVE

N ew recruits?" I sputtered. "As in, they'll only be allowed to join your club if they steal their assigned dog?"

Gertrude nodded. "Yes."

I snapped my fingers as a few missing puzzle pieces slid into place.

"The tire tracks!"

"What about them?" Vance asked.

"That's why they were all different!"

Vance was nodding, "Because each thief used a different method to remove the dog from the scene."

I looked at Gertrude, who refused to meet my eyes.

"Where do you get off taking dogs that don't belong to you? How would you feel if someone did that to your own dog?"

"I would feel terrible," Gertrude admitted. "But, I don't have a dog, and it had to be done."

"What had to be done?" Vance demanded. "Stealing the dogs? What right did you have to order prospective club members to commit a crime?"

"We had to know if we were allowing the right people into our club."

"How's this for prerequisites?" I snapped. "Do you own a small dog? Does it belong in the toy group? Presto, you're qualified."

Gertrude's nose lifted.

"That's why the Mini Me's are the best. All of our members are dedicated to preserving the toy group's status of being the best group, the best companions."

"There is no one group that's better than all the others," I pointed out. "Opinions vary. That's why there are so many different breeds of dogs."

"You own those dreadful corgis," Gertrude sneered. "I wouldn't expect you to understand."

"Dreadful?" I repeated, flabbergasted. "You're calling my two little dogs *dreadful*? Why you pompous, wrinkled, mal-adjusted…"

Vance's hand appeared on my shoulder as he pulled me away.

"That'll be enough, pal. You don't want to say anything that might incriminate yourself."

"What do you have against corgis?" I asked, in what I hoped was a tone that wasn't dripping with disdain.

"The Mini Me's deserve to be recognized everywhere, not two crime-solving herding dogs. We are sick and tired of hearing about how wonderful those two dogs are."

"They're smarter than your dogs will ever be," I proudly praised, lifting my own nose up into the air. "They're smarter than you, and they're smarter than me."

"Don't let her draw you into a pissing match, Zack," Vance warned. "We've got work to do."

"What do you mean?"

Vance walked back to the board and tapped the fourth line.

"Do you see this? This marks the entry for what I'm guessing is the terrier group. Looks like they've picked out a Jack Russell Terrier, only they haven't got him yet."

"No check mark," I breathed in amazement.

"Right. We need to find out who they've selected and warn him."

"Or..."

Vance looked at me, askance. All he would have had to do was raise an eyebrow and he would have nailed the Spock Stare. I started to pace.

"...we find out who the owner is and see if we can catch them in the act."

"Oooo," Vance cackled, as he rubbed his knuckles. "I like it. How do we figure out who they've targeted?"

I pointed at Gertrude. "We don't have to. She already knows."

"And why should I tell you?" Gertrude demanded.

"Because this sick, twisted game of yours has to stop, lady," Vance replied. He pulled one of the chairs out from the table, flipped it around, and then straddled it. "We need to be certain that the Jack Russell Terrier on the board doesn't suffer the same horrible fate as poor Sydney's beagle."

"What are you talking about?" Gertrude snapped. "That beagle is fine. Edith is…"

Vance smiled as a look of horror spread across Mrs. Barterson's face. My detective friend nudged me on the arm.

"See what I did there? Gertrude here just divulged that the captured dogs are not only alive, but more than likely still in town. And who might this Edith be, Mrs. Barterson?"

A thin frown appeared on Gertrude's face.

Vance stepped aside and pulled out his cell.

"This is Detective Vance Samuelson. I need a records check for anyone with the first name of Edith. I'd start by looking at everyone within a one mile radius of the park on 8th Street. If you don't find anything there, then start expanding the circle until you do."

Gertrude sobbed harder, suggesting we were on the right track. There had to be something I could do to speed this up. This was a little old lady, for crying out loud. Perhaps I could appeal to her sense of right and wrong?

"Remember, that beagle belongs to a little girl who desperately needs him back," I reminded the tight-lipped old woman.

"I will not turn on my friends," Gertrude finally said. Her face told me she was done cooperating.

"Edith," I repeated. The name did ring a bell. "Edith. Would that be the same Edith who filled her water bottle with coconut rum during your walk in the woods? Wasn't that the same time Vance and I were looking for the beagle? Oh, holy cow. You had the dog in one of those strollers, didn't you?"

Gertrude became tight-lipped again.

"How?" Vance demanded. "How could they have managed to get the dogs away without them freaking out? That's the part I'm having a huge problem with."

"Detective?"

One of the policemen had poked his head into the kitchen. He was holding a small white bag with some type of logo printed on the front.

"I think you should take a look at this."

"What is it?" Vance wanted to know.

The policeman handed Vance the bag and then continued his search.

"What is it?" I asked.

"I'll be damned. Ask and ye shall receive. So that is how you pulled it off."

Vance handed me the bag. There was a black and green logo, and the word 'Composure' displayed on the front. Then, in a smaller font farther down the bag, I saw the words, 'Behavioral Health'. My eyes widened with disbelief as I flipped the bag around and read a label which pointed out what effects the product guaranteed would happen. It couldn't be!

"The label on the back says that there are ingredients in here which facilitate calmer behavior and relaxation."

Vance didn't respond. He was still scowling at Mrs. Barterson.

"It also says that this stuff is safe for long-term use. So, this is some type of tranquilizer? Is that it?"

"It's a relaxant," Gertrude condescendingly informed us. "It's perfectly safe and it's 100% organic."

"A relaxant?" Vance repeated. "People actually make dog relaxants?"

I shrugged. "Apparently. This has got to be the stuff they've been giving the dogs. If these chews are anything like the bag claims them to be, then these more than likely calmed them. Calmed them enough to be willing to go off with a stranger, that is. Or, maybe it made them dopey, who knows?" I looked at Gertrude for confirmation, but she avoided my eyes.

"Where are they now?" Vance asked again. "Where's my dog, lady?"

"I'll bet they're with that Edith person. The one with the rum. Isn't that right, Mrs. Barterson?"

She may not have said yes, but Gertrude's eyes gave us all the confirmation that we needed.

"You can do us all a favor and tell us her last name," Vance told her. "Sooner or later, we're going to figure it out and it'll be that much worse for you."

"Well, she was one of those ladies we met when we were searching for Sydney's beagle," I recalled. "Remember when those women all passed around a water bottle full of rum? Edith is the one who did that. I'll bet you she's a member of the Mini Me's. There's gotta be some record of current members somewhere around here."

Vance pulled out his phone to relay the information. I sat back down at the table and looked at Gertrude. She had tear stains running down her face, her eyes were red and swollen, and she was gently rocking back and forth in her chair.

"Do you want this to be over? Come on, Mrs. Barterson. Deep down, you had to know what you were doing was wrong. Help make it right. Tell us how we can find this Jack Russell before he's taken. Do you want another child to go through what Sydney is going through?"

"He doesn't belong to a child," Gertrude softly murmured.

I leaned forward to put my elbows on the table.

"Who doesn't?" I wanted to know. "The Jack Russell? Who's the owner? How can we find him?"

"I've never met the owner," Gertrude admitted. "All I know is he usually takes his dog for a walk downtown every afternoon, weather permitting."

"You're going to try and take the dog while

they're walking down Main?" I asked, incredulous. "Gutsy. Stupid, but gutsy."

Gertrude shook her head. "No. I'm told he lives off of Blackstone. He walks his dog down 6th, passing the park on 8th. He always stops and sits on the bench while he throws a ball around. That's when they're planning on taking the dog."

"When is this supposed to happen?"

"Today."

"Gertrude, thank you. You've been a big help. Vance? Where are you?"

I left one of the cops with Gertrude and hurried outside. I found Vance talking on his cell, gesturing frantically, as he paced back and forth on the sidewalk. I waved at him to get his attention.

"Hold on, Captain. Zack? What is it?"

"We're looking for a guy who lives on Blackstone. At some point today, he's supposed to take his dog for a walk down 6th, on his way to Main Street. He's due to stop at the park on 8th for a bit. It's supposed to happen while he's there."

"*How* did you find this out?" Vance wanted to know.

"I got her to tell me."

"Way to go, Zack! Captain? Did you hear that? Good. Right. I'll meet you there." Vance finished the call and slid the phone back into a pocket. "Zack, I think we can take this from here."

"Do you want me to help with anything?"

Vance shook his head. "Buddy, you've already been a big help. Go home. Spend time with your dogs. We'll take care of this."

"How are you going to find the missing dogs?"

"That's easy. We'll pull the member list for these Mini Monsters…"

"Mini Me's," I corrected.

"Whatever. Anyway, all we have to do is find an address for an Edith. There can't be that many in this psycho club. If she's the one that's been taking care of them, then she's the one who'll tell us where they're being held. I want Anubis back. By God, I'm not going home today until I can give my family back their dog."

"If you need any help, then you know where to find me."

"I do. Thanks, Zack."

Several hours later, just before four in the afternoon, I got the call. Sure enough, it was Vance, and he didn't sound pleased.

"Hello?"

"Zack? I'm glad I caught you."

"Hey, Vance. How'd it go? Why does it sound like you're about to give me some bad news?"

"The Jack Russell was a no-show. We had undercover cops stationed all the way from Blackstone to the park. There wasn't anyone walking a Jack Russell Terrier today."

"Do we know if Mrs. Barterson is right? Is there someone on Blackstone Lane who owns a Jack Russell?"

"Yes. Myself and Officer Jones went door to door, asking if anyone knew of a Jack Russell Terrier living nearby. There is. His owner's name is Peter Woolson. He's single, retired, and has lived in PV for the last twenty years."

"Have you noticed anyone else scoping the area out?"

"Meaning, have I seen anyone with walkers or wheelchairs circling the block? No, I haven't."

"Well, it's easy to see why he didn't go to the park today."

"What? Why?"

"Think about it, Vance. If you knew there was a serial dognapper in PV, would you have willingly taken Anubis to the park?"

"Point taken. Damn it. I really wanted to catch these ladies in the act."

"What do you say I go for a drive with my two favorite canine co-pilots? I could let you know if they spot anything."

"Hmm. At this point, I'll take anything. Sure. Go ahead, pal."

I gathered up the dogs and loaded them in the Jeep.

"Okay, you two. Work your magic. We're looking for a Jack Russell Terrier. You know what they look like, don't you?"

I received two blank looks from the corgis. Now, I'm ashamed to say that I actually Googled the breed on my phone so that I could show my dogs a picture of another dog. Sherlock looked at me as though I had finally gone off the deep end. Watson simply ignored me.

We spent the next half hour driving around town. I was driving west, on Main Street, approaching 5th Street, when I got my first hit. Well, in this case, it'd be a *woof*. Sherlock sat up, woofed again, and then stepped up onto the window sill so he could see out the window. Intrigued, I checked to see what was around me.

I shouldn't have had to bother. This wasn't the first time Sherlock had woofed at this particular intersection. It wasn't the second, either. All told, it might be the fourth or fifth. Gary's Grocery was on my right, about a block away. The empty space that used to be the Square L was also there. Then there was Harry's office, the site where I had adopted Sherlock last year. And, of course, right next to Harry's office was Furs, Fins, & Feathers, PV's one and only pet store. As you may recall, Sherlock has a history there, too.

"You're gonna have to be more specific, buddy," I told the corgi. I started pointing at all the various places he's shown interest in before. "The grocery store is over there. The convenience store has been torn down, but it used to be over there. Then we have…"

I trailed off as I noticed Sherlock wasn't paying me the slightest bit of attention. He was staring straight at the pet store. Was there something in there that needed to be checked out? Or was he trying to gross me out by saying he wanted another of those damn 'pizzle' chews?

"Fine. We'll take a look. All I ask is that you stay away from aisle 2, okay? The last thing I need right now is for either of you to pick out another animal part."

Just then, a foul, putrid stench wafted in front of my nose. I cursed silently and unlocked the power windows so I could roll them all down. Watson was panting contentedly.

"That couldn't have waited until you were outside?" I asked the timid red and white corgi. "You haven't let one of those rip in a while, have you?"

Watson had a tendency to eat too fast. When she did, she inadvertently would swallow air. The correct medical term for what would eventually happen is 'flatulate'. In layman's terms, it means she'll end up farting to release the stored air. It's not pleasant, no matter how you look at it.

We were greeted by none other than the store owner himself, Justin Roesh. He had a huge grin on his face and instantly tried to direct me over to his aisle full of natural chews. Yep. Aisle 2.

"Welcome back, Mr. Anderson. I am very pleased to see you here. May I assume that your two adorable dogs enjoyed the pizzles and pig ears?"

"Yes, you may, but that's not why we're here. At least, I don't think that's why we're here."

"What are you here for, then?" Justin curiously asked. "I can assure you that I have been paying all my bills in a timely manner."

"I know you have. I just wanted to see if there was anything else in this store that Sherlock might want to check out."

Much to my dismay, Sherlock and Watson both headed straight to the store's second aisle. Watson trotted over to the whiskey barrel full of pig ears, selected one, and trotted back. Sherlock ignored the pig ears and, instead, thrust his snout into a different barrel, one full of those things.

"Dang, Sherlock. I swear you like those things only because I absolutely hate them."

Justin laughed and rang up the order. As we turned to leave, I saw another customer approaching the door, holding a leash. I pulled my own two dogs to the side and held open the door.

"Much obliged," the middle-aged man said, as he offered me a smile. "Come, Winston."

My jaw dropped open as a little Jack Russell Terrier trotted in after his owner. He briefly sniffed noses with my two corgis before disappearing into the store. I stared incredulously down at Sherlock, who chose that time to look up at me. I swear he had a smug expression on his face.

"How on earth do you keep doing that? Is that coincidence or did you know that was going to happen?"

Sherlock's jaws opened somewhat and he

panted. He gave himself a vigorous shaking and then, seeing that I still hadn't exited the pet store, slid into a sitting position. I stepped away from the door and pulled out my cell.

"Hey, Zack. Did you find something?"

"I think I have," I excitedly told my friend as I lowered my voice. "A guy with a Jack Russell Terrier just came in the store."

"What?! What store?"

"Furs, Fins, & Feathers. Sherlock wanted to come in here, and I'm not sure if he wanted another chew toy or if he knew that guy would appear. Either way, I'm almost ninety-nine percent certain that it's the guy we're looking for."

"Excellent work, Zack! I'll be right…"

"Oh, you gotta be kidding me!" I interrupted.

"What? What is it?"

"Vance, two older ladies just parked in a convertible VW Bug next to my Jeep."

"So?"

"They haven't got out of the car yet. They're presently staring inside the store."

"Do you think they're part of that screwball dog club?"

"Without a doubt. They look like … uh, oh. They just spotted me. Vance, they're leaving!"

"I'm heading out the door right now. Do you think you can follow?"

"I'm putting the phone down. I have to load Sherlock and Watson. Come on, you two. Daddy gets to be part of a high speed chase!"

Some high speed chase. Two old ladies in a Volkswagen convertible? I think their top speed was probably 25 mph. Plus, I don't even think they noticed I was following them.

"Where are you now?" Vance asked, nearly five minutes later.

"The same place I was the first time you asked. Traveling west, on Main."

"Main isn't that long. How can you still be on the same street?"

"Because they stopped at Wired Coffee & Café to get a latte."

"Ha, ha, Zack."

"Dude, I'm not making that up. They stopped for a friggin' latte."

"Do they not know you're following them?"

"I honestly don't think they have a clue."

"Any idea where they're going?"

"Actually, I have a pretty good idea where they're going. We seem to be heading toward Mrs. Barterson's house."

"Hah! I knew it! This isn't going to end well for them."

"Why?"

"Because I'm at Mrs. Barterson's house."

"Sweet. Hey, I see you now."

"And I see you. They haven't noticed me yet. When they do, I'll ... nope. There they go. They were starting to pull in and now they're heading back out. They won't make it far."

They didn't. Vance and his fellow officers had

the car pulled over in less than sixty seconds. He texted me to let me know he was taking them to the station. Then he invited me and the dogs to tag along. Who was I to turn down an interrogation? Especially when I wasn't the one being questioned?

Vance was waiting for me just outside of interrogation room 2. He didn't look pleased.

"Just got the call. Records says that there isn't anyone with the first name Edith living anywhere around that park."

"Damn," I swore.

"There are three Ediths living in the PV area. None are close to the park. We've already sent black and white units out there to check them out."

"Perfect. I hope they find something."

"Me, too." Vance looked at the closed interrogation door then back at me. "Come on. Let's go ruin their day, shall we? You watch from the viewing room."

"Got it."

"We're very sorry," one of the ladies said, once Vance had taken a seat at the table.

The bright lights of the bleak interrogation room shone mercilessly down upon the two senior citizens. From the other side of the glass, I shook my head. I don't think I've ever seen two people more out of place than those two. They looked like they should be playing bingo, or bridge, or any number of other activities that old people do. Then again, I really didn't know what senior citizens did for fun.

"It never should have gotten this carried away," the other added.

"Then why'd you do it?" Vance asked. He glanced once at the huge mirror where myself and several others were sitting and observing the proceedings. "And you'd better not tell me that you have no idea."

The two women shared a nervous look. Vance sighed, glanced once at the open manila folder sitting on the table, and then looked at the woman with her long white hair up in a high ponytail. He pulled out his chair and sat down.

"Mrs. Mary Murtaugh. Ms. Rochelle Lindstrom. Let's start with you. Ms. Lindstrom. Would you care to tell me why you were following Mr. Woolson?"

"We weren't going to hurt his dog," Mrs. Murtaugh haughtily exclaimed, before Ms. Lindstrom could utter a word. "Contrary to what you might have heard, we're not monsters."

"Oh, yeah?" Vance challenged. "Care to tell me where my dog is? Do you remember the German Shepherd? That's Anubis. He's my dog. Where is he?"

"He's safe," Rochelle said, in a soft voice.

"And how in the world did you manage to take Anubis without him putting up a fight?" Vance inquired. "I don't care if you gave him a whole bag of those dog relaxant chews. You'll tell me or else I'll…"

"You'll what?" Mary sneered. "Please, Detective. You can't threaten us. What do you possibly think you could do to the two of us? We're old. We've each had wonderfully full lives."

"They're not planning on divulging what they did with the dogs," I murmured. "Unbelievable."

Captain Nelson grunted as he entered the room from my left.

"So," Vance continued, "you're telling me you're willing to sacrifice what's left of your lives because you don't want to return these dogs to their rightful owners?"

"Those dogs are going to be well cared for," Rochelle insisted. Her voice had started to quaver.

Vance zeroed in on the change of tone and directed his full attention on her.

"Will be? *Will be?* So, that's your game. You plan on giving those dogs to someone else? I'll be damned. Zack was right all along."

"Damn right I was," I chuckled softly.

"For once," Captain Nelson muttered.

My smile disappeared. Thankfully, I heard the captain chuckle good-naturedly.

"We're going to get those dogs back," Vance vowed. "You're going to tell me where my dog is, as well as all the other missing dogs. And, you're going to tell me now."

Rochelle nervously looked at her companion, who frowned and shook her head.

"No, we won't," Mary argued.

"Get Mrs. Murtaugh out of here," Vance suddenly snapped. "I want to talk to Ms. Lindstrom by herself."

For the first time, Mary Murtaugh's composure slipped. For a brief moment, I saw a nervous, frightened old woman. Then she strengthened her resolve and the angry sneer was back.

"Where are the dogs?" Vance soothingly asked, once Ms. Lindstrom's struggling companion had been removed. "What's going on here? Why take all these dogs?"

"We were just following orders," Rochelle quietly began. "We were told the new recruits needed to prove their mettle. So, each recruit had to demonstrate they were willing to join the ranks of the Mini Me's."

"By stealing dogs," Vance guessed.

"One dog per recruit," Rochelle sadly confirmed. "Many of us were against it, but in the end, our objections were ignored."

"I wonder whose order it was," I mused to myself from inside the observation room.

Captain Nelson tapped me on the shoulder and pointed at the microphone. I do believe the good captain wanted me to be the one to relay the question to Vance! Excited, I seated myself before the antique-looking microphone and nervously hit the button.

"Who gave the order?" I asked Vance.

Vance briefly glanced at the mirror before dropping his gaze back to Ms. Lindstrom.

"Under whose order? The club president?"

"Mrs. Reezen?" I asked as I turned to the captain, appalled.

"Mrs. Reezen?" Captain Nelson repeated, puzzled. "I hope not. I know the Reezens personally."

"With the president out of town," Rochelle continued, "leadership of the club was temporarily handed to the vice-president."

I groaned. "Crap. It must be. The principal told me his wife was visiting a relative out of town."

Vance scribbled some notes and eventually looked up. "And that is?"

"Mrs. Gertrude Barterson."

"So, you're telling me this is all Mrs. Barterson's idea? Taking the dogs?"

Rochelle sadly nodded. "Mrs. Barterson has always wanted the responsibility of managing the club. Why, I'm not sure. It's a lot of work."

"Mrs. Barterson, huh?"

Rochelle nodded. "Yes. Do you know her?"

Vance briefly glanced up at the mirror before nodding, "We've met, yes."

"Mrs. Barterson didn't take the news too well that the reigning poodle failed to defend her title of Grand Champion last month during Medford's Dog Show."

"It's just a dog show," Vance exclaimed, bewildered. "Don't you think you people take

292

these things a little too seriously?"

Rochelle shrugged. "Perhaps. But then again, what else do we have to do? Practically all of us are retired. We needed something to do in order to keep us entertained."

"It's a lousy way to do it," Vance grumbled.

Rochelle immediately blushed, "I'm sorry, Detective. I didn't mean to imply that the only reason this happened was because we were bored. Mrs. Barterson claimed she knew of families in need. She knew of families who had children who desperately needed a family pet. So, we were 'killing two birds with one stone', she said."

"Let's go ahead and bring Mrs. Barterson in here," Vance said, as he looked up at the one-way mirror. "Ms. Lindstrom, go on."

"Once we received our sixth recruit, Mrs. Barterson claimed she had an idea about how to make sure the Mini Me's only accepted the most dedicated members."

"By stealing dogs," Vance whispered.

Rochelle's head hung in shame.

"I'm sorry to say that I went along with this ruse. I helped take the first dog, a beautiful chocolate Labrador. She was so friendly. I began to doubt our intentions as I heard her owner frantically calling out to her, but Mrs. Barterson assured me what we were doing was just."

"You mean, it was *just* plain wrong," I grumbled to myself.

Captain Nelson grunted once in agreement.

"How were you able to carry that Labrador out of the park?" Vance asked. "That dog had to be over 50 pounds!"

"She was such a friendly thing," Rochelle recalled. "All I had to do was slip a leash on her, give her a treat and a pat on the back, and she willingly followed us back to our car, in the other direction."

"And my Anubis?" Vance asked, his voice dropping to a dangerous level.

"Tell him to be careful," Captain Nelson quietly instructed. "Tell him if he can't stay objective, then I'll find someone else to conduct the interview."

"Watch yourself, pal," I told Vance through the microphone. "Captain Nelson says you need to stay objective at all times."

We watched Vance slowly nod and take a couple of deep breaths.

"Ms. Lindstrom? Please answer the question. How is it that you were able to persuade my German Shepherd, a dog whom I know doesn't like strangers, to go with you?"

"Oh, that was Mrs. Murtaugh's recruit. She told the rest of us that they weren't able to persuade your dog to go with them. So, he had to be carried."

"Okay, I'm having a hard time picturing that," Vance admitted as he sat back at the table. "No offense, Ms. Lindstrom, but you and Mrs. Murtaugh don't seem to be able to lift that much."

Rochelle Lindstrom nodded. "True. Thankfully, Mrs. Murtaugh's recruit was much younger and much stronger than any of us. She was able to carry him."

"And what about his bark?" Vance asked, bewildered. "There's no way Anubis would allow himself to be carried like that without putting up a fuss. I'm actually surprised he didn't bite anyone."

"The only thing I know is that he had to be muzzled."

"You *muzzled* my dog? I can't believe you muzzled my dog. I'm gonna personally..."

I felt another tap on my shoulder.

"You'd better remind him again," Captain Nelson advised in a quiet voice.

"Keep your cool, Vance," I repeated into the microphone. "Don't lose it now."

"I want my dog back, lady. So do the rest of the owners. Where are they?"

There was a light knock on the door. The captain and I turned to see who it was. A uniformed officer poked his head in the room.

"A woman is here to see you, Captain."

"Tell her I'm busy."

"She says it's urgent. It's regarding this dognapping business."

That got our attention.

Captain Nelson rose from his seat. "Oh? Who is it?"

"She says she's the president of the dog club."

"Mrs. Reezen is here?" I asked. "She must've just made it back to town."

Captain Nelson nodded. "Very well. I'll go out and meet her. Mr. Anderson, would you kindly ask Detective Samuelson to join us?"

"Vance, there's a lady here who wants to talk to the Captain," I relayed into the microphone. I watched Vance glance up at the mirror. "He wants you to go out there and meet her with him. She says she's the president of the dog club. I'm assuming she's referring to the Mini Me's."

Vance nodded, excused himself, and exited the room. I hastily switched off the mic and hurried out the door so I could enter with everyone else. Vance was just returning to the interrogation room, and this time, he was accompanied by the captain, a lady I didn't recognize, and the handcuffed Mrs. Barterson. From the way the newcomer was glaring at Mrs. Barterson, I figured this strange lady was the mastermind behind this whole foolish plan and was angry that she had been foiled.

I still couldn't believe this was Mrs. Reezen. She was much older than I thought she'd be. This was the principal's wife? I figured Don Reezen was in his early to mid-fifties. This woman looked to be in her mid-to-late sixties. Sure, I knew in this day and age a large difference in age between two consenting adults really didn't factor too much into the relationship, but I've never experienced it firsthand.

The woman was wearing a monochromatic gray business blazer with a pencil skirt, grey nylons, and black pumps. She had black leather gloves on (I'm not sure why—it's at least sixty degrees outside), and was holding a peach colored handbag. Her jet black hair was done up in a style I've seen Jillian wear before. I think she called it a long bob haircut. Anyway, this lady looked professional, classy, and angry. Very angry.

Rochelle took one look at the newcomers and sprang to her feet, as though she had sat on a tack.

"Mrs. Johansson! Ma'am! I had no idea you were back in town!"

Rochelle refused to look at either the newcomer or Mrs. Barterson. Vance pulled out the chair next to Rochelle and indicated Gertrude should sit down.

I stared at the stranger, totally confused. This wasn't Mrs. Reezen? But I thought Mrs. Reezen was the president of the Mini Me's? Then it hit me. Me and my lousy memory, that is. Mrs. Reezen was the president of the non-sporting group of dogs known as Paws & Effects. I had completely misremembered. That means this lady had to be the owner of Treasure Chest, the swanky gift shop that Jillian loves. Judging by the glare Mrs. Johansson was giving Rochelle, she was not a happy camper.

Mrs. Johansson placed her designer purse down on the table and pulled out a chair. I should also mention that she deliberately chose the same side of the table as Vance and the captain. She pulled off her leather gloves and gave Gertrude and Rochelle the coldest look I think I have ever seen anyone give another person. Aside from me and Abigail Lawson, that is.

"Mrs. Barterson. Ms. Lindstrom. Do either of you want to tell me what I'm doing here? I was about ready to board a cruise ship for Panama when I got the call to get back here. What do you have to say for yourself? What's been going on around here?"

"Ma'am," Vance began. "Both ladies here appear to be involved with a string of dog thefts."

Mrs. Johansson stared at Gertrude as though she didn't know her. She gave Rochelle an equally cold glare.

"Gertrude, would you care to tell me what's going on? I left you in charge of the Mini Me's. What in the world happened? What have the two of you done? What is all this business about stealing someone else's dog?"

"Dogs," Vance corrected. "Plural. And, unfortunately, that included a beagle belonging to a little girl named Sydney, who just so happens to be a certain someone's granddaughter."

Asta Johansson's eyes widened in horror as her gaze shifted to the stern-faced captain.

"Oh, please tell me that's not true. Tell me

nothing happened to that poor little beagle."

Gertrude's upper lip quivered as she let out a loud sniffle, "You were busy. You're always so busy! You never have time for us anymore. I asked you if there was something I could do to help take some of the burden off you. Do you remember that?"

Mrs. Johansson nodded. "Yes. I allowed you to oversee new members to the club. Is that what you're referring to?"

Gertrude nodded.

"What did you do, Gertrude?" Asta demanded. She was met with silence. "Damn it! Talk to me! What did you do?"

"We conducted a recruiting party, only the prerequisites for joining were the ability to prove they had what it takes to be a member of the Mini Me's."

"*By stealing dogs?*" Mrs. Johansson cried. "You openly encouraged women to take dogs belonging to someone else? What is the matter with you?"

"If it was up to you," Gertrude said, with a bit of heat coming into her voice, "then you'd let just anyone into the club. The toy group is the best group out there! We couldn't let just anyone in, could we? So, we had to be certain only the right people were chosen."

"Are you the ones responsible for those missing dogs in Medford, too?" Vance wanted to know.

"What missing dogs in Medford?" Asta asked.

"It happened three years ago," Vance explained. "Medford had a string of dog thefts, just like what Pomme Valley is currently experiencing. All different breeds, and all AKC groups were included, with the exception of one. Any idea which one?"

"Three years ago?" Asta repeated. Right about then, Mrs. Johansson's angry eyes jumped from Gertrude's over to Rochelle's, who had been sitting quietly with her eyes downcast. "Ms. Lindstrom, didn't you tell me you moved here from Medford a few years ago?"

Ms. Lindstrom refused to meet anyone's eyes.

"Oh, dear lord!" Asta exclaimed. "You masterminded those thefts, didn't you?"

Ms. Lindstrom kept her eyes trained on the table.

I saw the captain whisper something to Vance, who then, in turn, scribbled something on a piece of paper. He handed the slip of paper to the officer standing guard by the door.

"Were you the one who gave Mrs. Barterson the idea to steal dogs here in PV?" Vance asked, after the guard departed.

Rochelle's silence spoke volumes.

"No problem, Ms. Lindstrom. Take your time. I've got all the time in the world."

Ms. Lindstrom continued to sit in stony silence, letting out an occasional sob every minute or two.

There was a knock on the interrogation room door. An officer poked his head in the room and held out a manila folder. Being closest to the door, I took the folder and passed it to my right. Once Vance had it, he opened it and began to read.

"It says here that you were arrested three years ago, Ms. Lindstrom. Would you care to tell me about that?"

Again, more silence.

"Very well. Let's see. It says here that you have a felony on your record, Ms. Lindstrom. How very ... very ... un-grandmotherly. Would you care to expand on that?"

Ms. Lindstrom stubbornly refused to speak.

"That's okay. I've got everything here. Let's see. You were arrested for taking personal property. On multiple occasions."

"That isn't a felony," Rochelle Lindstrom softly whispered.

Vance shook his head. "Actually it is. Although, I can understand your confusion. Typically, taking another person's dog is usually classified as theft or grand theft. However, unfortunately for you, in the great state of Oregon, dognapping is considered a felony, which is why you were incarcerated for over two years. More than likely, that's why you moved here. You needed a change of scenery after you were released on good behavior, didn't you?"

"Answer the question!" Mrs. Johansson

snapped, after a few more uncomfortable seconds of silence had passed. "Ms. Lindstrom, was that why you moved to PV? To start fresh in a new area?"

More silence.

"Did you know she had stolen those dogs in Medford?" Vance asked Gertrude.

"I do not recall," Gertrude Barterson hesitantly answered.

"Oh, horse sh—," Captain Nelson muttered. "You were probably in on it then just like you are now."

"There's no proof of that, is there?" Gertrude Barterson coolly replied.

"What did those people ever do to you?" Vance demanded. "Whatever happened to those missing dogs? The police report says the dogs were never recovered."

"They were given new homes," Rochelle answered, becoming defiant. "Their owners didn't appreciate them."

"Who are you to judge who's a proper dog owner and who isn't?" Captain Nelson demanded. "It doesn't make any sense!"

"They had to be taught a lesson," Gertrude whispered. "The only dogs worth talking about are toys, nothing more. The other clubs needed to be taken down a peg or two. When Mrs. Johansson's poodle failed to defend his title last month at the show, I knew steps had to be taken so the Mini Me's could regain their glory. Plus, I was so tired of hearing about those two infernal corgis."

"Sherlock and Watson?" Vance asked, confused. "What about them? What did they do to you? They haven't been in any dog shows, as far as I know."

"And you'd be correct," I mumbled to myself.

"Herding dogs do not deserve more attention than the toys," Gertrude flatly stated. "So, once I was given control over the new recruits, I knew what I had to do. Plus, I made it fun for everyone. Each recruit was responsible for recovering one dog, only it had to be a breed belonging to one of the groups."

"You think yanking dogs away from their homes is *fun*?" Captain Nelson demanded, growing angry.

"Only the right people should be allowed to join the Mini Me's," Gertrude reiterated. The frown was back and her face hardened.

"What are you talking about?" Asta stammered. "It's a dog club! For crying out loud, if a person has a breed of dog that belongs to our specific AKC group, then they're qualified. That's it! End of story."

"Let's agree to disagree," Mrs. Barterson spat as her face suddenly twisted into a snarl.

Asta Johansson's eyes narrowed. She sat back in her chair and folded her arms.

"Gertrude Barterson, Rochelle Lindstrom, you're both relieved of your duties. Furthermore, the two of you are hereby expelled from our organization and are forevermore banned."

A tear rolled down Gertrude's cheek. Rochelle's nose lifted, but other than that, her face was devoid of emotion. Neither of the two women said anything.

"We need to know where those dogs are now," Captain Nelson announced. He consulted the file in front of them and tapped the page. "More specifically, we're missing a cocker spaniel, Detective Samuelson's German Shepherd, and my granddaughter's beagle."

Asta gave Gertrude another cold glare.

"Answer the question, Mrs. Barterson. Where are these dogs? They are going to be returned to their respective owners. Now."

Gertrude became tight-lipped and shook her head.

"Gertrude, this isn't a game anymore," Asta snapped. "These people need their dogs back. Tell us where you've hidden them."

Again, Gertrude shook her head.

"Can you tell us if there's a member of your club with the first name of Edith?" Captain Nelson suddenly asked.

Asta nodded. "Mrs. Edith Colley? Of course."

"And do you know where she lives?" Vance asked.

Asta shook her head "I'm sorry, I don't. Why are you asking? Has Mrs. Colley been pulled into this scheme, too?"

Vance nodded. "I'm afraid so. We suspect Edith might be the one who has the dogs. By any chance, do you know of anyone who might know where Edith lives?"

While Asta Johansson was scribbling down names onto a notepad, I nervously cleared my throat. Vance immediately looked over at me, as did the captain. I figured I really didn't have any business whatsoever giving a detective or a police captain suggestions, but I was an official consultant.

"Can I ask a question?" I then pointed at the list of names Asta Johansson had provided. "Was Edith Colley one of the three from that list you ran earlier?"

Vance flipped through his notebook and frowned. "No."

"Why not?" Captain Nelson demanded. "How did she slip through?"

"I'm not sure, Captain," Vance replied.

I pulled out my phone and quickly ran a few online searches for the last name of Colley in Pomme Valley. Within moments, I was looking at a list of three names. One of them lived right on 8th Street.

"I've got a hit," I quietly announced, as I held up my phone. "I've got a Beatrice Colley living on 8th Street. Coincidence?"

"Where on 8th Street?" Captain Nelson demanded. He had risen to his feet and looked as though he was ready to sprint out the door.

"It doesn't say," I admitted. "If I wanted to pay for the premium service, then it would give me their full address."

"8th Street is fairly long," Captain Nelson mused. "However, I can pull enough people to search every damn house on that street if needs be."

Vance placed a restraining hand on the captain's shoulder.

"Captain? You won't have to. May I make a recommendation? Let's do this the easy way. Zack? Would you and your associates care to head up the search party?"

"When do you want us to start searching?" I asked.

"Right now, thank you," Vance answered. Captain Nelson nodded his agreement.

I hurried home to get the dogs. Sherlock and Watson were in the midst of a tug-of-war battle for a knotted piece of rope. As soon as I walked through the door, Watson dropped her end so fast that Sherlock ended up falling down onto his rump. With an exasperated snort, he spat the rope out and looked up at me, as if to say, I meant to do that.

"Would you two like to go for a ride? We've got some dogs to find."

Fifteen minutes later, we were cruising north on 8th Street. The windows were open, the fresh air was blowing, and I was scowling up a storm as I noticed I was going to have to get the Jeep washed. Again. Both dogs had their heads sticking out of the driver side windows and were spraying saliva all over the outside of my Jeep. Ugh, drops of dog drool had even sprayed up onto the back windows.

"That's disgusting, guys. Come on, Sherlock. Do your thing. Doesn't anything look appealing?"

We drove on, in silence. It wasn't until the second pass, heading south on 8th, while the dogs had their heads out the windows once more, when I finally got a hit. I heard the best noise in the world: a soft woof.

"What is it, boy? What do you see?"

I pulled the Jeep over, clipped leashes on the dogs, and set them on the sidewalk. Sherlock and Watson immediately pulled me over to the western side of the street. Both corgis surged forward, as though they thought they were pulling a wagon. I had to be careful, since the last thing I wanted was for either of them to end up choking themselves. So, as a result, I increased my pace.

So did the dogs.

That meant the pull on the leashes returned. Cursing mightily, I increased my pace to a light jog. The corgis reciprocated, increasing their own pace so that it was still faster than my own.

Now I was in a full-blown sprint. Naturally, both dogs easily out-paced me. When we arrived at a vacant lot between two houses, I was out of breath and panting so hard that passing motorists probably thought I was a chain-smoking asthmatic trying out for a decathlon.

The dogs led me to the back, where all the houses were sitting up against the border of the woods. Sucking as much air into my lungs as possible with each breath, I knew I must've sounded like a fat, overweight guy who had just sprinted after an ice cream truck. However, I was trying to catch my breath just as soon as possible, and I wasn't having much luck.

"What are we doing back here?" I whispered, as we approached a thick clump of wild manzanitas.

I ducked down, out of sight, and looked slowly around. The two houses situated on my left and right appeared vacant. Plus, I didn't see any evidence of any dogs anywhere. No sheds, no outdoor kennels, no nothing. Were we in the right place? What had caught Sherlock's attention?

"I don't think this is right," I whispered to Sherlock. "I'm feeling an awful lot like a Peeping Tom right about now. Come on. Let's go back to the Jeep. We'll try again."

Just then, we heard a car approaching. I heard a squeal of tires and then a car door slam. An elderly woman with frizzy white hair appeared and hurried toward the house. Her head was down or else she would have seen us. I immediately dropped to a crouch and held my finger to my lips, as if the dogs would know what that gesture meant.

"Quiet guys. This has potential."

The woman hurried to the back of the house on my right, walked up to one of the back walls, and then slowly, almost painfully, squatted down on her knees. It looked as though she was either fiddling with something on the ground or else she was contemplating relieving herself. I sure hoped it was the former.

"Well, well, guys. Look at that. It looks like that house has a root cellar."

The old woman struggled to pull open a large metal door and then descended down into the depths of the house. Just then, I heard the jingle of a collar, as though a dog had just shaken. I looked down at the corgis. They had both heard the noise, too, because both of their ears were now sticking straight up. I should also point out that all four ears were angled straight at the house. I pulled out my cell.

"Bingo, buddy. I think we've found them."

"Where?"

I gave him the address. I swear, the PVPD must've been circling the block, just waiting for a phone call. The instant I hung up, I heard signs of cars approaching. Vance and three other officers appeared on the sidewalk. I held a finger to my lips and waved them over.

"Whatcha got?" Vance quietly asked as he dropped down to a squat next to me.

I pointed at the open cellar doors.

"I watched an old lady open those doors and go down into that cellar. I'd also like to point out that she got here in a hurry. Screeched her tires and everything."

"You think the missing dogs are down there?" Vance asked.

I nodded. "Yep. As soon as she disappeared from sight, both the dogs and I heard the jingle of a collar, much like what it sounds like when Sherlock gives himself a good shake."

To demonstrate the point, Watson shook her collar. I pointed at the red and white corgi.

"That. It sounded just like that."

"And you're sure it came from over there?" one of the officers asked.

"One hundred percent positive," I confirmed.

"That's all the validation I need," Vance softly said. "Very well, we'll take it from here. Stay put, Zack. We need to see if we can catch these people red-handed."

Vance's sidearm appeared in his hand. He and the three officers quietly advanced on the cellar. Once all were in place, and leaving one officer at the top of the stairs as a lookout, Vance and the two remaining cops quickly descended into the cellar. Shouting came next, followed thereafter by...

Barking! I heard several dogs barking!

Several minutes later, the elderly woman appeared, with her hands cuffed behind her back. It was Edith, all right. The policeman at the top of the stairs took possession of her and led her away. As for the other two cops, they were each holding a dog. One was a dark brown cocker spaniel, and the other was a beagle.

Vance appeared last, holding the leash to a large prancing brown and black dog. It was Anubis! As soon as they made it to the top, Vance dropped to the ground and wrapped his arms around his dog. Anubis, for his part, was whining with joy and practically beating Vance senseless with his powerful tail as it wagged back and forth.

EPILOGUE

Y ou're telling me you did all this in less than two weeks? So, what did you do, wait for me to go out of town before springing this surprise?"

I grinned at Jillian. "If you want to get technical, this really only happened in the last week or so."

"And how long have you known you were planning on expanding the winery?" Jillian asked.

"Ummm, for a week?"

Jillian laughed, slipped her arm through mine, and started to walk with me. I led her north.

"See that farmhouse there? That's the Parson's place. Their farm borders our winery on the north and west, from there to right over there. All that land now belongs to Lentari Cellars. Pretty cool, huh?"

Jillian had gone strangely silent. I gave her a few moments, but when she didn't say anything, I pulled her to a stop.

"Are you okay?"

"You said *our* winery."

Surprised, I was taken aback.

"I did?"

"You did."

"Umm, I'm sorry. I didn't mean anything by it."

"Mm-hmm."

I nudged her shoulder with my own.

"Hey, don't you read too much into it, either."

Jillian gave a slight giggle and gave me a million dollar smile.

"I still can't believe I missed all the excitement. And here I was, spending time with my parents in Arizona, while you almost singlehandedly broke up a dog-smuggling ring."

"Oh, please," I scoffed. "You make it sound as if a gang of ruthless thugs were involved. They were little old ladies, that's all. But enough about me. Let's talk about you! I'm surprised you didn't let me know you were coming back early." We turned east, toward the buildings that made up the winery. "I would have picked you up at the Medford airport."

"I know you would, and it means a lot. However, the decision to come home early was a spontaneous one. I'm still not sure what prompted me to push my return date forward by a full week. Maybe I was tired of living in my parents' RV? Perhaps I missed my bed. Perhaps … perhaps I missed you."

I felt my face flame up. Darn that woman and her ability to make me blush. What was I supposed to say to that?

"Don't say anything, Zachary," Jillian instructed. "Your face has told me everything I needed to hear."

"Umm, is that good or bad?"

Jillian rested her head on my shoulder.

"Good. It's very good, Zachary."

I heard a car horn honk behind us. We both turned to see Caden's gray Toyota 4Runner pull up to the winery. My winemaster exited the car, saw the two of us slowly coming toward him, and waved.

"That reminds me," I whispered to Jillian. "I've got a surprise in store for Caden. It's almost noon, so they should be here at any moment."

"Who?" Jillian wanted to know.

Living out in the quiet countryside, I heard the approach of a car before I could actually see it. There, about a quarter mile down the road, I saw the truck and trailer. My eyes widened as I saw what was strapped on the back of the trailer. *That* was my tractor? The friggin' thing was huge! It even had an enclosed cab! Intensifying my surprise was the front loader attachment installed on my tractor, turning it into a loader.

Jillian noticed I was staring at the approaching truck and gasped with astonishment, "You didn't!"

"I did. There's Lentari Cellars' newest piece of equipment."

"It looks so huge! Are you sure that's going to work for the winery?"

"The salesman at the John Deere dealership measured the width of the tractor. It's classified as a narrow tractor, especially made for wineries. The salesman assured me it was used so little that it ought to be."

"Wow! Have you told Caden?"

We both looked over at the winery. Caden had just unlocked the store's main front door when he paused as he caught sight of the truck. It was approaching our driveway and was slowing. A look of incredulity appeared on his face.

"You wanted one, now you've got one," I told him as Jillian and I joined him at the front door. "It's not brand new, but the salesman gave me a fantastic deal on it. I will say, for the record, that he didn't tell me it had an enclosed cab, nor that it had a loading bucket on it. That's pretty cool, right?"

Caden still hadn't uttered a word. Together, the three of us watched the huge truck head toward us. I could see the driver gesturing at me, wondering where I wanted the tractor to be delivered. I looked over at Caden and nodded toward the truck.

"He wants to know where to put it. Well, let him know where you want it."

"Holy cow, Zack. I ... I ... I have no words. You seriously bought this thing? For me?"

"For the winery," I corrected. "And, I'll need you to learn how to drive it so you can teach me. I can't wait to see what it can do."

Caden suddenly thrust out his right hand. Not sure why he suddenly wanted to shake my hand, I hesitated.

"No, come on, Zack. I want to shake your hand. Thank you. Thank you for showing me you are willing to invest in the winery."

"Make me proud, buddy."

As Caden moved off to deal with the delivery of the tractor, my cell phone started to ring. A quick check of the display showed that the number was unknown. I sighed. This must've been another one of those stupid crank calls. Should I, or shouldn't I?

Unable to resist the chance that there might actually be a human I could tell off on the other end, I decided to take the call.

"Hello?" Silence. "Who's there? Haven't you got anything better to do than to bug me? And, for the record, you're a number of hours early. Aren't you the one who typically calls me in the middle of the night? What, around 3:30 a.m.?"

For the first time, I finally heard something. I could hear someone softly sobbing.

"Who is this?" I asked again. "I can hear you crying. Are you okay?"

"It wasn't an accident," the voice softly informed me, between sobs.

"*What* wasn't an accident? Explain yourself."

"Your wife. Her death? It wasn't an accident. Why else would I call you at 3:30 a.m.? I'm sorry. I have to go."

The line went dead. I'm sure I turned as white as a sheet. Jillian hurried to my side and took my hand in hers. She even had to give it a slight shake to get my attention.

"Zachary? What is it? What's wrong? You've gone so pale!"

I had to take a couple of deep breaths.

"Those calls? The ones that always call in the middle of the night? That was another one of them. This time ... this time there was a voice. A female voice. She said that Sam's death wasn't an accident!"

Jillian gasped with alarm. "Did you recognize the voice?"

"No. Whoever it was talked in nothing more than a whisper, as though she was afraid of being overheard."

"What are you going to do?" Jillian asked.

"I need to go find Vance. I ... I think I want to have my wife's case reopened."

Well, so much for my plan for the year. Ever hear of the phrase, 'Biting off more than you can chew'? Well, that was me. Sadly, it's been almost a year since Holiday Hijinks was released.

Okay, that won't happen again. In fact, I even have the next CCF book 95% finished. As you may or may not know, I participate in November's NaNoWriMo challenge, which is to see if an author can write a 50K story in only a month. I've tried a few times before, but to no avail. This time I made it. That's right! 50 thousand words in one month! Well, there's more than that, if you take into consideration the progress I've made on the 2nd Pirates of Perz story.

So, the plan is to get Muffin Murders (CCF5) polished up and ready to release, only — after careful consideration — I've decided to release it possibly at the end of January. It all depends on when I can get Pirates #2 done. I'll stagger the new releases, thereby giving the impression that I'm on a fairly consistent release schedule.

So, what's next for Pomme Valley? Well, the next book will be called *Case of the Muffin Murders*. It contains multiple murders, lots of finger pointing, and one dog owner scrambling to prove his girlfriend's friend innocence. All with the help of two gifted dogs, that is.

Thank you very much for reading the book! I only ask that if you enjoyed it, then I hope you'll consider leaving a review wherever you purchased it. Amazon, Barnes & Noble, or Kobo, it doesn't matter. Every review, be it bad or good, will always help out the author, especially an indie author, such as myself.

Happy reading!

J.

August, 2017

THE CORGI CASE FILES SERIES
Available in e-book and paperback

Case of the One-Eyed Tiger
Case of the Fleet-Footed Mummy
Case of the Holiday Hijinks
Case of the Pilfered Pooches
Case of the Muffin Murders
Case of the Chatty Roadrunner
Case of the Highland House Haunting
Case of the Ostentatious Otters
Case of the Dysfunctional Daredevils
Case of the Abandoned Bones
Case of the Great Cranberry Caper

Sign up for Jeffrey's newsletter on his website to get all the latest corgi news: www.AuthorJMPoole.com

If you enjoy Epic Fantasy, check out Jeff's other series:
Pirates of Perz
Tales of Lentari
Bakkian Chronicles

Made in United States
Orlando, FL
28 December 2021

12618363R00193